THE GIFTED

ANNA KATHRYN DAVIS

TATE PUBLISHING
AND ENTERPRISES, LLC

Published by Tate Publishing & Enterprises, LLC
127 E. Trade Center Terrace | Mustang, Oklahoma 73064 USA
1.888.361.9473 | www.tatepublishing.com

Tate Publishing is committed to excellence in the publishing industry. The company reflects the philosophy established by the founders, based on Psalm 68:11,
"The Lord gave the word and great was the company of those who published it."

Book design copyright © 2013 by Tate Publishing, LLC. All rights reserved.
Cover design by Rtor Maghuyop
Interior design by Jake Muelle

Published in the United States of America

ISBN: 978-1-62295-149-9
1. Fiction / Fantasy / General
2. Fiction / Fantasy / Paranormal
12.12.28

Sometimes, when the world sets you apart, the only way to save it is to come together.

ACKNOWLEDGMENT

Special thanks to: God, for giving me my voice; Mrs. Cline, for showing me I had it; Maddie and Maacah, for supporting it; and my mother, Lori, for always putting up with it.

PRELUDE

S ometimes things happen that can't be explained. I am one of those things. I'm not exactly human; I'm evolved into something else, but what that is I don't know. My parents were human, but they're long gone now…a trend that everyone in my life seems to have followed.

I am nothing like you know. My beginning is not unlike yours, though my end is another story.

I've never been normal, even as a baby. I was—I am—beautiful, beautiful in a way you can't even comprehend. From the moment I entered the world, the curse of my face has haunted me with more troubles than it's worth. People lose their minds when they look at me. Even my own parents weren't above it; they fought over my attention like dogs. As I got older, I understood what it meant to be the object of everyone's desire: a life of constant idol worship that left me feeling dirty and more alone than anyone could really comprehend.

On top of that, I'm also physically and mentally more advanced than most people. I can fight too, and not just karate or kickboxing. I'm talking swords, shields, and serious hand-to-hand combat. I didn't learn most of this, though, until I went out on my own. It's surprising the kinds of trouble a teenage girl can find even when she's not looking for it.

I never asked to do the things I can do, and I certainly never wanted everything it's caused in my life. I don't know why I am the way I am. All I do know for sure is that it's been four years since I left society, and since then, it's started to fall apart.

PART ONE

The weak can never forgive. Forgiveness is the attribute
of the strong.

—Mahatma Gandhi

CHAPTER ONE

The thought made me so nervous I fingered the blades at my hips. Nallah, my Bengal tiger and best friend, seemed to feel my anxiety, for her tail flicked with tension. I exhaled and rubbed the spot between her ears. She sat beside me as I stood still, staring at the edge of the forest. This was as far as my world went most of the days of the year. Nallah nudged at the back of my legs as if she was daring me to go. I glared down at her and asked, "Do you want me to make a rug out of you?" She looked up at me with her big blue eyes, unflinching. I held her gaze in a deadlock until I blanched. "Fine," I groaned, "I'll be back before dark. Go enjoy your tiger time while I'm miserable." I took one heavy step out of the edge of the wood and set off toward town. I took my time with the walk. I had a lot to think about, like how I was going to deal with anyone I met. I wasn't afraid of getting hurt; I was more concerned with being seen. My boots scraped against the pebbles sprinkled along the asphalt as I came to stop just outside town. I couldn't believe how much everything had changed.

The road was spotted with abandoned cars and debris littered the patches of grass lining both sides of the road. In the distance I could see smoke rising above the town's profile, thick and dark as it swirled into the sky. An ominous wind swept through the air, and for a moment I was unsure if I was in the right place. It was a ghost town.

I touched the blades at my waist and approached a convenience store. By accident, I caught glimpse of myself in the dirtied window and gasped at my reflection. I hadn't seen myself for four years, and for a split second, I thought the tan girl with thick lips and long black hair was someone else. I leaned in toward the glass and looked closer, remembering then why I avoided mirrors.

I dropped my gaze, embarrassed, and approached the front door. I hesitated, took a deep breath, and then pulled the handle. I was hit with a stench of cigarette smoke and rotten milk. I scanned the cluttered aisles to assess the number of people present, but there was no one. I wasn't even sure if there was anyone working the counter in the back.

I groaned.

I sure as hell was not coming back tomorrow just because no one was working the cash register. I got a buggy, the only one with all four wheels, and pulled the notebook from my back pocket. I gathered soap, a couple cans of food, and everything else on my list before making my way to the back counter. Old, rotten food was stacked along the rear wall, and flies buzzed around the moldy plates. I grimaced and then looked for an employee.

"Hello?" I called out, my voice loud in the silence. "Is anyone here?"

A few seconds passed before an older man poked his head from a small room behind the counter. He was overweight and balding. His dull, grey eyes glazed over, and he scurried to me. I shifted awkwardly under his brainless gaze.

"Hi," I began, looking away from him. "I'm ready to check—"

"Beautiful goddess!" I watched his pupils dilate.

"Oh, lord."

I braced myself as he crawled over the counter and landed by my feet. He bowed to his knees, his belly fat hanging over the rim of his khaki pants. "You have finally returned to marry me!"

I looked away. "Um, no I'm actually just here to—"

"Why?" He let out a pained sob and grabbed at my feet. What was left of his greasy hair touched the thigh of my right pants' leg. He begged, "Please. Please, oh, Aphrodite! Oh, beautiful angel, goddess of the sun. Marry me!"

I shook him from my leg, returning him to his bow. He continued to sob dramatically as I looked around the store. There was still no one inside.

"Where is everyone?"

He seemed not to notice. I sighed and tapped him on the shoulder. I repeated my question. He smiled a yellow grin, and said, "My goddess, the disappearances have stopped many people from leaving their homes. That, paired with the invasion threats—"

"Invasion threats?"

"Yes, oh beautiful angel of life! The army approaches!"

"What army are you talking about?" I furrowed my eyebrows at the stubby little man.

"Marry me! Marry me, please, will you? You are so beautiful."

I rolled my eyes.

"Why? Why do you torment me so?" He began sobbing again, causing me to sigh.

I was not getting any more information out of him. As I looked away from him, I saw a newspaper behind the counter.

I read the front headline: "Invasion Continues: Middle America Is Taken."

"Hey, thanks." I grabbed the paper, tucked it under my arm, and looked back up at the man. "What do I owe you for this?"

"Nothing, you owe me nothing! It is I who owe you…"

He continued ranting as I exited the store, murmuring my thanks. The guilt bore down upon me as I began the ten-mile walk home.

I'd gone into the store with no intention of paying; I had no money. The poor man couldn't have denied me, even if he'd wanted to, and I took advantage of him. I knew I needed this stuff to live, yet all the same, the logic of it didn't make me feel any less horrible about doing it. The fourteenth of May sucked.

My mind wandered to the overall lack of activity at the store. Never had it just been me and the owner. This had always been a quaint town, not the sort to be quick to change. How could *so* much have changed in just four years?

The light scrape of gravel against stone broke through my thoughts, jarring my heart into a race. I kept walking but lowered my hands to my knives. My breath deepened as I tensed and then turned around

The road was empty.

I couldn't shake the eerie feeling that I was being watched, though. Goose bumps crept up my back as I replaced my knives and turned back to my buggy. Just to be safe, I set off for home at a pace no normal human would be able to match.

CHAPTER TWO

N allah jumped around me as I pushed the buggy into the clearing, pausing to cover the tracks it made every few feet. I smelled the blood before I saw the two mangled deer lying beside the fire pit. I smiled, turning back to Nallah.

"Did you get both of these today?"

She frolicked through the underbrush, her tail weaving around like a snake. I grinned like a proud mother and petted her head.

"You're such a good huntress, aren't you?"

She nipped at my hand in response.

I hummed as I unloaded the items, slowly transforming the barren shelves of our cupboard into fully stocked layers. When I was done, I took a small jar of jam and a loaf of bread from the top shelf and then closed the doors.

"In celebration of my successful trip into society, tonight we dine like gods!"

Nallah growled suddenly and crouched, baring her teeth in the retreating sunlight. The growl grew from her throat until it erupted into a roar. I finally saw what she was cornering: a young man.

Or at least that's what I thought it was. He seemed almost transparent, like he was more of a shadow than a person. What was clear was that he was about my age with the reddened skin of someone who spent too much time in the sun. His mischievous eyes were light blue, possibly a shade lighter than the sky. His cheeks were freckled, and his dark-brown hair stuck to his sweaty face. He was taller than me by a good foot, and I could tell that, under his black t-shirt, he was muscular. I was caught off guard when I realized the boy's eyes were wrong. They *weren't* dilated;

in fact, they were startlingly clear and met my gaze. He laughed as if he could read my expression, and winked. Then his flickering appearance vanished into nothing.

My jaw dropped.

"Andare!" I called to Nallah, signaling for her jump forward, but where he had just been, her massive claws hit nothing but a tree trunk.

"Can I ask a question?" I heard the voice, but as I spun to face it, I found nothing.

There was only the empty clearing.

"Where did you find a Bengal tiger in Mississippi?"

The sound came from my right, but he wasn't there. I shook my head to steady my nerves. Nallah stooped beside me, a growl emanating from her lips.

"Show yourself." My eyes darted around wildly.

"Why? So you can sic Cujo cat on me?"

I turned to my left this time, but when he spoke again, he was behind me.

"Or so that you can thrust one of those knives into my gut?" The boy's tone was playful.

"If you just…" I spoke so quietly this time that if he replied, I would know he was within a foot of me.

"Just what?"

I kicked in his direction, and my boot struck bone. His image flickered, him grabbing his jaw with a surprised look. Then he vanished again.

The world slowed, and my senses heightened. I felt him next to me, the air leaving his lungs, the faint scratch of metal against leather. I understood then, and blocked his dagger with my right knife. He reappeared, smiling, and dove at me. My knives closed together like scissors, immobilizing his dagger and the hand holding it. He surprised me and spun the blade, knocking it from his hand, but knocking my knives away as well.

No one had ever taken my knives from me before.

He grinned and kicked the blades away, leaving us only with our fists. I dove forward and came up at his feet, knocking his ankles from under him. He fell hard to the ground, though my glory didn't last long before he knocked me to my back.

My stubbornness took over, and I rolled to my feet. We exchanged punches, his hits hard and direct. I got a strange sense of exhilaration from the challenge he presented, and before long I found myself laughing as I struggled to gain the advantage.

He dove at me, but I moved so he would hit the ground instead. I never saw his body touch, though, for he disappeared before he made contact. My whole world shimmered with tension as I waited. I stood still, my breathing deep and heavy, and then I saw it: the slight bend of a brown leaf about three feet to my right. He made his mistake: the only one he would get.

I jumped and crashed into an invisible opponent. His body reappeared under me, and by some luck we'd landed only a foot from our dispelled weapons. I grabbed one of my knives before he could reach them and pressed it hard against his trachea.

"I win."

His eyes sparkled, and a smile broke his face as he raised his hands in surrender. I pulled another four blades from his belt and one from his boot before I was certain he was bare, though I wondered why he hadn't used them in the fight. As I pressed against him, I realized this was the closest I'd been to another human in four years.

I shook the thought from my head as I sat back, allowing him to sit up. I kept one blade ready in my hand. "What are you?"

He rubbed his jaw where I had clipped him with my boot, but he still smiled. "I could ask you the same question."

I met his eyes, shaking my head as Nallah paced anxiously around us. "No, you couldn't. I'm the one asking questions."

"Fair enough, I guess." He wiped his hands on his knees. "I'm the same thing as you."

"You turned invisible."

"And you look like a wonderful acid trip," he joked, though when I looked away, his voice softened. "I just meant that your Gifts are different than mine. Ultimately we're the same."

I shook my head, "You shouldn't exist."

"Ouch." He laughed. "Is that my cue to disappear?"

"You shouldn't be here. How did you find me?"

"I followed you from town." He was nonchalant.

Immediately I thought of the pebble I'd heard scrape the ground and wanted to slap myself for being so dumb as to not investigate further. "I ran too fast for anyone to follow me."

He shrugged. "Anyone but me apparently."

"You can do what I can do?"

"I told you that we're the same. Why shouldn't I be able to?"

I groaned, rubbing my eye with one hand. "Why do you keep saying that? I'm not invisible. Normal people don't disappear like that."

He smiled mischievously. "You think you're normal?"

I stared at him a moment. "You don't know anything about me."

"I know enough."

I stood up. "Look, you can show yourself out."

I turned to leave, but he stepped before me, and my chest collided with his. Nallah let out an angry roar, and my voice hit ice.

"Get out of my way, or I will kill you."

"Are you sure you could?" He grinned.

I pushed him. "You need to leave. Now."

He caught my wrist in his hand. I spun back onto him, raising my fist at his face, but he caught it with his other hand and smiled.

"Nice right hook, but I'm a little too tall for you to try that angle."

I yanked my fist stiffly from his grasp.

"Look, give me five minutes to say what I need to. Then I'll leave."

"Fine," I said, "but if you touch me again, I'll shove a knife between your ribs."

He smiled and followed me over to my table. I sat on top of the slab as he took the only seat. Nallah took an anxious place behind him, her eyes never leaving his form.

"First, your name."

"Parker."

"Why are you here?"

"I've been looking for you for the past three years."

"I've never seen you before in my life."

"Of course you haven't." He smirked as his appearance began to fade.

My snarl apparently stopped him from going completely invisible, though, because he said, "You're name is Rose, and you were born in the June tornado that tore up north Mississippi sixteen years ago, right?"

"How do you know—"

He reached in his pocket and pulled out a piece of paper. It was worn, yellowed, and torn. He handed it to me. There were five zodiac signs drawn around a sun.

"You're showing me my horoscope?"

"No." His expression flattened. "Look under the signs."

Under each of the symbols, a small paragraph was written.

"That first one, the lion? That's mine. I'm a Leo. Go ahead, read what it says under it."

"No." I looked back at him.

He sighed. "Why not?"

"Because this isn't what I asked for. This is some stupid newspaper clipping."

"Look, the sooner you read it, the sooner I'm gone."

I yielded and read it aloud, "The Leo son, with a lion heart, has the strength of a tiger, and the charm of a lark. Seen like the wind, calm through what transpires, the young lion prince, leads the others from the fire. Sharp with a blade, and sharper with wit, his pride is strongest, but his loyalty unbent. Desire shall strike him, in the form of a moon. She is his downfall, but will save him from doom. Strong, he shall lead; prideful, he will fall. With the others, he is victorious; alone, he is nothing at all.

"What the heck does this mean?"

He tapped the paper. "Look at the next one. The woman's face? That's Virgo. Read it."

I sighed heavily and read, "The Virgo daughter, with the winter's breath, has the innocence of a dove, but shadows of death. Around her, people calm or darken to her will. Inside she is jaded, and gloomy with chill. Pure, her heart is. Kind, she wants to be, but a darkness in her soul, keeps her different than you and me. The objects she desires shall move without her touch, and when the secrets come full circle will be when she knows too much."

I looked up from the paper and said, "This one sounds creepy. Can she really move stuff without touching it?"

He smiled. "Yes, Lila is very capable of telekinesis."

"Lila?"

"Not yet. Now the one at the far right."

"The horse?"

"It's a ram," he said flatly. "But yeah, that's Capricorn."

"The Capricorn son, with the eye of the raven, has the sight of hell, but the warmth of a haven. Forever in the future, while never leaving the past, this young ram is both the first and the last. His blade forever sharp, though his wit may be dull, his intelligence is commendable, and his heart, even more so."

"I suspect you expect me to believe this is a real person as well."

"His name is Brad, and he's the reason I knew where to find you."

"How did he know where I was?"

Parker grinned and said, "Not yet, you've got two more. You see the one under Capricorn, the scorpion? That's Alexa."

"The Scorpio daughter, with the heat of the flame, has the power of wit, and the knowledge of the game. Her heart set ablaze, and her passion unyielding, her jealousy unmatched, and her anger never shielding. A weakness inside, hidden beneath the cracks of the stone, jaded she stands, fallen from her entitled childhood throne. Accurate is her arrow, sure is her mark, never shall it fail, as sure as a lightning's spark. Strong, she is vulnerable, and weak, she is hard. Understanding her true nature is a part of the scorpion's charm."

"Jealous and angry? She sounds like a gem."

He laughed and said, "Yeah, Alexa is...a character."

"Well, this is all very entertaining, really, but this has nothing to do with me, and it's been way past five minutes so I think it's time—"

"You haven't read the one about you yet."

I looked at the last symbol painted on the paper. Down at the very bottom, set apart for the other four zodiacs, was a small, blue crab.

"So what if the last sign is mine?"

"Read it and decide for yourself."

"The Cancer daughter, with the fate of the moon, has both the certainty of life and the promise of doom. Her face, like an angel, and her mind quick and true, her Gifts are like the ocean, both violent and beautiful, too. Like the stages of the moon, her abilities will forever change, one day she is sun, and another she is rain. One path she may take, and live a life in the sun, or another she may walk, and from shadows, she shall run. Uncertainty is her fate, and hardship, her name, but in herself she finds strength, and learns to play the game. Darkness haunts her, and follows her in the sun, but in the shadows she thrives, like the moon's only sun. Victorious and content, she will meet her demise, but honest and haunted, she will live, with a debt behind her eyes. She is the key, the master to the game, but only if she learns the rules, and lives to see the day."

I looked at him and said, "*If* she lives? What is this?"

"It's a chart."

"Cute."

"Look, it means that you are the Cancer the chart is talking about."

"Oh, is that what it means? Because I was hoping it'd tell me why there is a stranger who can turn invisible following me home from the supermarket and why he knows my name."

Parker sighed and said, "I'm trying to explain this to you, Rose. You're not normal."

I laughed dryly. "*I'm* not normal? You're the one who is ranting about zodiac signs!"

"I'm trying to tell you that there's nothing wrong with you, Rose. The way you look isn't your fault. Nothing you can do is an accident. You were *made* for this." He pointed to the piece of paper.

"But what is this?"

"This is the chart of the Gifted. And you are the last one we were supposed to locate."

"You're crazy."

"Rose! Have you noticed anything different about the world lately? Like everything seems to be falling apart?"

I thought of the newspaper headline.

He said, "That's the Infestation. That's why we're here."

"The infestation of what?"

"It's a foreign species. We think it evolved from something else, something introduced by the government that went horribly wrong. They get inside the body, and... Look, I can't just tell you. You won't believe me."

"This is so beyond ridiculous."

"I know it doesn't make much sense, but you are the fifth member of the Gifted—the only thing that stands in the way of everything falling apart. We can't do it without you." He pleaded.

The look in his eyes made me question myself. I stared down at the paper, trying to understand. This couldn't be real, though.

"What is it you're thinking?" he asked.

"I don't know."

"Of course you don't. How can you not know what you're thinking?"

My anger peaked, and I shoved the paper back at him, turning away. He grabbed my shoulder.

"Think, Rose. You know the world is changing, and it's not for the better. Can you seriously deny that you've never wondered why you are the way you are? This is why, Rose. It's because you are destined to help save the world."

I spun around to face him. "No, I'm not. I don't know how you found me or why the hell you're trying to mess with me like this, but it will stop right now. I am not some delusional teenager who thinks she is a superhero."

He looked up warily at the sky. Storm clouds churned in the distance. "You don't believe me."

"No, I don't."

"Then will you do me one favor? Will you come with me to town tonight, after dark?"

"What?" I raised my eyebrows.

"I've got to show you something that just might change your mind. Please, just tell me you'll come."

Curiosity got the best of me. He breathed with relief when I nodded, and the boyish grin returned.

"I'll be back at midnight." He winked, and then he was gone.

CHAPTER THREE

Parker led me silently up the interstate as bitter, shrill winds circled around us, making my eyes water. His steps were as silent as my own yet broader and more unevenly spaced. The glow from the approaching town cast his shadow back in a distorted, haunted figure that danced with every step he took. The closer we got to town, the more anxious he became.

"Why are you so apprehensive?" I finally asked.

He stopped walking and turned to face me. His hands were buried in his pockets, and I could see the worry in his blue eyes. "Rose, I need you to do exactly what I say when we enter town."

"What?" I pushed past him. "I don't take orders."

"Listen to me!"

I turned, realizing how tense he was.

"Do you feel that?" He asked.

"Feel what?"

"Close your eyes."

I reluctantly did.

"Do you feel that sticky feeling of tension? That knot forming in the pit of your stomach?"

"No?" I opened my right eye skeptically.

He sighed. "You're not trying. Just relax a second, and then tell me what you feel."

I shut my eyes, and for a moment I felt nothing. Nothing but the cold, that is. Then it happened: the faintest hint of *something* tickled at my stomach.

I hesitated, unsure if I really felt it, and then inhaled. The tickle grew larger. I was certain I felt it then: the cold, haunting sensation of fear crawling into the pit of my belly. It lingered, knotting and twisting itself into grotesque formations, and slowly built the maddening awareness of tension in all of my limbs. Gooseflesh rose up my back, and I felt the sudden urge to scream. My heart raced. Millions of urges to run, to flee bombarded my mind, and the only thing I could process was danger. Danger was near. Danger was coming. Danger. Danger. Danger.

But then it was gone.

"What the hell was that?"

A car's headlights appeared in the distance.

"It's our body's warning system that they're coming."

"That who's coming?"

Parker pulled me into a ditch off the side of the road. Nallah crouched behind us.

"The Infestation. They're what we are fighting."

A small van was swerving down the interstate. I gasped, watching it collide with a tree on the other side of the road. When it came to rest, I saw a woman in the front seat, her body shaking violently. I stood to go to her, but Parker grabbed me by the wrist.

"You can't go out there."

"Why not? She's hurt!" I yanked my arm free, even as he desperately tried to pull my shirttail, and ran to the totaled van. I could hear Parker calling my name over the hissing coming from under the hood, but I didn't stop.

The driver was a small brunette woman collapsed against the wheel, motionless.

"Ma'am?" I reached out to her, "Are you all right?"

The woman lifted her head, and where her eyes should have been were empty, black sockets. I stepped back, my eyes wide, as the woman's skin ripped from her face in a horrific, bloody mess. Her shrill scream gave way to a croaking call similar to a cicada. I tripped over my own feet and stared up from the ground as a giant insect-like creature emerged from her skin.

It looked down on me—its large, black eyes slick as ice—and I felt my heart stop. Its body was a single, oblong torso, gleaming slick and black like oil. I was so close I could see the individual scales on its chest. Its long legs, skinny and coated in tiny hairs like a cockroach, were directly attached to its upper body. Its face was triangular and as black as the eyes that dominated it. Instead of a mouth, there were two pincers. They opened and released a single piercing siren that stabbed at my ears. The scream bombarded my mind, cutting into it like shards of glass. I writhed in pain, grabbing at my head, until I heard Nallah roar.

I opened my eyes just as she struck the creature in the chest. She wrestled it, throwing it against the pavement, its body cracking with each hit. I regained myself, rising to my feet as it threw Nallah against the side of the van, tipping it over. It moved closer to her, its pinchers spreading. I pulled my knives from their sheaths and whistled. It turned to me, its soulless, black eyes piercing into my face. I spun the knives in my hands and said,

"Come and get me."

The creature tried to open its pincers and then realized what Nallah had done. The left claw was gone, completely taken from its face.

It moved forward, its legs clicking against the pavement like high heels on a marble floor, before it jumped, throwing itself at me. I fell to my back and pushed with my legs, throwing it through the air. It landed smoothly, the vibrations from its chest growing louder.

"It's calling backup." Parker was suddenly beside me, a dagger in his hand.

"Where did you get that? I disarmed you."

"Not the time!" He shrieked as the insect charged at us.

I ducked, thrashing into its torso with my knife. Smoky green blood splashed across the road. I jabbed with my left knife, barely missing its shoulder. It turned toward me, but Parker thrust his dagger in its back. I jumped as hard as I could, spinning my heel into its face. A sickening crack ended the clicking as its head spun from its body.

The creature dropped to its knees and fell to the ground.

Parker stood over it, breathing heavily. My hands shook as I stared at the dead thing. I turned and retched onto the pavement

As I squatted, my hands covering my face, I felt the soft brush of fur against my side. I dropped my hands to see Nallah standing by me, her chest matted with blood.

I pulled her into my chest and stroked her softly.

Parker rested his hand on my back and said, "We need to leave. I'm not sure if its call made it to any of the others."

"There are others?"

"There're thousands of them. Welcome to the Infestation." His joke fell flat.

I stood, looking at him—the teenage boy with warrior's eyes— and I suddenly felt very sad. I knew, then, that it was all true; the world really was changing, and I was at the center of it.

Everything was cold.

"We're really supposed to fight all of them?" My voice shook.

"We have to. We're the only ones who can."

"Where exactly are we going?" I asked as I sped up to follow him.

He said over his shoulder, "We're going to the camp."

"No, we're not. My camp is about a four hours' walk in the other direction."

"I didn't say your camp, did I? You need to learn to pay attention to details."

I made a mocking face that he didn't see and said, "And you need to learn that no one talks to me like that. I don't care if you're some zodiac superhero or not. I don't take orders."

He continued without looking back. "I'm taking you to the camp. It's hidden in the Smokies, kinda near where Alabama, Mississippi, and Tennessee all meet."

"How long do you think it'll take us to get there?"

"Ehh." He paused to look up at the sun. "If it were just you and me? I'd say tomorrow. But since we're dragging along a three-hundred-pound fur rug, I'd say we'd be lucky to get there by Saturday."

"Four days isn't that bad to travel halfway across a state." I paused. "And besides, Nallah only weighs two hundred, thank you very much."

He laughed. "Well, still. We'd move a lot faster if we ditched the fur ball."

"You'd also be two members shorter. I don't go unless she goes."

"Yeah, I kind of figured that. What was it you said? Oh yeah." He mimicked my voice. "Nallah isn't just a pet, Parker." He laughed. "Where'd you find her anyways? It's not like Bengal tigers are just roaming all around the southeast."

"You really wanna know? It's not really a short story."

I looked back at Nallah as I spoke. She'd finally captured a butterfly, crunching it between her paws.

He laughed. "Well, now that you put it that way…"

I smiled. "And it's kind of embarrassing."

"Oh, then I definitely want to hear."

"You have to realize, I've been living all by myself in the woods since I was about twelve. That gets lonely."

"So you, what, ordered a tiger off of eBay?"

"No," I said flatly. "On my thirteenth birthday, I'd been feeling especially low and really just wanted to see someone else's face. For a long time I'd had people worship me, and cutting off into the woods was major shell shock; it took me a while to get used to being alone."

"Then why'd you go into seclusion like that? With a face like yours, I bet you got whatever you wanted."

I tried not to blush at the way he said "a face like mine."

"It never felt right. People shouldn't be put on pedestals just because they have a pretty face. Idolization is unhealthy, especially when it's based on something as superficial as appearances. Besides, I never really liked being worshiped like that. It made me feel dirty."

He walked a few minutes without making another comment. Then he said, "So how does that explain you ending up with a tiger?"

"Oh yeah." I touched the flaking trunk of a dogwood. "Well like I said, I was having a particularly lonely thirteenth birthday, so I convinced myself that it would be all right to go to the zoo after dark and just see the animals."

"You like animals."

"Yeah, animals are easy. There's no sugar coating or sucking up. Animals see through you."

"How?" He stopped walking and turned to look down at me from the top of the ledge I had yet to climb.

"I dunno." I took a handhold and hoisted myself higher. "I guess I mean that they don't care what you look like. If you're a good person, they like you. It's like they see what really makes a person who they are, rather than all the junk on the outside."

He reached a hand down to lift me up to his level. "Spoken like a true philosopher."

"Huh?" I ignored his hand and hoisted myself up on the rock next to him.

"Cancers tend to be more philosophic, deep thinkers." He sat down on the edge of the rock, his legs dangling over the edifice.

"And what about Leos? They all deep thinking, too?" I dug the apple out of his pants' pocket, smiling as he jumped in surprise.

"Nope. We prefer the literal."

Nallah approached us with a limp squirrel in her jaws. She sat, munching on the carcass as I attempted to ignore the sounds of bones crunching.

"Apparently the world's most pampered feline will eat raw game." There was a smile in Parker's voice.

"I guess traveling suits her."

"So you got her on your thirteenth birthday?"

"Oh yeah, I never finished. I snuck into the Jackson Zoo and wandered around for a few hours until I came up on her. I've always liked big cats, so when I came to the tiger exhibit and she was all alone in the corner, I had to get closer."

"You climbed into a wild tiger exhibit," he said flatly.

"Are they really considered wild if they were bred in captivity?" I smiled. "But yeah, I did. She was still a baby then, barely a few months old. You know that's the time in a cub's life when they're supposed to be close to their mothers, but she was completely secluded. I don't know what it was, but we clicked. She let me come up to her and pet her, and she looked at me with those big, blue eyes and—"

"And you realized then that a tiger would be the ultimate fashion accessory?"

"No." I stood and dusted myself off. "It was like when I looked in her eyes, I was looking at home. I've never really had a home, so I wasn't about to leave her."

"So you stole her?" He stood up next to me.

"Stole is such a harsh word." I laughed. "I like *adopted* better."

"Of course you do." He stepped in front of me, taking the lead once more.

About six hours in, my feet were hurting, and once we hit twelve, I was certain they were bleeding. I could ignore the pain, but I wasn't happy about it. Parker didn't show any sign of fatigue. Though he actually seemed to be moving *more* quickly the longer we walked.

"All right, we're stopping." I leaned up against a tree and felt a twang of guilt at seeing Nallah tiredly trying to keep up with Parker's pace.

She walked with heavy limbs, as if the exhaustion in her body was so great that it filled her bones with concrete. She reached me and fell on the ground, wheezing with weariness.

"Seriously?" Parker asked.

"Yep."

Parker sighed, pinching the space between his brows and said, "All right, I guess this is as good a campsite as any."

I exhaled before sliding down the base of a tree. I tilted my head back against the trunk and closed my eyes, the exhaustion tingling in my bones like fire ants.

"You did well today."

I squinted and saw Parker pulling his boots off and laying down against a tree four feet from me.

"Ya know, for you," he added.

"Nah," I whispered, my eyes almost closing. "I did well regardless."

I heard him laugh before turning his back to me. I breathed out and almost felt like I didn't have to touch the blades of my knives before shutting my eyes for good.

<hr />

"No!" I groaned and pushed Parker as hard as I could. Nallah was like a furnace beside me, still deep in sleep.

"Come on." He nudged me again, "We need to stay on schedule."

"Screw your schedule." I shut my eyes tighter.

"Look, I let you sleep in. It's nearly five."

"Sleep in?" I groaned, wiping at my face. "We walked for eighteen hours yesterday, and you think getting two and a half hours of sleep is sleeping in?"

He sighed, making me wonder if it was a habit for him. "It is for you. You don't technically need sleep at all."

My expression fell. "You must be dense. Just because I don't need it doesn't mean I don't still feel exhausted. And Nallah actually needs sleep, you know, to *survive*."

He looked frustrated. "We have to give up certain luxuries while travelling."

"Apparently like getting sleep and eating and bathing." I stood up reluctantly, my joints popping.

I looked down at my sweat-dried t-shirt and grimaced. "Seriously, when can I bathe?"

"When we get to the camp," he said as he motioned for me to wake Nallah.

"In four days?" I said and leaned down, patting Nallah. "Come on, sweet girl, the tyrant is calling."

Parker snubbed my comment. "Actually, if we make the same time as we did yesterday, we should be there the day after tomorrow."

———⬥———

Parker was so intent on making his schedule that we alternated between bursts of speed and walking. Nallah was alright at first, keeping up with Parker and I fairly well as we blurred through the paths, but eventually it became more and more difficult for her to keep up. Watching her become as fatigued as she did with no sign of Parker relenting made my mood deteriorate.

"All right, Parker," I said, wiping the sweat from my forehead, "I need to pee."

"Charming. Pick a tree and hurry up. We have to get goin'."

"We have to get goin,'" I mocked. "You can be so annoying."

I wandered through the trees to get as far away from him as possible as I looked for a good place to do my business. Nallah roamed in my vicinity as I chose a nice oak tree to defile. After the business had been done, I stood and buttoned my crusted jeans in disgust.

"Nallah?" I called out, scanning the vicinity. I stepped forward without looking and slipped off the edge of a mossy rock, tumbled down the small hillside, and landed in a thicket of barbs.

I groaned and brushed my forehead. I could already feel the blood starting to trickle down my leg. I peeked down and saw a huge hole in my jeans, exposing an angry gash on my knee. "Great." I tried to stand, but my leg screamed out in protest.

Nallah came bounding up beside me, sniffing my wound. "Thanks for showing up now," I said, leaning against her body to stand. "You all right?" Parker peered down from the top of the hill.

"Oh, I'm just peachy." I spat bitterly. "No, I fell into a freaking thorn patch."

"Ew. How bad did it get you?"

"Umm." I looked back down at my leg and was surprised to see just how big the bloodstain was. "Well, it's bleeding pretty badly."

"Here, lemme see." He came down and helped me over to a large rock so he could look at the cut.

"Hmm." He tore the lower half of my jean leg from the rest of my pants.

"Really?" I said.

"What?"

"These are the only pants I have, and you just made one half of them Capri's."

He rolled his eyes and ripped the denim into strips. He used a few of the strips to wipe away the blood, revealing a jagged slash deep in my knee.

"Ehh, it's not so bad."

I grimaced as he used the remaining strips of fabric to tie like a bandage. "All right," he said with a smile, helping me to my feet. "Let's keep going."

I stared at him.

He raised his eyebrows. "What? You thought I'd carry you to the Smokies?"

The bursts of speed after that grew shorter and shorter, and only partly because of Nallah. My leg was stinging, and I was getting tired of having to follow Parker. The few times I'd tried to speed ahead of him, I'd gone in the completely wrong direction and had to backtrack a good mile or so. The smug look on his face every time I had to come back was enough to make me puke. I settled myself to sullenly following after my last detour put me five miles in the wrong direction.

"Come on." Parker looked back at me. "You're superhuman. You shouldn't be moving this slow."

I grunted and followed him up another hill. "Oh, you're right. It's not like I have a gaping wound in my leg or anything."

"Stop being such a baby. Look, it's stopped bleeding."

"If you are trying to convince me that everything's good because I've stopped leaking my DNA, I'm not buying it."

"You're right. Things were so much better when you were leaving a blood trail," he said as he smiled and reached down to help me climb the last few steps of the hill.

I ignored him and instead grabbed the nearest tree branch, hoisting myself to his level. We stood at the top of a precipice above a large field of ivy. It stretched on and on, the other end of the forest tiny against the horizon.

"Whoa." My jaw dropped. "That is a lot of empty space."

He smiled. "It's that crazy kudzu weed. The stuff just took over. We go through there, and we bypass a day's worth of traveling through the woods."

We made the slow decline into the forest of weeds. As we hit the field, a pungent plant odor filled my nose. I laughed when I saw Nallah's head periodically appear above the green tangles, chasing God-knows-what.

"So tell me about yourself." Parker's voice contrasted with the sound of leaves rustling as we walked.

"What?"

He looked back at me. "Well, I mean, we are going to be spending a lot more time together. It'd be nice to know something about you."

"Like what?"

He chuckled. "I already know you treat that tiger like it's a person, you stole said tiger from a zoo because you think animals can see people's souls, you whine a lot, and you talk in your sleep. That pretty much sums it up."

"I talk in my sleep?"

"Well, you more, like, mumble." He laughed. "I couldn't understand a dang word of it, and believe me, I tried."

"I never knew that," I said, and then paused, thinking. "I don't think it's fair that you know so much about me, but all I know is your name."

"Me?" He thought for a moment. "Where do I start? Hmm… Well, I don't have any pets, but if I did, it would be a wolf, 'cause let's face it. I can't just say a dog, because you have a freaking tiger." He grinned.

"I lived on my own for a while before I met with the other Gifted. I never knew my dad, but I was real close to my mom before she died." He swallowed before looking distractedly up at the sun. "I like mornings a lot, and I am a Leo."

"I already knew the Leo part, and I kind of figured the morning thing. So, why, out of all the animals, would you pick a wolf?"

"I guess I really like the whole traveling-in-packs thing. It's like a big family, kinda like the Gifted."

He didn't have to mention how nice the whole "family" thing was. Even I didn't want to live alone forever. "So what's with this Gifted? Are you like the alpha male or something?"

He grinned. "Yeah, I guess. It just kind of felt right for me to take control. Brad's a good guy, but he's never had the sensitivity to lead the others, and Lila is just too young. She's only twelve."

"And what about the Scorpio, Alexa?"

A sly look crept into his expression as he said, "I'll let you decide for yourself why she couldn't take charge."

"So they're cool with you leading them? They never question it?"

"Yeah, they're not like you; they trust my judgment."

"Uh-huh."

"Uh-huh what?" He turned back to me. "Are you saying I'm not an alpha?"

"I didn't say that. It's just that alpha's are supposed to be all regal and junk. You're just kind of bossy."

"I'm not like that all the time, just with you. I'm 'regal' with the others."

"Hey, whatever you say," I teased.

As we climbed higher on the bluffs, I heard the faint trickle of water nearby. I fantasized about convincing the tyrant to let me take a quick bath, but stood speechless when we reached the highest peak of the bluffs.

A valley of green stretched far on both sides of my periphery. Little puffs of oak trees and red dogwoods painted the ocean of foliage. Four peaks caged in the valley, explaining why so much of the journey had felt like we were climbing mountains.

"Welcome to the Smokies." Parker was calm as he looked out over the expanse.

"Does this mean we're here?"

"Not quite." He pointed to a small area snuggled between two mountains in the distance. I could make out the faint whiteness of a waterfall.

"The camp is real close to there. With any luck, we should arrive by noon tomorrow."

Parker's hand rested on the small of my back. A chill of exhilaration raced up my spine before I could silence it, making me feel betrayed by my own body. I reared back and pushed him away.

"What the heck was that for?"

"Didn't I tell you not to touch me?" Anger pulsated behind my eyes, anger so strong it hurt. I wanted to push him again.

"I was just getting a bug off your shirt. Chill out," he said, causing me to stop dumb.

I was angry because I wanted it to be more than that, and now I was disappointed. Looking at Parker now, I blamed him. He was the reason I was so irrational, so out of myself. I couldn't help it, so I punched him.

A few times.

"Hit me back." I seethed.

"No."

I swung harder, but he caught my fist in midair.

"Go screw yourself, Parker." I pushed past him, but he grabbed my wrist. "Let go of me."

"Not until you tell me why you're so mad."

I yanked my wrist from his grasp and turned to walk away for the second time. He reached for it again but Nallah jumped between him and me, her teeth bared.

He looked up at me. "Well, aren't you gonna call her off?"

I smiled down at her and said, "Good girl."

His expression flattened. "Seriously?" He reached into his pocket to retrieve his dagger, the handle pointed toward Nallah as if he would stun her with it.

"Do it, and I really will kill you."

He dropped his knife to the ground, the blade ringing as it vibrated against rock. Then he went invisible and walked away, the bushes rustling as he left. I counted to ten before following in silence.

Well after midnight, Parker and I crept through the darkness of the valley with Nallah separating us. My temper had gotten the best of me, making me petty and irritable.

"I'm not going any farther." I planted my foot on a grassy knoll.

"What do you mean you aren't going any farther? You're not the one in charge here."

I snorted. "Well, I am now. Consider yourself impeached."

"You said you'd do what I asked. Remember what happened last—"

I cut him off. "Last time we were being attacked by oversized cockroaches. Seeing as this is not that situation, I'm saying we don't go any further."

"Why do you insist on being so difficult?"

"And why do you insist on being such a tyrant?" I folded my arms. "I'm not moving."

He exhaled, annoyingly dramatic, as he stomped his foot on the ground. "No, we keep going! It's barely two."

I half-laughed and raised an eyebrow. "I'm sorry, did you really just *stomp* your foot at me?"

He stretched his arms out to both his sides. "What is the big deal? If we want to make it to camp by noon—"

I put my hands on my hips. "You don't get told no a lot, do you?"

He turned his back to me, wiping his hand down his face. "Has anyone ever told you how ridiculously stubborn you are?"

I sneered. "Oh yeah, it's what all the trees say to me. What the heck do you think? I've been living alone in the woods for four years."

"Well, that's obvious. Your people skills suck. You've done nothing but treat me like a criminal this whole time."

"Oh I have not, you big baby." I scoffed. "I haven't done a single thing toward you that wasn't precautionary."

"Okay, so having Nallah nearly attack me on the bluffs because I tried to swat a bug off your shirt? That was absolutely precautionary? Or how about ignoring me whenever I tried to help you? Or how you argue with me over every single path we take, even though I'm the only one who knows where we are going? Every time I try to help you, you push me away like I'm out to get you. What the heck is your deal?"

"In my own defense, *Parker*, I don't know what boys like you do with your hands when they're not stretched out trying to help me up a ledge."

He rolled his eyes. "Oh, real mature, Rose. You going to stick your tongue out at me now and take my lunch money?"

"Ha!" I barked. "Well it's not like you'd need it, would you? Nooo, cause you don't even want to stop for lunch. You just keep pushing us on like a freaking slave driver. Can you not see how worn out Nallah is or how tired I am?"

He scoffed. "You're a warrior. You're made for this type of stuff."

"No," I corrected. I sat down and crossed my legs. "I'm a teenage girl traveling in the middle of God-knows-where with some pigheaded, teenage Nazi."

"Nazi? Really?"

"Oh, I'm sorry. Would you prefer power-obsessed dictator?"

"I am not power-obsessed. You're just whiny."

"Whiny?" I mimicked him. "Get up, Rose, I don't care that you've only had two hours of sleep after nearly being killed by a homicidal bug. Oh, you're hungry after walking for nearly eighteen hours? Too bad! And you fell and scraped your knee? That sucks, 'cause we ain't stopping to clean it up, because we have to make it to some camp that I won't tell you the directions to before Saturday, because I'm obsessed with my made-up schedule."

"Oh we are doing impressions now, are we?" He coughed and closed his eyes, reopening them with a fake, prissy smile on his face. "Hi, my name's Rose, but I won't tell you any more than that because I don't trust anyone! And don't try to touch me either, even if it's just to help me up a cliff, because then I'll sic my jillion pound Satan-tiger on you and gripe when you try to defend yourself against her."

"Oh, don't you call Nallah Satan, you jerk." I stood up, my hands shaking.

"Well, it's the truth. Every time I get near you, she flips out and tries to tear me apart." He stepped closer, Nallah rising to her feet as he did. "Oh, there she goes."

"Excuse her for caring about my safety, unlike you, apparently. We need you to help us defeat these alien freaks, blah-blah-blah. What a joke." I stepped closer, only four inches away from his chest.

"You're right. I care absolutely nothing for you, and that's why I jumped onto the back of a giant bug that was about to kill you." He stepped forward too, our chests now bumping.

"I hate you!" I screamed, baring my teeth at him. We were standing so close his breath burned my cheeks like fire.

His hands closed around my face, pulling me toward him. His lips collided with mine. It was a brusque impact, almost painful, but then my body responded. I reached above me to drape my arms across his shoulders when I realized I had tears falling from my eyes.

He pulled back. "Ah, hell, you're crying." He wiped at his face. "I shouldn't have done that."

I shook my head, swallowing.

"I'm sorry." He stepped back. "I...I...I don't know what came over me."

"I do." I felt small as I looked away from him in disgrace. "I need some air," I said and turned to walk away.

"No, Rose...please?"

I looked over my shoulder and then broke out into a run. I moved through the trees so quickly that they blurred.

Nallah was struggling to keep up, but I couldn't slow down. I entered a clearing and then collapsed onto a rock in the center. The moon shone down on me like a hot spotlight as I buried my head in my hands. My chest heaved as I cried, the teardrops falling from my eyes like blades.

Nallah uneasily approached me, nudging her head against my knee, but I pushed her away. She tried again, this time more fervently, before I looked up. Her large, blue eyes bore into mine. I wiped my nose against my sleeve. I stroked her coat, taking slow, deep breaths to calm myself.

"He's ruined everything. I thought I'd finally met another person who wouldn't go crazy just because they looked at me." I shook my head in defeat. "But now he's done this."

Nallah purred as I collected my thoughts. The moon drifted a good bit in the sky before I was finally ready to go back to where I'd left Parker.

He sat with his back against a tree, his head resting on his folded arms. I crept into his vicinity, hoping he was asleep. He looked up at me.

"I'm so sorry," he whispered, barely louder than the crickets.

Crying had drained me, leaving me cold and tired. "You couldn't help it."

"Of course I could have helped it. I'm supposed to be in control, be a leader..." He furrowed his brows, and for the first time I let myself admit how beautiful he was. The moonlight shone bright on his coppery curls, and every shade of the ocean glowed in his eyes. I felt empty looking at a face that only a few hours ago held such promise.

"You're not going to be able to understand, but believe me when I say it wasn't your fault." I sat away from him against another tree. "It's just what my face does to people." I couldn't believe how small I sounded.

"Rosie," he said, scooting near me. "This isn't your fault. It was a stupid thing for me to do, because you're obviously not ready, and I just..."

"What do you mean *I'm* not ready?" I lifted my eyes to meet his. "Parker, you don't get it. *You* will never 'be ready' for *me*. You can't just get used to the way I look. It's not how my stupid Gift works. Every time you look at me, you will get caught up in my face all over again. It's just how it is. It's a sick joke nature played on me," I whispered. "Everyone I meet wants to spend forever with me, but it was made so that none of them ever can."

"Rose." He reached forward to place his hand on my knee.

I pushed it away. "Just go back to your spot, Parker." I turned my back to him. "I'm sure we only have a few hours before we need to get up, anyways."

He hesitated, but I eventually heard him walk back to his spot. Nallah laid down with her back to mine, but even with her so close, I'd never felt more alone.

CHAPTER FOUR

I never actually fell asleep. I'd lain awake all night, listening to Nallah's breathing and Parker's snoring. I was too consumed with my thoughts about him to fall asleep.

I couldn't get over my disappointment that Parker had fallen for what every other person did. I was upset that he was normal. What I couldn't wrap my head around, though, was *why* I'd hoped he would be different. Why had I put him at higher standards than everyone else? Was it because I really did like him, even despite all the grief I gave him? Or was it because I'd put so much faith in him before he failed me?

Parker was a good person. I didn't know a lot about him, but I knew that. He cared about other people more than himself; I could see that in the way he talked about the other Gifted. He was strong too, stronger than even me, and that was something I'd never expected. But what I sensed most about him, despite having no real evidence, was that he had a good heart. There was a look in his eye, a feeling when he smiled that made him seem good. Parker was a better person than I was.

And yet he'd still fallen for the spell.

That was why I was so upset. I wasn't going to find what I'd wanted in him and that hurt.

I was still thinking when the sun began to rise, so I gave up on sleeping and made myself stand and dust off my pants.

Parker looked up at me sleepily. "You're up early."

"Yep," I said, turning my back to him to wake Nallah.

"We need to talk about last night. We can't just pretend—"

"Let's just focus on getting to that camp today, all right?" I said. If it was up to me, never talking about it again would be too soon.

"Whatever you say, Rose," he said, shaking his head. "Whatever you say."

He started walking west of where we'd been sleeping. "It's about a straight five-hour hike that way."

I nodded and set off beside him.

The temperature steadily rose as the day passed along with Parker's mood … By the time we heard the loud roar of a waterfall, he was almost happy.

"We're nearly there," he said, beaming at me. "Just over this hill."

I swallowed, nervously touching my blades. It had been one thing being with Parker, but it was a different situation entirely being with a group of people I'd never met.

Anxiety heated my body. Nallah sped up to walk by me; she'd grown accustomed to my moods and was able to discern the good ones from the bad ones.

"Parker!" A young girl called from the top of a hill.

Parker laughed and ran up to her, leaving me awkwardly at the bottom with Nallah. The girl's sandy blonde curls bounced as Parker spun her. He put her back on her feet she linked her small, pale arm through his.

She smiled, her grey eyes shining behind thick lashes. She dragged Parker down to me.

"Hi." She had a quaint southern accent. "You must be Rose."

"Um, hi," I said, trying not to fidget with the hem of my sweaty shirt. "Yeah, I am, and I'm guessing you're Lila?"

She beamed. "I should have known Parker would tell you about us. He goes on like we're his children or something." She rolled her eyes and patted his shoulder. She saw Nallah and gasped happily. "Is this your pet?" She kneeled and said, "Brad said you had a tiger. I've never seen one up close before. She's beautiful."

"Oh be careful!" Nallah didn't really have the best people skills, and I could almost see her attacking the little blonde like a hunk of rib eye.

But it was too late. Lila had already stretched her skinny, little arm toward Nallah and—Nallah let her pet her between the ears, purring like a house cat.

"She's friendly," Lila said, giggling. "What's her name?"

I shook my head. I shouldn't have been surprised to see my two-hundred pound tiger roll over for a girl to rub her belly.

"Her name is Nallah," Parker said, "What I probably forgot to tell you, Rosie, is that Lila here has a funny way of charming animals. None of us know why."

"I can tell you why." She looked up, still rubbing Nallah's belly. "Because I have a dazzlingly wonderful personality."

Parker laughed and said, "Well, that makes sense, since Rose here thinks that animals see people's souls."

"And you don't?" A male's voice, a little deeper than Parker's, came from behind us at the top of the hill.

I turned to see a tall teenage boy come trampling down the hill. He was dark skinned with shaggy blonde hair and green eyes that sparkled in the sunlight. He was muscular with broad shoulders. He came crashing into Parker. Parker stumbled, and the boy laughed, slapping him good-heartedly on the shoulder.

He turned to me, and his eyes widened to the size of saucers. "Geez, Parker. You think you could have gotten her here in any worse condition?"

I blushed, and Parker shrugged the boy's arm off his shoulder. "Brad, she can hear you. She's standing right there."

He just seemed to realize that and smiled, reaching for my hand. "Sorry about that. Sometimes I forget people hear what I say."

I looked at Parker, confused, and he just shrugged.

"Don't worry about it," I said, surprised by my own shyness.

"Alexa isn't going to like this at all." He shook his head, looking at Parker like I wasn't there again.

"What won't she like?" I asked.

"Well, you're way more beautiful than I led her to believe, and there's the fact that you and Parker kissed."

"They did what?" A female's voice came loud and angry from the top of the hill.

Every one of our eyes darted up to the girl glaring down at us. She was Latina with dark sandy skin and long brown hair blowing wildly around her face. Her lips were thick and dark, and she had deep-brown eyes. She was tall, a few inches taller than me, and she was more than curvy.

Parker smiled up at her. "How've ya been, Alexa?"

"I've been well." She smiled at Parker and then blatantly sized me up. "But Brad thinks you guys have been better. What happened to her pants?" She asked Parker, ignoring me.

"It's actually a funny story." Parker started to laugh, but it died in his throat when he saw Alexa's expression. He coughed uncomfortably and said, "On second thought, it's not funny at all. No reason to even talk about it."

"Parker kind of ripped them off me," I said, then realized how it sounded.

She faltered and then sneered. "Well, it's not like it matters if he did, does it? I mean, it's not like you actually paid for them. Brad tells me you're quite the little thief, taking advantage of innocent people left and right."

I was taken aback. She didn't know the first thing about me. Did she really assume I enjoyed taking advantage of people to survive? I hated that.

Parker stepped between us and laughed uneasily. He said, "Okay, let's all take a breather, and—"

Alexa interrupted him, "I don't like her."

"What?" I asked, my anger flaring. "What's your problem?"

A cool chill crept down my spine, and instantly I felt calm. I looked over at Lila, who was sitting on the ground, her eyes closed with her fingers over her ears and a look of hard concentration on her face. When she opened her eyes, the cool sensation snapped like a rubber band. I was myself again.

"Alexa, do I seriously need to go over what we talked about again?" Parker asked.

"This is ridiculous," she said and then stomped up the hill.

"I'll go after her." Parker hesitated when he saw the alarm in my eyes. "You'll be fine."

"Sorry about that." Lila took my hand and led me forward.

"What's her deal?" I asked.

Brad hurried to walk on my other side. "I'd guess she hates you."

"I don't even know her."

"She knows you," Brad said.

"How?"

"Genius, here," Lila said as she motioned toward Brad, "has been trying to woo her by feeding her obsession of knowing everybody's business."

"Huh?" I asked.

"Basically he's told every vision he's had about you to Alexa whenever she asked."

"Why'd she want to know about me?"

Brad was quiet as Lila talked. "For one, she's had Parker to herself for a few years. Let's face it. I've just barely begun puberty. Alexa hasn't had much competition for attention."

"But I don't want to compete with her. I don't care—"

Lila interrupted me. "No, *she* doesn't care that you don't care, because she's Alexa, and she's jealous of, like, everything."

"That's ridiculous."

Lila snorted. "Welcome to what I've been saying."

"Look, I don't want any drama. Parker said I was here to help, and—"

"Oh, she knows we need you." Lila waved her hand dismissively. "But you're the biggest obstacle to get to Parker."

I snorted. "I can almost promise you that after last night, Parker and I will never be anything more than what we are now."

"I wouldn't bet on it." Brad grinned.

We reached the top of the hill and looked down the other side. Nestled inside the forest, unobtrusive to the trees' designs, were five small cabins making a circle around a large, open space. A fire pit stained black with ash was in the center, and off to the side was a long table with five chairs. I heard the faint roar of a waterfall, and I saw a worn path in the trees leading into the distance.

"Down through there are the bathrooms and the gully where we bathe." Brad pointed down the trail. "And if you take a left at the fork, you'll be at the sparring grounds."

"Y'all have sparring grounds?"

Lila grinned. "What? You think we could take down alien bugs without a little training?"

"How did y'all build all of this?"

"Three of the cabins were abandoned mountain climber's refuges," Lila said. "You know, for in case there was like a snow storm or something. We made sure they weren't on any of the maps before we added onto them. Then we built the bathrooms. Everything else was pretty much already here, though. We just cleaned it up a little bit."

"Wow," I said, unsure what else to say.

"I would stay and chat some more," Lila said abruptly, "but I'm going to go see what happened to Parker and Alexa." She turned and bounded down the hill.

I noticed the solid disappointment in Nallah's eyes, and had to shake my head. Of course my tiger would melt at the first sign of slate-gray eyes and curly pigtails.

The tall grass at the bottom of the hill tickled the cut on my leg. I wiped at it agitatedly.

Brad looked down at it and said, "You're probably going to want to wash that."

I wasn't sure if I was supposed to laugh, so I just nodded my head. He laughed.

He led me around the campsite, skirting the cabins, and then down the trail. For a moment the only sounds I heard were the crunch of our boots on the leaves and the gurgle of a waterfall.

"You know, Parker said not to tell you any of the visions that I've seen about you," he said, looking ahead of him, "but I'm more inclined to hear what you think."

"I think that Parker has let this leader status go right to his head."

Brad smiled back at me.

"If it's about me, then he has no say in whether or not I hear it."

Brad shook his head and laughed. "Man, that's refreshing."

"What? He doesn't get opposed much?"

"Not really," he said. "Lila usually just goes with the flow, because she hates confrontation."

"What about Alexa?"

He laughed. "She likes to play, but honestly, she'd probably throw herself off a cliff if Parker said it was right."

I ducked under a low hanging branch. "Well, I'm not about to blindly follow someone because of who they are. If the logic isn't there, than neither am I."

"It's good he likes you. You'll keep that monster ego of his in check."

"Don't say stuff like that."

His smile returned. "What? You said you wanted to know."

"I meant the visions about me."

"They're all about the two of you. So that pretty much means you're not ready to hear any of them"

"Ready to hear? Of course I'm not, since I obviously know nothing about what I can handle," I said flatly. "What is it with y'all telling me what I am and am not ready for? It's getting kind of ridiculous."

"You're probably right. I just find it hard keeping things to myself sometimes. But I can take a hint. You don't want to hear any more about all that I've seen between you and Parker."

"Brad, I honestly don't want to hear about it, because *if* Parker felt anything at all for me, it's not for the right reasons."

"He kissed you, didn't he?"

My stomach fluttered. I hoped Brad wouldn't notice the rush of color to my cheeks. "How did you know about that?"

"Psychic, duh?"

"Of course," I said, rolling my eyes. "But you don't understand. He didn't really have a choice."

"What? Did you force him?"

"No." I laughed. "My face got to him. It was bound to happen eventually."

"You don't know, do you?"

"I don't know what?"

"Rose." He paused. We were standing where the trees became a dense thicket. "We're immune to each other's Gifts."

"No," I said so quickly that he had barely enough time to smile. "No, that's not true. When I first got here, Lila changed my mood."

Brad shrugged. "Lila's a freak. Her Gift is the only one that seems to have any effect on us, and even then she has to stay really focused on it for anything to happen, and it drains her pretty bad."

"Well, if hers works on you, how do you know my face doesn't too?"

"I'm not falling to my knees and worshiping you, am I?"

"The way I look has no affect on the four of you?"

"Not in the way you're thinking." He smiled.

"So when Parker kissed me—"

"It had nothing to do with the way you looked."

Brad pushed against the brush to reveal a blue gully straight out of a fairytale. Moss carpeted the land nearest the water, and large boulders surrounded its edge. An immense waterfall made of piled stones cascaded into the far end of the pool.

"Wow," I breathed out.

"It's amazing isn't it?" a voice said from directly beside me.

I jumped in surprise.

Lila was standing beside me.

I furrowed my brows and looked behind her. "Where'd Brad go?"

She shrugged. "No telling. I just heard you coming."

"I thought you went looking for Parker and Alexa?"

"I did."

I waited for her to say more, but she didn't. "Okay, then…" I said awkwardly.

"Oh, you brought Nallah!" Lila exclaimed.

Nallah ignored my stare, showing her betrayal, and bounded over to her.

Lila laughed and hugged her neck. "She's such a friendly cat. You did so well raising her."

"Yeah, well, she hasn't always been this agreeable."

"Oh, no." Lila looked up to me. "I've seen what she thinks. She's not really all that aggressive by nature. The main thought she keeps playing in her head is you."

"You mean I make her aggressive?"

"Not on purpose, no, but she can sense when you're uncomfortable, and that's when she gets defensive. Naturally, she sees you as her cub."

"*Her* cub?" I laughed. "I was the one who raised her."

Lila giggled. "That's not the way she remembers it."

Lila stood and dusted her hands on her pants. "I'll let you get to your bath now." She began walking away. "Oh, wait." She paused by the thicket "We usually use our own bath stuff, but you can use some of mine. It's in the yellow tub." She turned to leave but stopped one more time. "Oh, about your clothes…"

I looked down at my bloody, sweat-hardened garments and realized there was no fixing them. "I'll just go get some of Alexa's old stuff and leave them on the other side of the door."

"Door?"

"Oh, that's what we call the thicket." She patted the wall of brush and said, "See, it's all connected to this vine. Parker made it swing open. Pretty cool, huh?"

I looked at the invention, impressed. "Yeah, I would have never thought of that."

She smiled. "Yeah, Parker has his moments of genius. But anyways, I'll leave the clothes on the other side of it. No one will bother you as long as it's closed."

She left and Nallah watched her go with sad eyes.

"Traitor," I muttered.

I stared at the water for a few moments. Nallah didn't share my hesitation; she ran past me, and leaped into the water. The splashing from her jump soaked me straight through.

"I guess it doesn't matter now," I said dryly, and took off my clothes. I forced myself to take off my knives last. It was only when their leather pouches were sitting on one of the few dry rocks that I felt truly bare.

Nallah looked up at me from one of the rocks and tilted her head.

I covered my chest with my arms and crossed my legs awkwardly. "Excuse you."

I dipped my toe into the gully and shivered. This water was colder than the river at home.

I scolded myself for being such a baby, took a deep breath, and then dove in. I sank to the bottom and sat cross-legged on the pond's bed. The mossy floor pressed against my bare thighs. My hair floated around my face like black seaweed.

I opened my eyes to the world underneath the surface of the gully. The water was a brilliant aquamarine with slivers of sunlight piercing through. I looked up and saw Nallah's chest as she broke the surface with her clumsy paddling.

I lazily kicked my way to the top and silently broke the surface. I would have called to Nallah then and ended her search for me, but I fell silent at the sound of boots on stone.

Then I saw him.

Parker was undressing on the side of the gully. I didn't know what to do. If I called out, he would know I'd been watching him undress, but if I said nothing, I would probably end up seeing more of Parker than either of us ever intended. I ducked behind one of the boulders and watched him pull his shirt from his sticky limbs.

He had strong shoulders and a well-defined torso. His skin, like his face, was a little red from sun exposure, and he had soft, brown freckles across his shoulder blades. Around his neck he wore a cross pendant hanging from a thin gold chain.

With the sunshine lingering in his hair, I saw all the different colors. Before I thought it was a single shade of brown, but now I could make out the lighter shades, like the faint strands of caramel and the few pieces of gold. His eyes sparkled too. They were so light, lighter than the gully, even. I had never seen someone with such dark skin and hair with such wonderful eyes. It was then that I finally *saw* him. He was truly the most beautiful person I had ever seen.

Nallah had finally seen him too. I sensed the tension in her limbs; she was about to growl. I ducked under the water and swam to her, praying Parker wouldn't hear me when I resurfaced. I came up directly behind her and froze. Nothing.

I sighed, sending up silent thanks. I rested my palm on her furry backside. She hesitated, looking back at me, but the desperation in my eyes silenced her.

"Hey, Rose, I'm going to leave the clothes out here, okay?" Lila called to me, blowing my cover.

I closed my eyes and laid my forehead against the moist rock before me. If I heard her from here, there was no chance that Parker hadn't.

"All right, Rosie," he said. "I see your knives now. You can come out. I know you're here."

"I'm, uh, naked."

I peeked around the rock and saw Parker looking at my crumpled pile of clothes.

He scratched the back of his neck and uncomfortably shifted his weight, "Uhh...I brought this towel for me, but you can use it if you want."

I rolled my eyes. "Look the other way. I'm sorry, but no peep show tonight."

He chuckled and closed his eyes. I paused, watching to see if he would peek, and then hastily ran and grabbed the towel from him. I wrapped it around me tightly and then reached for my clothes to make a quick escape.

"Rose, please don't go yet." I turned to scold him for peeking, but he wasn't.

"You heard my steps."

"I made the door myself." He grinned. "I know the sound it makes when it opens."

"Oh."

"Can we talk?"

"Can I, um, at least put some clothes on first?"

His gave me a lopsided smile that made my stomach jump. "If you must."

Alexa's clothes fit relatively well. I had the strange feeling though, that no matter how well they fit, she would not enjoy my wearing them.

"All right," I said and sat on one of the rocks. I set to lacing my knee-high boots. "I'm decent."

He turned to face me, and his breath caught in his throat. I pretended to be absorbed in the lacing of my boots, hiding my embarrassment. There were times where even I got overwhelmed by the sight of me, but it didn't make it any less awkward when it happened to someone else.

"I'm sorry," he said, digging his hands into his pockets.

I tried not to focus on the flexing of his arm muscles, but that pretty much failed.

"You take some getting used to."

"Maybe I should just wear a bag over my head so I won't be so appealing."

"It'd have to cover your whole body for that to work." He laughed uncomfortably, but it died in his throat when he saw I wasn't amused.

"Yeah." I walked past him to get my knives.

He sighed and dropped all attempts at banter. "All right, tell me what to do."

"Whatever do you mean?" I said.

"Look, can you drop the attitude and talk to me for real for a half a second?"

I crossed my arms and sat on a rock, facing him. "Fine. Tell me what you want to say then."

"First, I get that you're pissed off because I kissed you." His expression changed. "No, you know what? I don't get it. Why in the world would you be pissed about that?"

"I don't know."

"How can you not know? It's just a kiss, Rose—"

"Parker," I said and stood, hooking the knives around my waist. "Let's not do this now."

"Then when, Rose?"

"Honestly, I'd be perfect with never."

"Of course you would," he said flatly. "But no, we will talk about this now."

He grabbed my wrist, and I looked down at it. The heat his skin brought against mine made my heart beat faster. I hated that he could do that to me so easily.

"You have about four seconds to get off my case." I yanked my hand away from him. "And stop touching me."

"Or what, Rosie—you going to beat me up?"

"Parker, seriously. I'm not in the mood."

"You seemed to be in the mood when you were talking to Brad."

"Oh my gosh. You're jealous."

He was taken aback, embarrassed. "I never said that. I just—"

I laughed. "No, you're jealous that I gave Brad attention earlier. Admit it," I said, poking his bare chest.

He didn't step away. "You would like to hear that, wouldn't you?"

I shook my head and said, "Probably more than Alexa."

He stepped back then and sat on the rock. "You two should really consider being more civil. We are a team."

I shrugged. "I'll let you be jealous of Brad if you let me hate Alexa. Fair trade."

He held my gaze for a second before he faltered, a smile breaking through. "You drive a hard bargain...Would it be petty of me to ask what Brad and you did?"

"Probably."

"Never mind, then."

I laughed and then said, "We just talked. No big deal."

"About what?"

"Stuff."

"Stuff like?"

"Like...the fact that my face doesn't do anything to you. It doesn't make you crazy."

He laughed and said, "A lot of things about you make me crazy, but your face isn't one of them."

I bit my bottom lip and hesitated, unsure if I should ask him what I was thinking.

"Say what you want, Rosie. I can tell you're holding something back."

I said, "Why did you kiss me if it wasn't because of my face?"

"Why do you think?"

I sighed. "Parker, you can't have feelings for me."

"Why?"

"Because."

"Why would that be so bad, Rose? Would it really be the worst thing for someone to care about you?"

"Yes." My palms sweated, and my face was hot.

"But why?"

"I don't want to talk about it." My mouth was dry.

"Rose, talk to me, please."

"No."

He was getting frustrated. "I just don't understand why you can't let me in long enough to understand *why* you won't let me in. I'm not asking for a lot, Rosie, just some answers."

"No, you're right," I said. "You at least deserve that."

"Well?"

It took me a second to find my voice. When I did, it was small. "Everyone who cares for me dies, Parker."

He deflated. "What?"

I looked away, uncomfortable, and swallowed again. "It's not safe. People die when they get close to me."

"What? Who are you talking about?" His warm hand closed over my shoulder, but I shrugged him off, crossing my arms.

"It doesn't matter now. They're gone."

"Talk to me, Rose," he said quietly.

I shook my head. I had to get away from him, away from his perfection before I could really become unglued. I took off as fast as I could run, away from him. The forest blurred past me.

Alexa stepped in my way right as I entered the camp. "First you steal my boyfriend, and now you think you can take my clothes?"

"Alexa, move," I said through clenched teeth.

Parker ran into the clearing, shirtless, calling after me.

A fire burned deep in Alexa's eyes as she looked at him and then back at me.

Her eyes enlarged to the size of my fists.

Behind me Parker said, "Alexa, don't—"

But her hand came hard across my face before he could finish.

I laughed, shaking my head and touching the cheek she'd hit.

"What's so funny?" she asked, bitingly.

"Oh, I was just picturing the look on your face after I do this."
I slammed my fist into her jaw and pulled my knife as I pinned
her to the ground.

She struggled underneath me, but the fat of my blade was
pressed to her neck. Parker jerked me away, and Brad rushed
to Alexa.

"Geez." Brad helped her stand. "I've never seen anyone move
that fast."

I shrugged Parker off me and stalked away. Nallah just then
emerged from the clearing and fell in step beside me. I kicked in
the door to the first cabin I saw and slammed it shut behind me.
I paced, and then kicked the small dresser in the corner. I sunk
into the thin mattress and dug my hands into my eyes. There was
a small tap at the door. Then it slid open just enough for Lila to
peek inside.

"Are you all right?"

Nallah pushed the door open and squeezed beside Lila's legs
into the room. Lila came to sit by me. A coolness kissed my spine,
and I exhaled, letting her relax me.

"I've been better." I grimaced.

"I've got a feeling Alexa isn't really the problem."

"Of course she's the problem," I bit, but Lila's unwavering
stare made me sigh. I ran my hands through my hair and said,
"Okay, she is *a* problem, but yeah. She's not really the main issue."

"Is it what Parker said to you?"

"I guess I shouldn't really be surprised that you already know
about that."

She shrugged. "Hey, there're really no secrets with us."

"I just…don't know what to think. I hardly know him, yet—"

"You feel something." She smiled.

"I don't know what I feel." I sighed and ran my hands through
my hair.

"Things are different for us, Rose. Time isn't a factor in how
we form relationships."

"I don't believe that."

She paused. When she finally spoke it wasn't like she was talking to me; she was in her memories, her awareness distant. "I was five when Brad and Parker found me. I was comatose in a children's psychiatric ward in Pensacola. I had been placed there after my parents died, because I was 'unresponsive.'" She turned to look at me. "You know, I don't just feel the emotions of the people around me, I *become* them.

"I sat there as they were dying, bleeding to death from those gunshots, and I became every ounce of fear in them. The fear of death is the worst feeling a person can experience. It consumes every ounce of their mind and rages within them like a caged animal... It took me nearly a year to come back from being that fear. I was lost to it until Parker and Brad found me."

She said, "I don't know your story like Brad and Parker do. I never asked. But I do know that the kids here, even Alexa, know you better than anyone ever will. We all have shadows in our pasts, and we all share the same future.

"We are in the middle of a war, and all we have is each other. Stop worrying about what makes sense and what is possible, because it doesn't matter. The only thing that matters is that you have us—all of us—even if it doesn't make 'logical' sense."

A silence passed over us, and I said softly, "I'm sorry about your parents."

She shrugged. "Every one of us here is an orphan."

I sighed heavily, rubbing my eyes. "Why couldn't Parker just like someone else?"

She laughed. "Well it's only half his fault. The other half you can blame on Brad. He's never been good about keeping what he sees to himself."

"His visions?"

"Yeah, I won't get too into it—"

"No, please." I wanted to hear.

She paused and then said, "Brad has been having visions about you since the day we started looking, nearly three years ago. It started out with him telling us all about the beautiful girl with violet eyes, but it became so much more to Parker.

"He's the leader, and a lot of the time I feel his loneliness even when he's with us. He's always felt he has to protect us, but with you, it wasn't like that.

"Brad told him everything about you. He got to see you just as a person and not as someone he was responsible for. He couldn't understand you. You made no sense. You did things like refusing to live amongst people yet counting every day you were away from them and going to extreme measures to never have to see your own face despite being so beautiful. You were a puzzle he couldn't figure out, so he made Brad tell him more and more until somewhere along the way, he fell for you. In Parker's mind, he's known you for three years."

I sat quietly, drowning in my own thoughts. Parker knew so much about me, so much more than I knew about him. I wanted to feel angry, angry that he had spied on me for so long and learned so much about me without my even knowing he existed...and I did, but I felt something else, too. Something that told me I couldn't put off the truth any longer and hide behind the plague of my Gift—someone had feelings for me based on me as a person.

"There's another reason why Parker feels the way he does."

"Hmm?" I looked back at her, my eyes refocusing.

"It's the same reason why you're sitting here talking to me as if you've known me forever. There is a preset plan for us all, Rose," she said and stood from the small bed. "Not even Brad knows it completely. The truth is that we all play our own part in this master scheme, and no matter what we do, our part has already been decided for us.

"We were all fated to come together, and so we did. We are all fated to band together and fight this Infestation, and so even now, in the beginning, we feel the pull of our future friendships. We may not come out alive on the other side, but whatever happens, it's already set. We can't change it."

I didn't know what to say, so she left me with an unnerving chill glued to my skin. There was something about Lila. She spoke as if she knew what she was saying beyond a doubt and that she accepted it with an unwavering clarity.

I turned to Nallah and saw how worked up she'd become. She was responding to my own anxiety, pacing in front of the cot. I sighed, grabbed the spot between my eyebrows, and shut my eyes. I couldn't ever remember being this tired. I lay back against the wall and brought my knees to my chest. Nallah sniffed the bed cautiously, but I ignored her, knowing she would settle in a moment. I closed my eyes, inhaled, and ran my hands through my hair.

Was it possible that I was not here by accident? That I was destined to see that thing hatch from that woman and then, in fright, follow Parker all the way to the Smokies so I'd end up in this very spot? My head spun.

The wear of the four-day journey lingered in every inch of my body. I relaxed and let my mind wander. I saw the woman's face from the van just before she was ripped in half; the memory played on repeat behind my lids.

CHAPTER FIVE

My parents had never been late picking me up from school before. I shrugged my pink jacket off and slung it over the back of the recliner. I looked around and wondered where everyone was. Our living room looked normal enough. The blue couch was still in its honorary spot—directly in front of our small television that only picked up three channels. The potted plant in the corner drooped, dying. Mom never could keep plants alive; I was too much of a distraction.

"Bruce," my father said from somewhere down the hall.

That was odd; my father golfed on Mondays. I crept up the hall toward the voice. The door to my little brother's room was cracked open just enough for a sliver of light to spill into the hall. I pressed my eyes to the crack to peek in.

I could see Bruce sitting in the middle of the floor, looking uncomfortably down at his hands. My mother paced in and out of view, while my father leaned against the powder-blue walls. His head hit just under the train border Bruce refused to be let taken down despite being too old.

Bruce wasn't like me. According to the doctors, Bruce had severe autism. They said he'd never be as functional as the rest of the population—that he would be slow to understand. I knew they were wrong, though, because I knew Bruce. He wasn't stupid; he just thought differently. Bruce was the only person who actually listened to what I had to say. That was why I loved him the most.

"Bruce, what did we tell you about being with Rose?" said my mother.

Bruce looked to the floor and mumbled too quietly for me to hear.

"We told you to stay away from her," my father said.

I shook my head, angry with myself. It wasn't unusual for my parents to act like that. My face was like a drug; when people got used to seeing it, it became a fix they couldn't be without. I'd known I'd been ignoring my parents lately to spend time with Bruce, but it was just so tiring being around them. Being with Bruce was easy, and I didn't have to think.

My father spoke. "I don't care what you want, Bruce. We talked about this."

"Your sister is special. She deserves to be shared with everyone. It's not fair for her to spend all her time with you, now is it?" My mother spoke down at him.

"Rose is my friend, though." He looked to the corner of the room.

My father sighed. "Fine, Bruce, you leave me no choice."

Everything happened so fast. My father lowered to his knees in front of Bruce, and I thought he was going to hug him. He didn't, though. I heard my brother gasp.

My father pulled back, a bloody red knife in his hand, and said, "It had to be this way."

I threw the door open and ran at them. My father and mother looked up. They smiled stupidly, and my father dropped the knife.

"Don't worry, pumpkin," my mother said. "Everything will be fine in a moment."

Bruce whimpered behind them, his skin going white. He looked down at the blood seeping through his shirt and began to cry. I panicked. I jumped forward and grabbed my mother by the shoulder, pulling her away from him. I flung her back and then kicked my father out of the way when he stepped toward me. I dropped to my knees beside Bruce and cradled him in my lap.

He looked up at me, his breathing gurgled and heavy. They'd punctured his lung. I stroked his blond hair from his face and cried.

He smiled up at me, and managed to touch my face. His bloody fingerprints burned my skin and mixed with my tears. I felt his small heart stop beating and watched as his green eyes closed for the last time. I wailed and rocked him in my arms. Something warm dripped on my shoulder. I looked up and had to push Bruce from me so I wouldn't vomit on him.

Blood dripped from the ceiling and was spattered on the walls. My mother's body was impaled on Bruce's bed frame. My father was worse. I kicked him so hard, his ribs collapsed, leaving his chest shrunken and deformed. How could I have not noticed how badly I hurt them? I didn't know I was capable of this.

I stood with blood dripping from my fingers and retched again. I couldn't cry for my parents, though. Crying meant feeling, and if I felt anything more at that moment, I would have lost control. I stood up and forced myself to breathe. My parents killed Bruce because of my face, and so I killed them. I killed them with my bare hands.

⸻

I opened my eyes, and my heart was racing. Nallah slept beside me. I shook my head, breathing out. I needed air; the flashback had been too real. I walked to the gully and climbed the tallest rock and lay down.

"Hey."

I jumped, startled. Parker appeared next to me.

"It was almost a perfect night," I mumbled.

"I'll go if you want me to."

"No," I said, and he lay beside me. "I'm almost glad for the company."

"I'm surprised you're still here. I was sure you would leave after Alexa hit you."

I smiled. "It would take more than that."

"Well, you also had a serious talk with Lila, which could freak anyone out." He laughed. Then he fell quiet, and all we heard was the gurgle of water. Then he said, "Why are you still here, Rosie?"

I rolled to my side and looked at him. "This is where I need to be, I guess. And I don't want to leave yet."

"You feel it, don't you? This bond? It makes it so easy for all of us to connect."

"Well, maybe not Alexa."

"Yeah, maybe not Alexa." He grinned. "But you feel what I'm talking about. It's that way for all of us."

"The way Lila worded it—"

"You're not going to understand what she said, Rose."

"Why not?"

"Lila isn't all…human."

"None of us are."

"Well, Lila isn't like the rest of us. She's not some twelve-year-old kid, even with her Gifts."

"I noticed."

"She knows more about all of this than even Brad. Sometimes I think she knows how this will all end up, and she just isn't telling us."

"She told me that our paths are already decided, that there's nothing we will do that hasn't already been planned. We just don't know any of it. It's scary."

"She likes you." He smiled. "Lila doesn't usually talk to any of us about serious things. It's a good thing, I think."

I agreed. We didn't want to know everything she knew. "She… she also mentioned something about us."

"I'm not going to lie to you, Rose, so be sure whatever you ask me next, you really want to know the answer."

"As stupid as it sounds, I just need you to promise that you won't fall in love with me."

"I can't do that."

"Parker. I'm not a good person to care about."

He snorted. "That's all right. I like my women with a little fire in them."

"I'm serious."

"Look, it's dangerous to lead a group of teenagers with superpowers too, and you don't see me throwing in this towel."

I lay silently beside him for what seemed like a long time. Our breaths were the only sound other than the water.

I finally whispered, "If you won't promise me that, will you at least promise that you won't treat me any differently than you treat the others? It's my one rule."

"You are the only woman I have ever met who wants to be treated average."

I swallowed and said quietly, "Maybe that's because all I've ever wanted to be was average."

Parker looked at me and reached for my hand. I let him take it.

⊰•❧•⊱

A knock at the door woke me. Nallah growled and dug her head into my side.

"Please don't be naked," Brad said, opening the door. A flood of light blinded me.

"What the hell do you want?"

"Hmm, I thought you'd at least look a little worse when you first woke up. Guess not."

"Brad, get to the point, or I will sick Nallah on you."

He looked at my pet that lay sacked out, dominating most of the small bed. "Yeeeeah, I'm real scared."

I gave him a flat look.

"All right, I came to wake you up."

"I figured as much. Why?"

"Why? Because today you start your training!"

He shut the door behind him, and I dug my face into my pillow and groaned. Nallah yawned beside me.

I stood up and stretched. "I don't wanna hear it. You weren't the one up until three last night."

I slid on a pair of shorts and a faded sweatshirt that was about two sizes too big. I opened the door and shielded my eyes from the light. Birds chirped and, on the other side of camp, Lila laughed.

"Rise and shine, sleeping beauty!" Parker called from the cook fire.

I smiled and smelled something delicious. "Where in the world did y'all get bacon?"

"Deer." Brad said, biting into a sandwich.

"You can't get bacon out of a deer, can you?"

He shrugged. "You can get it out of a turkey."

"So, how'd you sleep?" Lila smiled and motioned for me to sit by her.

"Okay, considering, I guess." I took the plate Brad passed me.

"Yeah, I would have troubles sleeping at night too, if I were you." Alexa didn't look at me, but I could see where I bruised her jaw.

"How's your face healing?" I grinned, and she snarled.

"Oh, you two stop it." Lila bit into a piece of bread. "It's too early for me to try to focus on mellowing y'all out."

"White bread? Where did y'all get this stuff?"

"Places," Brad said through a mouthful of food.

"Places…"

"You know. Here and there."

"We go to grocery stores," Alexa said, giving Brad a weird look.

"In the middle of the Smokies? It would take you a week to get to some place that sells it and to get back. The food would have spoiled by then."

"Nah. There's a small town about a mile away from here. We walk to it on Saturdays."

I turned and glared at Parker. "So much for no other human contact."

"Oh come on, Rose." Brad laughed. "People aren't so bad."

"You haven't been around them when I was there," I muttered.

I gave the second half of my breakfast to Nallah. She sniffed it and then swallowed it in one gulp.

"Ya ready?" Lila stood from the table, stacking her plate among the others in the center.

I wiped my mouth on the edge of my sleeve and piled my plate with the others. "To train?"

"Come on! I have seen grass grow faster than y'all move." Parker stood, crossing his arms at the opening of the trail.

Lila and I walked over to him, but Brad waited on Alexa. He held his arm out for her to take, but she walked past him.

"Let's get this over with. I think it's time someone showed the new girl how it's done," Alexa said.

"Well, we all know it won't be you. I already won that fight."

"Ohhh, burn!" Brad burst out laughing but swallowed when Alexa shot him a glare.

"All right, all right, all right. Children," Parker said, "we are going to the sparring grounds now, but everyone has to be on their best behavior, or I swear, I will turn this group around."

Everyone laughed but Alexa.

We passed the gully and kept walking until we came to a large circular clearing with three archer's targets spaced evenly around the edge. In the center there was an area boxed in with faded wood that smelled faintly like old maple. Also, near the left side, there was a cupboard, holding the weapons and a small oak table with an empty bowl atop it. The ground was sandy, giving a little under my boots and working the muscles in my legs as I walked. No wonder they all stayed in shape. Even the ground was a work out.

Lila picked up the large bowl, and then passed me, going back the way we came.

Parker said, "It's her turn to get the water for us."

I watched Nallah stare after her with disappointment.

I sighed. "Fine, go."

She hesitated, looking back at me, and then bounded off after her.

I turned to face the group again but everyone had dispersed. Alexa and Parker were unlocking the cupboard, and Brad stood in the middle of the center square, motioning for me to join him.

"I'm glad I finally get someone to train with. It's been basically me beating up trees for a while."

I laughed, and Parker looked over at me. "Why didn't you just train with Parker?"

"He likes to throw things."

"Like rocks?"

"Nah, he's been working with knives since he mastered hand-to-hand. Though he has thrown rocks before," Brad said. "Actually, he threw a rock at me like a week ago. I think it left a bruise." He turned awkwardly to show me the back of his arm.

"What about Alexa?"

"Arrows." He pointed over to Alexa, who lazily aimed and fired a perfect bull's eye.

"Can she fight hand-to-hand as well as she shoots?"

"She beat me." Brad smiled. "But you're going to beat me too."

"If you think you're psyching me out, you're wrong."

He winked. "I've already seen this fight, and believe me, you don't make many mistakes."

"Then why fight me in the first place?"

"Because it helps me to get better. I remember how to move correctly if I get a bruise in the process. And hey, maybe I'll teach something to you?"

I laughed again. "Like what?"

Brad moved so fast I couldn't see him and kicked me in the side. The air escaped my lungs, and I flew sideways, toppling over the edge of the wooden barrier.

"First, don't ever let your opponent take you by surprise, and second, leaving the square is forfeit."

I pulled myself up and walked, hyperaware of the throbbing in my side, back to where we began.

"Are you ready?" He didn't wait for an answer before he kicked me.

I caught his ankle and slammed him into the ground. He jumped back up without even a grimace of pain. He was strong.

"You're pretty good. But I'm better."

I saw his openings—his neck, the soft part of his nose, the temple—but I was going to fight fair, so I left the death blows out.

I got him hard in the side with a roundhouse kick, and he doubled over. I didn't hesitate. I kicked the backs of his knees, and he fell forward, his face hitting the wood border of the square. I held him down by pressing my knee between his shoulder blades and pulled his head back by his hair.

He struggled and then laughed. "I yield."

I smiled and collapsed next to him on the ground, breathing heavily. Sweat poured down my body inside the sweatshirt. It was too hard to breathe with it on, so I took it off. I balled it up and collapsed against the dirt again.

"I don't understand," He said between gasps.

"I told you I would win."

"No, I knew that would happen. What I don't get is why you waited to take your shirt off until *after* we wrestled."

I threw the jacket at him and it hit him in the face, making me laugh.

He cradled his nose. "Ah!"

"Here, let me look at it."

He hesitated, and then sat straight when I came closer.

I looked at his nose, already bruising, and sighed. "I'm sorry about this. Do you want me to set it?"

"Yeah, go ahead. It's not the first time this has happened."

I looked at him sympathetically. I'd broken my nose once when I fell from a tree. Of course, mine never swelled or bruised, but it had hurt like hell.

"All right. One, two—" I didn't wait for three before I snapped the bone back in place.

He winced, pulling his head from my hands, and grabbing at his nose. Blood dripped from his fingers, but he smiled through watery eyes. "Well, that's a great start to the day."

"Rose's gift evolved," Lila said, reentering the area, carrying the sloshing bowl of water. She rested it on the table and dusted her hands off on her pants.

"Huh?" I asked.

Lila pointed at my side, "Brad clipped you there, enough to break the skin, and you're not even bruised. You healed yourself."

I grabbed at my side and realized she was right. My jaw dropped. I'd never been invulnerable to bleeding.

Parker walked over, his eyes wide, looking at my exposed side. "That's amazing."

"Great, so it looks like she beat me to a pulp and I just stood there," Brad complained.

"What's it matter? It's not like you were going to beat her in the first place. Who cares if you left a mark?" Parker joked, shoving Brad playfully, but Brad winced and grabbed his nose.

"Hey, take it easy with the touching." He gingerly touched his nose. It was already turning purple.

"Maybe you should go ice that thing." Parker grimaced.

Brad waved his arm dismissively and left.

Parker glanced back over at my abdomen, and I felt very self-conscious in only the sports bra. I cleared my throat and slipped the sweatshirt back over my head.

Alexa called as she shot a perfect bull's eye, "You took your clothes off the first time he singled you out?"

"No, I took off *your* clothes." I smiled, and Lila giggled.

Alexa rolled her eyes and pretended to be absorbed in her archery. I turned back toward Parker and saw him giving me a look.

"Oh please." I snorted. "She deserved that one."

The sun passed overhead, and the hours trickled by slowly. Brad eventually came back, but Parker was right. One look at his nose, and I knew he wouldn't be fighting anytime soon. I really was sorry I'd broken it.

With my sparring partner gone, I filled my time with observing Parker. I wanted some kind of knowledge about him to try to even out all he knew about me. He behaved differently with each person but, at the same time, always stayed himself. He never lost his composure, and he managed to keep smiling even when Alexa tried to get a rise out of him.

It didn't take me long to understand why he was the one who led them. Parker was just the kind of person that was born to lead. He saw everyone's strengths and applauded them while still being aware of weaknesses and encouraging improvement. He was the perfect blend of friend and mentor, even to Brad, who was a whole year older than him.

By sunset, everyone was covered in a hearty mixture of sweat, dirt—and with the exception of me and Lila—blood. Parker was nursing a bruised jaw from Alexa kicking him in the face, but she hadn't escaped from their spar unmarked. She favored her ankle when we walked back to camp.

"Hey there." Parker sat down beside me on our rock by the gully.

"Is this going to become a nightly thing for us?"

"Well, to be fair, I was here first."

It was chilly out, and I'd forgotten a jacket again. I shivered.

"Would you say it was breaking my promise to you if I told you that you look beautiful tonight?"

I snorted. I was wearing one of Brad's old t-shirts that said something about monster trucks and a pair of Alexa's oversized pants. "I know this outfit is every man's idea of sexy, but yes, that's against the rule."

He chuckled. "Just checking… You did really well today, by the way."

I turned and looked at his face in the moonlight. He was beautiful even with a ripening bruise on his jaw. I reached out and touched it, the skin of my fingers meeting the stubble on his chin. He stopped talking, and our eyes locked. He placed his hand over mine and leaned into my hand.

I jerked and pulled away. I looked down at my knees, but I could still feel him watching me. When I looked up, he leaned in and cupped my face. I held my breath and he kissed me.

"That was definitely breaking the rule," I said, but I was smiling.

"I won't tell."

"I still mean what I said. Tell me you're still going to follow the rule."

"I cross my heart and all that jazz." He smiled.

"Good, because—" A wave of nausea rolled into my stomach, and I gasped. I gripped my torso, and my eyesight shook. I recognized the sickness, and I was afraid. I didn't want to look up. I didn't want to see, but I had to. I lifted my head and froze at what I saw staring at me from the other side of the gully.

There, standing behind a tree on the outer edge, was a barefoot man.

CHAPTER SIX

The world slowed, and all my attention focused on him. He was tall, over six feet, and also gangly. His arms and legs were pale and skinny. He smiled and then leapt with a speed he shouldn't have possessed. I ran, my instincts taking over, and jumped, crashing into him.

We hit the ground and rolled, separating through the brush. He was back to his feet faster than I was and was at me again before I could stand. He dove on top of me, his hands finding my neck. It felt like iron rings closed around my airway, and no matter how hard I punched, his grip never faltered. It didn't make sense. I never struggled when I fought; I never came close to losing.

Parker rammed into him like a train, pushing him from me. They rolled, the barefooted man struggling to get a good a grip. Parker flickered in and out of vision as they wrestled, preventing the man from getting the upper hand.

I stumbled to my feet while they grappled like wild dogs, and caught my breath. I watched the fight and realized Parker wasn't going to win. The barefooted man was too fast. I had to do something.

I whistled and grabbed the barefoot man's attention.

I jumped forward so quickly I knew I was a blur. I crossed my knives like scissors, and when our bodies met, I sliced through him like he was made of paper. He collapsed with my knee digging into his abdomen. I'd pierced his lungs. He had less than three minutes to live.

Parker appeared beside me.

The man's eyes were fading, but he still gave me a bloody smile. "It seems you have bested me." He laughed when I jumped. "Oh, yes, we can speak when unhatched."

"Unhatched? What are you?"

"I am the beginning of the end, for you," he said, smiling.

"Why are you here? How did you find us?" Parker demanded.

"We've always known where you hide, but Rose is what we waited for."

My stomach dropped. They had come because of me. "Why do you want me? I'm nothing to you."

"Oh, but you are everything to us."

"Who is us?" I asked.

His head lolled to the side.

"Oh no, you don't. You don't get to die yet." I thrust the blades farther up, shocking him.

"Beware, girl." The light in his eyes flickered. "It's almost time."

"The time for what?" I lifted him by the collar of his matted brown t-shirt.

"We're coming for you." He smiled, and his eyes closed.

I screamed and shook him, but he was gone. I stared down at him, at the blood and at his face. Everything fell to silence.

"Rosie." Parker touched my shoulder.

I shrugged away. "Come on." I pulled my knives from his chest and stood. "It's time we tell the others."

"Holy hell." Brad stepped from his cabin in a pair of boxers decorated with cowboys. He gaped at my bloody clothes. "What happened to you?"

As the rest of the group emerged from their cabins, I sat on the table twiddling my thumbnail with the tip of the blade that had just ended a man's life. Nallah sat by my feet and snuck whiffs of the blood on my clothes. I could only imagine how it must smell to her.

"Is everyone here? No one is gone?" Parker was a ball of tension beside me.

"Holy moly, Rose! What the heck happened to you?" Lila said.

"Where was it?" Alexa folded her arms and gave me a hard look.

"Where was what?" Parker asked.

"I know that blood. I can smell it." She looked back at me and said, "Where'd you fight it?"

"At the gully. He appeared while we were talking." I said.

"You knew it was a he? It was still unhatched, then. They only look like humans before they hatch, then they look like the giant bugs you saw before," Alexa said.

"How'd you know about them staying unhatched? Even I didn't know they could do that." Parker said, looking at Alexa skeptically.

"Parker, believe it or not, I did know about the Infestation before you found me. You didn't teach me everything I know about these things. I might not have known why I was killing them until I met you guys, but they still died all the same."

I said, "I spoke to him before he died."

"Him as in the bug, or him as in the host?" Brad asked, leaning against the table.

"Is there a difference?"

Alexa answered me. "The bugs take the soul of the human they're in, feeding off of them and draining them like a parasite. That's why we call humans with bugs inside them 'hosts.' The bugs don't have souls themselves, so that's why they need the hosts—to steal them. They're unhatched when the thing is still in the body. It hasn't subdued the soul yet. Somewhere inside, a human soul still lingers. It's possible for the human soul to talk to you if the thing inside it was dying."

I hardened. Inside the bug I killed was an innocent person. "I spoke to the bug, not the man."

"What'd it say?"

"It said to beware, because more were coming."

Everyone was silent, and for a few, torturous moments, only the crickets were heard.

"Where will we go?" Lila's voice was small.

"Where can we go?" Brad crossed his arms.

I couldn't stand the sadness in their eyes. They hadn't been ready for this, yet I brought it to them. The regret made my chest hurt. I looked away. "We can't stay here."

Parker nodded heavily and said, "We'll leave at dawn."

I turned and walked away with heavy footsteps. Nallah crept beside me, and we disappeared into the woods; I wouldn't have paused even if they had asked me to stay. But they hadn't.

Everyone moved with tired steps and spoke in hushed tones. I doubted any of them got much sleep last night.

Lila placed boxes of food and a few of her shirts into a small backpack. Brad packed and unpacked the same backpack three times because he couldn't fit all his clothes *and* his daggers. Alexa had disappeared into her cabin earlier and hadn't returned since. Parker was the only one already packed, and his was the only bag not bursting at its seams.

"You're not taking anything?" Alexa asked, stepping from her cabin.

I shook my head. "I've got nothing to take, but I volunteered to carry the weapons. Parker said he wanted to pack them himself, but I think he just wanted some time alone to say good-bye to the place."

She shrugged. "This is home."

"I'm sorry, Alexa."

"You don't have to be sorry. It's not your fault. We should have been ready, and we weren't. It's that simple."

"You're being nice."

She ran her hands through her thick mane and said, "Look, I don't like you, and you don't like me, and that's okay. But that doesn't matter now. A lot of stuff is about to happen. We're really in it now. The war is starting. That also means I can't ignore the fact that you can *actually* fight.

"The others"—she hesitated—"aren't as experienced with it as we are… They haven't killed. They could hesitate, even Parker. Basically, if it comes down to a blood bath, you don't have to worry about finding one of my arrows in your back."

I stared at her, unsure if I'd actually heard *her* say what I thought she did.

She glared at me and said defensively, "What? You think I can't be sensible?"

"It's just… Thank you, Alexa."

She wiped her hands on her pants and moved away from me. "That being said, you're now a part of this, so don't even think about running."

"All right." Parker walked into the camp, lugging an athletic bag. "Is everyone ready?"

Brad finally zipped his bag completely and exclaimed, "Yes, it all fit!"

Parker gave him a look, and he cleared his breath and said, "Yeah, I'm good."

"Lila?"

"Yeah, I had some room left over in mine, so I brought some food just in case."

Parker nodded. "And Alexa? You good?"

"Good? No. Packed? Yes," she said.

Parker slung his backpack over his shoulder and smiled at the others. He turned, his eyes meeting mine, and, for a split second, he faltered. That smile was a lie. "So, Rosie, where do you want to go?"

"It doesn't matter. Wherever ya'll want." I picked up the black duffle bag with the weapons. My back screamed in protest, but I hung it across my body anyways. This was going to be a long day.

"The only rule is that you get as far away as fast as you can. In what direction means nothing to me."

"Can I pick?" Lila asked.

Parker grinned. "Sure, squirt. Lead the way."

—————

"You cannot be serious," I said to Parker, looking out over the bustling city.

"This place has a really crowded bus system. We could get all the way to Phoenix without being spotted."

I shook my head and said, "This is crazy."

"No, this is Chattanooga." He smirked.

Alexa walked behind him and rested her hand on his shoulder. "Parker, I think you forgot one teensy little fact. How do you expect to get a tiger onto a bus?"

Parker looked from Nallah to me, but my glare stopped him from asking the obvious. His shoulders deflated, and he said, "Well, then I'm out of ideas."

"Why don't we just stay in town tonight and figure it out?"

Everyone turned to Brad.

Lila giggled and reached up to touch his forehead. "Did the sun get to you?"

He shrugged. "Why not? I mean, we're already here. It wouldn't be that hard to sneak a tiger into some cheap motel. I'm sure the people working there have seen weirder."

"Weirder than a tiger?" Alexa looked at him.

Parker raised his brows. "No, stop. This might work."

"It'd be nice to take an actual shower." Lila smiled, and the others agreed.

"You people have gone mad. How do you expect to pay for a motel room? And what about all the *things* down there that might recognize us?"

"They won't recognize us."

I knew I'd lost when Brad said it. No one doubted the psychic kid.

"The last place they expect to see us is in a big town like Chattanooga. We'll just disappear into the crowds for tonight," Parker offered.

"There's still the matter of the paying for it?"

"That's not a problem." Alexa sat down her backpack and fumbled through it. She pulled out a platinum card. "There should still be some money left on this. I mean, I haven't used it in years, but it's worth a try."

"Come on, Rose." Parker nudged my shoulder. "It's just for one night. We'll find a way out of town tomorrow."

I sighed in defeat. It was my fault they were in this predicament in the first place. The least I could do was let them have one night in town. "Alright."

I dropped my shoulders, and they burst into cheers.

"But let it be known that I do not have a good feeling about this."

CHAPTER SEVEN

"Pssst, Alexa!" I crouched behind some shrubs just outside the small bank. I was covered in dirt and reeked of sweat. Parker, Brad, Nallah, and Lila watched me through the trees behind the parking lot. Alexa had gone around the corner of the bank to withdraw money nearly twenty minutes ago. I got sick of waiting and volunteered to see what was taking so long.

I swore under my breath, stood from the bushes, and darted around the corner of the building. It was late, but there were still cars zooming down the road. I glanced around as I ran, unnerved by the shadows in the parking lot. Alexa wasn't at the ATM. I was confused until I heard her swearing from around the corner. She was on her knees, clawing at the dirt in the plant bed.

"Alexa, what the hell are you doing?"

She jumped and then snarled. "Digging."

"I can see that. Why?"

"We need money, don't we?"

"Yeah, but the debit card—"

"Look, I can't actually use that, but I have money here. I buried it a while ago."

"Why did you bury money?"

She wiped sweat from her forehead. "Are you going to help me?"

"What?"

"If you don't, I'm going to do it by myself anyways and take twice as long."

"Fine." I dropped to my knees beside her and started scooping dirt. "But seriously, why did you bury this?"

"I was planning to run away for a while, and I knew I needed some cash. I panicked when I got it, though, and buried it, thinking I'd come back for it. I didn't get the chance. Parker found me first."

A car honked in the distance, and I pulled the sweatshirt's hood down closer to my face. "Why did they send *you* to check on me?" She asked.

"They were worried. You've been here like half an hour."

"So they sent you?" She snorted. "What? Did they think the mob you would create would provide enough distraction for me to escape?"

"Fine, I got tired of waiting and ran over here before they could stop me. Happy?"

She opened her mouth to reply, but stopped when I pulled a plastic bag from the hole.

"Aha!"

She grabbed it and pulled out a leather purse, asking, "How much do we need?"

"I dunno. How much do you have?" I looked over her shoulder and gasped. "Holy hell, Alexa. Did you rob this bank?"

She snapped the purse closed. "No. Now, how much do we need?"

"All of it?"

She grabbed the wad of bills from the bag, and then threw it in the shrubs. She jammed the money into her backpack and slung it over her shoulder before looking at me. "What?"

"What kind of kid runs away with thousands of dollars without anyone noticing?"

"Me, obviously," she said, pushing past me. She ran back across the parking lot towards the others.

"What took you so long?" Parker asked, stepping from behind a pine tree.

"I had to wait in line." She zipped her card back into her backpack.

"Why are you covered in dirt, then?" Brad asked as he bit into a bright, red apple.

Lila looked at him sideways. "Brad, where did you get that?"

He shrugged, and took another bite.

Parker shook his head, a dismissive look on his face, and then said, "Alexa, how much do we have to work with?"

"I only had a little more than four hundred left on the card." She shot me a glare that dared me to say otherwise.

"Four hundred?" Brad's eyes shot open. "That's enough for us to stay in one of these places for days!"

I thought I might choke on my own gasp, but Parker stopped him for me. "It is, but we aren't going to. We'll save whatever we don't spend on a room for our getaway. Who knows, maybe we can rent a car or something?"

"You need a license for that. You know? Photo identification? I'm assuming none of you have one," I said.

Brad grinned and dug around in his backpack for a faded plastic card. "I do," he announced proudly.

"Brad, a library card from the fourth grade doesn't count as picture ID," Alexa said.

He took it back defensively. "Well, it has a picture on it."

"All right, focus." Parker took a handful of bills from Alexa, though it was smaller than how much she had.

She was keeping the actual amount from the others, and I could tell by how she avoided my eyes that she knew I was aware of it.

Parker folded the money and put it in his back pocket. "Let's go."

We walked through the trees lining the road until we arrived at a small motel. It was only one floor with ten rooms. The parking lot was deserted and littered with trash. It was dirty but cheap, and that was what we needed.

I stooped behind a dumpster in the parking lot with Nallah by my side, waiting for Parker to give me the all clear. Seconds passed before he turned and waved me towards him.

"All right, big girl, let's go." I stood and looked around me. I took off in a break-neck run for the door. I was at the room almost instantly and went crashing through the doorway.

To my surprise, I ran straight into a lamp. I blinked, and my eyes adjusted to the dim lighting. I had run into a small desk with a lamp on top of it. The lamp hadn't budged.

I burst out laughing. The lamp was actually bolted to the desk. Apparently the staff was worried about someone stealing the horrendous thing.

"Wow, that's so classy." Alexa rolled her eyes and sat heavily on one of the two polyester quilted beds. It squeaked from her weight and then started vibrating. Her eyes widened, and she jumped from it like it was a bed of snakes.

Everyone laughed until tears fell from our eyes.

—⋙•⋘—

We walked across the street to the dimly lit Waffle House. The parking lot was even dirtier than the motel's. All of that was forgotten, though, when slid into a booth in the corner, the smell of browning potatoes making our mouths water.

"I want one of everything," Brad said.

I was almost worried he would eat the menu, but Parker took it from him.

"Well, considering we are on a budget, I'd say stick to the kid's menu," Parker said.

Waffle House booths weren't made to hold five teenage kids. I was pinched up between the glass of the window and Brad. Parker sat across from me with Lila squeezed between him and Alexa.

"Rose, come on, chill out. You're all tensed up." Brad nudged me, and I tried to smile.

I couldn't stop thinking about Nallah, though. I'd never left her alone out in public before. What if something happened? The door to the motel wasn't that strong. What if she got through it?

I looked up from the menu I'd been holding and froze. There was a man sitting in a booth opposite ours. His head hung low, and his eyes were hidden by the green hat he wore over his grey hair, but I knew he had been looking at me. My stomach flipped, and I became nauseous.

"We need to leave," I said to Parker.

He looked up with a mouthful of biscuit and said, "Why?"

"Something's off about that man over there." I motioned to the other booth.

"What man?" Parker looked behind me.

I looked back up, but he was gone. "Where'd he go?"

"Where'd who go? Rose, we're sitting by the door. No one left. I would have seen them."

"I swear there was a man..."

"You're just hungry." Alexa shoved the plate of bread at me. "Eat something so I don't have to hear about your stupid hallucinations." Her expression didn't match what she was saying, though, and I wished I knew what she was thinking.

I didn't press it further. I sat silently as everyone chattered and ate their food.

After everyone was finished, I signaled for the waitress to come back. If the old woman thought it was strange for me to be wearing a guy's sweatshirt and sunglasses at two A.M., she didn't show it.

"What else can I get ya?" Her voice was raspy.

"Can I have a bag of sausage, please?" Her eyebrows rose, but she wrote down the order when she realized I was serious.

"Come up to the counter, and you can pick it up with your check." She waddled back behind the divider that separated the diners from the staff.

"Rose and I can handle the tab if y'all want to wait outside. Maybe look around for that man she thinks she saw?"

Alexa stood and pulled me from my side of the booth.

Parker's eyebrow rose, but Alexa gave him a look that stopped him. He went with the others to the parking lot without question.

Alexa put a hundred dollar bill down on the counter, and the waitress asked, "Is this the smallest bill you have?"

"No, I just thought I'd pay with the largest bill I have because I like to carry excess change."

The waitress looked at her sourly and then disappeared in the back.

"Look, I'm going to the bathroom. Wait here."

"Do you really think we should separate?"

She gave me a weird look. "Chill out. I just want to wash the syrup off my hands."

With Alexa in the bathroom, I was the only one in the restaurant. I walked over to the window and saw Brad eating something but then stopped when something in the reflection caught my eye. Behind me was a bulletin board with newspaper clippings pinned to it.

"Local Heiress Goes Missing. Assumed Dead," one of the headlines read. The article was dated October 28, 2005. A picture of Alexa with shorter hair and a rounder face was in the center.

"Eleven-year-old Angelina Louisa Fernandez, heir to the Fernandez motocross dynasty, went missing yesterday, only a few weeks after her parents' unexpected death. Search efforts are underway, and a reward is being offered for information on her disappearance. Fernandez was last seen leaving her family estate. Bloody clothes found four miles from her home were positively identified. However, a body has not been found. If you have information, please contact the local police department," the article read.

Alexa walked up, wiping her hands on her pants. "They don't even have paper towels, just one of those cheap air-blowing things."

"Who's Angelina Fernandez?" I asked.

She paled, looking past me to the board. She touched the faded paper.

"Did you lie about your name?"

She traced the round jaw in the photograph and said softly, "I'm not the same person I was then. Why keep the same name?"

"Do the others know?"

She shook her head. "I didn't want them to treat me differently. You won't tell them, will you?"

"It's not my secret to tell."

She smiled wearily. The waitress came back, holding a stack of change. She didn't try to hide her disgust when Alexa counted it in front of her and then shoved it in her front pocket. I grabbed the bag of sausage from the counter, and we went outside.

"Well, that took long enough," Brad said.

"They had to find some change."

When we got back to the hotel, I was excited to see Nallah again. I hoped the bag of sausage would make her forgive me for leaving her. I slid the metal key into the lock. The door drifted open. I was hit with a roll of nausea and whispered, "No."

I dropped the bag in my hand and turned on the light. The man from the diner was standing in the middle of the room, covered in blood. I could smell it from the doorway.

I pulled my knives out and leapt over to him. I screamed and stabbed into his chest. I couldn't make myself stop, even after I knew he was dead. The knives dropped from my stiff hands when I finally looked at Nallah. It looked as if she'd been eaten. I cradled her like a child and cried into her. I laid my head back against the cool wall and screamed. My best friend was dead.

Parker was beside me, lifting me from the floor. I didn't want him to touch me. I fought against him, crying and holding onto Nallah. He stopped and said something to the others, but I didn't care. Then he sat beside me on the ground, his hand on my back, and let me cry.

CHAPTER EIGHT

The lights flickered in the small subway car as we passed through another terminal.

We'd chosen a car with only one woman on it, and she left shortly after we arrived. I wouldn't have stayed on a car with five straggly teenagers this late of night either, especially if one of them was covered in blood. It was just us now, sitting solemn faced and straight backed in the cold, metal chairs. The car shook beneath our feet. We came to a stop.

I didn't quite register what was happening. I looked up, dazed, and saw that other people had boarded our car.

It was only now that I saw how tense my group had become. Parker sat beside me, leaning forward awkwardly so his body blocked me from the other people on the car. Lila clutched her knees so hard her knuckles were white. Alexa sat, straight-faced, across from me, and Brad sat tensely beside her. What had I missed?

We hurried off the subway at the next stop and weaved our way through people in the station. Parker had to guide me, because I'd lost the ability to think coherently. It was like my thoughts were short circuiting, stopping all rational ideas from breaking through.

I walked directly into two people before Parker grabbed my arm and said, "Rose, I get that you're upset over Nallah, I do, but get it together. You're acting brainless."

I squinted, squeezing my eyes shut. The dim light in the subway tunnel bore into me like the headlights of a street car. I nodded dumbly and allowed myself to be lugged, useless, like another suitcase. My brain felt like it was oozing from my ears, as if knives had chopped it up and made it so that it would seep from my head like an infection.

"Whererwegoinnm?" My words slurred, and my steps were as wobbly as if I'd had an entire keg of liquor.

"Whoa, Parker." Alexa grabbed my face. "She's really messed up. Look at her pupils."

I tried to stop but bumped into Parker. He held my face still and examined me, his grasp sweaty and cold.

"Someone is going to see her face, and I won't be able to protect her," Parker said.

I tried to say, "No one is going to see my face. Stop worrying." But it came out incoherent.

"What'd she say?"

Parker looked at me skeptically as he spoke over his shoulder to Alexa. "She didn't say anything."

"What do we do?" Brad asked.

Parker let go of my face but grabbed my hand. "We are going to go catch the bus as planned. I don't know what's wrong with her, but whatever it is won't be fixed without sleep. We've caused too much disruption here already."

"But she can't even walk straight."

"Let me worry about her. All of you just follow us. The Greyhound station is just up the block. Come on, stay close. We need to make sure she doesn't make a riot break loose before we get there."

"Sstop fussinovermeh."

"Rosie, shut up."

My feet skidded on the pavement as Parker dragged me. The bright lights of the bus station hit me like an anvil, and my head filled with the murmur of voices.

I covered my ears and groaned.

Parker rubbed my back, pausing. "Tell me what's wrong, Rose."

"E-e-everyoneisssoloud."

"It's quiet out here."

I shook my head in disagreement, but he pulled me forward. Parker opened the door and ushered everyone inside. The voices were louder now. I dug my head into the back of Parker's neck.

"I need five tickets to..." Parker scanned the board behind the teller's head. He turned and looked back at the rest of the group. "Where are we going?"

"Hawaii?" Brad asked, seriously.

Alexa ignored him. "Vegas. It'd be easy to disappear there."

"Let's go to Washington, DC. We could see the White House!" Once again, Brad looked hopeful.

I lolled my head and wiped my mouth on my sleeve. My eyes focused on one thing—Phoenix, Arizona. "Phoenix!" I yelled.

Everyone stop jabbering and look at me.

"What's in Phoenix?"

I shook my head. "Not...important."

"Oh come on..." Alexa whined.

Parker hesitated and examined me. He paused and then pulled the rest of the money from his pockets and slid under the counter. "I need five tickets to Phoenix, Arizona."

The bald man yawned, counting the money. "You're short twenty-five."

"That's all we have left."

"Sorry." The man started to hand it back to Parker.

Parker slammed his fist against the counter and turned back to me. "We can't afford to go to Phoenix. Pick another place."

I shook my head. That wasn't right. We *had* to go to Phoenix. This man was standing in the way of that. The incredible pounding in my head peaked. Hot tears fell from my eyes. I was almost certain the pounding was so loud the others could hear it. I pushed past Parker and met the teller eye-to-eye. His expression went slack, and his eyes widened.

"You are going to give me the tickets to Phoenix. You *want* to give them to me for three hundred and twenty-five dollars. No more and no less."

Speaking to the man somehow dulled my pain. He dumbly slid five yellow tickets out to me. I took them and gave them to Parker.

He stared at me. "How?"

I shrugged, rubbing my temple. The throbbing had gone down drastically, though it was still there. "We need to get on the bus. The station is getting crowded."

Parker was the last on the bus. We slid our way down the aisle to the last few rows of seats. The whole bus smelled of cheap window cleaner and fast food, but it was quiet, which I was grateful for. Parker slid in beside me, pinning me between him and the window. Behind us Brad, Alexa, and Lila sat in the only three-person row.

"Turn around if you can hear me."

"You need something, Lila?" I turned, and Lila jumped, surprised.

"Why would she need something?" Alexa asked, looking at me like I was crazy.

"She told me to turn around if I could hear her?"

"I didn't say that." Lila's eyes zeroed in on me skeptically.

"Oh, um, never mind." I sat back in my seat, but I felt Lila's accusing glare boring into the back of my head.

A few more people boarded the bus, but they all sat near the front. Maybe they didn't want to sit so near to the bathroom, or maybe our ragtag appearance scared them off. The bus began to move, and the parking lot became the open road. I looked down and saw Parker holding my hand. I pulled it from him and saw the worry in his eyes.

"Please stop," I whispered.

"Stop what?"

"Stop *that*, that looking-at-me-like-I'm-going-to-shatter-at-any-moment look. I hate it."

"Your headache scared me."

"It scared me too… It was like my head was splitting open."

"But it's better now?"

I nodded. "After I talked to that teller, it faded. I can still feel it, but it's like white noise."

"I have a theory." He stopped and peeked at the others behind us.

They were all fast asleep. We hadn't even been on the bus twenty minutes.

"What's your theory?"

"When we were on our way to the station, you read my thoughts."

"What?"

"Remember when you told me that no one was going to see your face? That I should stop worrying?" I nodded. "Well, I hadn't said anything about anyone recognizing you. I'd been thinking it, and then you reassured me."

I looked away. It wasn't possible to read thoughts, was it? "You've evolved again." Parker's lips didn't move.

I stared at him in shock before burying my face in my hands. "Oh God. I can read people's minds."

"It's amazing." Parker smiled as he thought it.

"Stop that!" I hit his shoulder. "So not only do people lose their minds when they look at me, but now I can hear their insane ranting too. Great."

"Well, look at the bright side. At least we know why you got the weird headache."

"Yeah. That makes everything better."

"Hey, what if you can control minds too?"

"Mind control?" I snorted. "That's a little too sci-fi, even for me."

"No, just think about it. You told the teller that he wanted to give us those tickets, and he did, just like that."

I paused, remembering the slack look in his eyes when I'd began talking. I bit my lip and swallowed. "Will you do me a favor?"

"No, I will not take my pants off!" He said loudly, and a few people from the front of the bus turned to look back.

I sank lower in the seat, embarrassed, and punched him.

He laughed and rubbed his arm. "All right, sorry. Being serious."

"Will you, you know, not tell the others about this, just for now? I don't want anyone thinking I'm going to be going all mind control on them."

"Cool. Our own dirty little secret."

I ignored him and looked out the window. "Do you think it's possible that the teller just did what I wanted because of my face?"

"I don't think so." Parker stretched and yawned. "I saw the guys on the subway when they looked at you. But that man…he was just empty. Like the only thing in his head at that moment was what you were saying."

"Freaky." I yawned too.

"Get some sleep, Rosie. You look awful."

I smiled widely and kissed his lips. "Thank you."

He laughed. "You are the strangest woman I have ever met."

I smiled and rested my head on his chest. His breathing was deep and steady, and the warmth of his body spread even through his shirt. I sighed, content, and closed my eyes for sleep.

Images of red assaulted me. I could taste the blood, hot and salty on my face, from where I stabbed into the man. Nallah. Nallah was gone. Nallah was dead. I'd brought her death to her. I shuddered, a coldness enveloping me.

Parker squeezed me closer. "It's been a hard day, Rose. Just let me take care of you."

I hesitated, images of Nallah in the back of my mind. I softly kissed his shoulder then pulled away and rested my head against the cold bus window.

I closed my eyes, feeling his disappointment, and whispered, "It's because I care for you that I can't."

"Rose," Parker whispered in my ear, waking me.

I sat up and wiped my eyes; my hand came back wet. I'd been crying in my sleep. Wonderful.

"We're stopping for lunch. I got you some clothes. I didn't realize how stained your stuff was."

Stained? Then I remembered. I was still wearing the clothes covered in Nallah's blood. My chest ached.

I grabbed the clothes from Parker and mumbled, "Thanks." I stumbled over him into the small bathroom.

I latched the door behind me and stripped off the bloody clothes. I numbly pulled my knives still crusted with blood from my waist and dropped them to the floor as if they were white hot. I stood in front of the mirror and barely recognized myself. My skin looked the same, the coloring unchanged, but something was different about my eyes. They were wilder, raw.

I gripped the sides of the sink so hard my knuckles were white. Images flashed behind my lids: blood, the man, Nallah. I grimaced. It was hard to breathe. My hands shook as I turned the faucet. Cold water filled the sink, and I splashed my face with it.

The water dripped from my skin, coppery red from the blood it washed away. I scrubbed myself hard, as if by washing away the blood I could scrub away the previous day. I held my head under the hand-dryer mounted on the wall and then put on the clothes. I took a deep breath, looking at my knife belt on the floor. I forced myself to pick it up and buckle it around my waist, feeling ten pounds heavier because of it.

There was a hard knock at the flimsy bathroom door. "Come on, princess melodramatic. Some of us actually have to pee."

I grabbed my clothes from the floor and unlocked the door. Alexa rushed in and pushed me out. I slid my old clothes into the weapon's bag and looked up, feeling self-conscious because Brad was staring at me.

"You're kind of naked."

I looked down at myself. It was true that I was showing a fair amount of skin; the shirt was short sleeved, and the shorts were, well, short. I hadn't considered it to be a real problem, but then again, we weren't alone in the forest anymore.

"She'll be fine." Parker motioned me to the seat by him.

I sat down beside him and heard his voice in my head. *If you don't want anyone to notice you, tell them not to.*

I stared at him. "Parker, that is not fair. I don't know if that will even work."

"If what will work?" Brad asked.

You'll be fine. I promise nothing will happen. I believe in you, but if something goes wrong, I can protect you.

I snorted. "As if I'd need your protection."

"Whose protection?" Brad's brows furrowed. Lila looked amused.

You're going to have to stop replying verbally to what I think. It makes people think you're talking to yourself. He smiled wryly.

"Well, you should stop thinking it then," I said back dryly.

Brad threw his hands up and sat down. Poor guy.

The bus made a sudden sharp turn and pulled into a fast food parking lot. Our group waited until the rest of the bus unloaded, and then we followed. We were somewhere in Oklahoma, still a good sixteen hours from Phoenix, but my legs ached from being inside the bus for so long.

Small bells jingled above the door when we entered the crowded restaurant. I staggered, a sudden force hammering at my brain. It throbbed with the immersion into so many consciences, and for a few desperate seconds, I thought I would drown in it.

"Everyone stop *thinking*." I bit. I closed my eyes and focused on breathing.

Everything went silent. I opened my eyes. The entire restaurant was frozen with every eye focused on me. They sat, shocked and staring, as if I was a four-headed clown. I widened my eyes, surprised it worked. I turned to look at Parker, and he just shrugged.

I stepped forward and cleared my throat. "You, um, don't see anything unusual about my appearance. I am an average-looking teenage girl. No, no, wait! You think that I am one of the ugliest girls you have ever seen."

Parker burst out laughing behind me, and I had to look down to keep my composure.

"Alright, um, go back to doing whatever you were doing."

As if nothing had ever happened, the entire restaurant went back to their busy conversations.

"What just happened?" Alexa looked around, confused.

A teenage guy passed and actually grimaced as he saw my face. I snorted and waved.

Lila smiled and said to Alexa, "Well, isn't it obvious? Rose is controlling minds now. Probably reading them too."

"What?"

I punched Parker's shoulder. "So much for our secret, jerk!"

"Ow!" He rubbed his arm. "I didn't tell her."

"Well then how does she know?"

"I figured it out myself, Rose. It wasn't that hard to put it together once you turned around after I told you to in my head. That and you got us those tickets."

"Are you hearing what I'm thinking now?" Alexa looked at me nervously.

"It doesn't really work that way."

"Well, then, how does it work?"

"Does this place have hot dogs?" Brad scanned the menu above us, oblivious.

Alexa sighed and pulled some cash from her backpack and shoved it at him. "Five burgers and Cokes."

"You had cash? You told me—"

"I, uh, found some more." Alexa cut Parker off. "So tell me about this brain thing. Are you going to be spying on everyone now?"

We jammed into a booth by the door.

"No. I think I have to *want* to hear y'all to get anything."

"So you only hear thoughts when you want to?"

"Not exactly. Like for instance when we walked in, I noticed that guy right there." I pointed to a man sitting by himself in the booth across from ours. "He thought his burger tasted strange. I heard that thought without trying to, but now that I'm adjusted to the room, I've kind of like tuned him out. I could still hear him if I wanted, but I don't have to."

"They didn't have any hot dogs." Brad returned, disappointed.

Alexa rolled her eyes and passed out everyone's food. I grabbed my burger and bit into it.

"Is it the same to hear our thoughts?" Alexa asked.

"I want to say no, because I can only hear Parker's thoughts when he wants to me to, but yesterday I heard something he was thinking about me, and then I heard Lila on the bus asking me to turn around."

"Oh yeah, I meant for you to hear that. I was already guessing when you got that headache and then made that guy give us tickets. Sorry, my bad," Lila said.

I took another mongo bite. "All right then, apparently I can only hear you guys' thoughts when you want me to, or if you just happen to be thinking about me."

"I think what we need to keep in mind is that this is still new to her. It still has its kinks, so no one can be angry if Rose accidentally hears their thoughts. Agreed?"

There were nods around the table.

"If it makes any of you feel better, I promise not to go *trying* to read any of your thoughts either."

"I've always pictured my mind as a desert. Thoughts just kind of roll in like tumble weeds and then leave the rest of the place sunny and warm for the majority of the time," Brad said with certainty.

The Gifted 103

Alexa stopped chewing and turned to look at him. "That is the stupidest thing I've ever heard."

Brad shrugged and took another bite of his burger. Everyone else laughed.

Parker stood and said. "Alright, guys, time to go. The bus is about to leave."

Brad looked around and panicked. He shoved the rest of his burger into his mouth and jumped up to follow us.

When we got back on the bus, it was easier to think. There were fewer minds than there had been in the restaurant. Something had changed, though. There was one more mind on the bus than there had been this morning, and it didn't feel human.

CHAPTER NINE

I sat up higher in my seat to see her. She was about Parker's age, maybe a little older. Her skin was a soft chocolate color, and her black hair was cut almost as short as a boy's. I couldn't see her eyes now, but I remembered seeing them when we'd stopped for dinner in Texas. They were the color of caramel, so light they were almost golden.

She was average build and average looking, if not even a little below average on physical appearance, but there was something in her demeanor: she was hard. She didn't smile, even when someone smiled at her, and she walked with an intensity in her step, constantly looking over her shoulder.

It was dark outside the bus's windows, and the infrequent glow of street lights blurred together in a sleepy line in my head. I was tired, but I wouldn't let myself sleep. We would get there sometime around two a.m., and until then, I wasn't letting the dark girl out of my sight.

Parker shifted in his seat, his blue eyes opening sleepily. He smiled and whispered, "You should probably get some sleep. I can take watch if you want."

I shook my head. "You took watch for me last time, remember? I got a few hours. You've barely had six."

"More than enough." He stretched. "Now you sleep."

"Look, I'm not going to sleep again on this bus, but there's no reason for you not to."

He sat straighter in his seat. "You forget I'm just as stubborn as you."

"Oh, how could I forget that?"

He turned to look behind us. The others were all sleeping stacked upon one another like puppies in a clothes basket.

Parker turned back to me and whispered, "Looks like our flock just might make it to Phoenix."

I tried to smile, but an uneasy wave rippled in my stomach. Of course we would make it to Phoenix, but that meant the girl at the front of the bus would, too.

"What are you thinking about?"

I bit my lip. "Now don't freak out, but do you see that girl up there in the front? Right row, maybe four seats back?"

"Why? Is she cute?"

"Shut up and be serious for a moment."

He sighed and peaked over the seat in front of us. "Fine. The one with the short hair?"

"Yeah."

"Okay." He sank back down beside me. "What about her?"

"She makes me feel uneasy. Her thoughts are weird."

"Like follow-us-into-a-dark-alley-and-hack-us-into-little-bits weird?"

"Stop it. I'm being serious."

"So am I. Are you sure you aren't being a little paranoid?"

I hesitated, unable to excuse the uneasy feeling in my chest. "Remember what I told you about me just knowing things?"

Parker sighed. "Alright, so you *know* this girl is off?"

"She doesn't feel completely human. I think." I hesitated. "She may be a host."

"Wait, seriously?" He sat up higher to look at her again, but I jerked him back down.

"Yes, seriously. I don't think it's noticed us yet, though."

"What are we going to do? I mean, we can't exactly jump her on the bus."

"We aren't going to *jump* her at all. We're going to get off the bus and disappear for a little while. If she finds us, then we do something. All I know right now is that she gives me the heeby jeebies."

"Heeby jeebies?"

"Shut up."

"So you want to get off the bus?" Parker asked.

I nodded, swallowing. Parker exhaled and said, "All right, next stop, we'll get off and leave this host lady in the dust."

"What if she notices us before then?"

Parker shrugged, "We'll cross that bridge when it comes."

"Okay," I said, nodding.

Parker took my hand in his. It was warm, and he ran his thumb across my skin. I looked down at our intertwined fingers, and my chest felt heavy. Why couldn't he just get over the fact that I couldn't be with him?

I whispered, "Parker. I don't think this is following the rule."

"Screw the rule."

I pulled my hand from his and scooted away. His jaw tightened, and he sat up straighter. I'd hurt his pride…again.

You know why we can't break it, I thought the sentence to myself angrily, wishing he could hear it.

No, you *know why we can't break it. You never tell me anything.*

I turned my head sharply. "Did you just hear *my* thoughts?"

"What?" he bit, but then stopped. His eyes widened. "Wait, I did. It was like you said it in my head. Try again!"

I closed my eyes and thought, *I'm thinking about blue elephants.* I opened my eyes, and Parker looked disappointed.

"I didn't hear a thing."

I slumped, discouraged. "Huh." Then it hit me. What if he hadn't read my thoughts? What if I had *sent* the thought to him? I concentrated hard on his face and thought, *If you get this, I am now even more of a freak.*

Parker's eyes softened. "You're not a freak, Rose."

I threw my head back dramatically. "So now I'm *sending* my thoughts too?"

"Telepathy, looks like you can add that to your list, Rosie," he said smiling.

I buried my face in my hands and groaned. The next stop to get off this bus couldn't come any sooner.

CHAPTER TEN

"I still don't understand why we got off the bus," Alexa said for the fourth time

"Because, Alexa," Parker said and wiped sweat from his forehead, "Rose got a bad feeling about one of the people on there."

"Okay, but that doesn't explain why we're now wandering in the middle of the freaking desert?"

I breathed out hard, trying to control my temper and said, "Brad said he had a feeling about going this way. Do you want to doubt the psychic kid?"

"No offense, but Brad has feelings about a lot of things that never happen."

"You know I can hear you?" Brad said defensively.

I glared at Alexa. "Look, stop complaining. We're all hot and tired, but if the psychic kid says he thinks the best path we should take is directly into the desert, that's where I'm going. So please, just shut up."

Alexa scowled and took a step toward me. "Don't tell me to shut up."

I took a step toward her. "Or what?"

Parker intercepted me. "All right, guys, just knock it out."

He turned to Brad. "How much farther do we have to go? I feel like another mile and these two may just commit murder."

I shook his grip from mine. He wouldn't have to wait for another mile if he got in my way again. It was too hot for us to be out here in the first place; I'd told him that. I'd said that we should have waited until nightfall for the temperature to drop and *then* set out to follow Brad's hunch. But had he listened to me? No.

So now, here we were, walking in circles, carrying twenty pounds of junk in the desert. My face was hot as an inferno, and my lips were so dry they felt like they might crack. I was lucky they couldn't bleed, though, because Lila's had started not long ago and wouldn't stop. She was silent, barely keeping up. Alexa, on the other hand, seemed to get whinier as the hours passed.

"I dunno." Brad squinted and peered over the never-ending desert. "I kind of feel like we should have gotten there by now."

"Where is 'there'?" I asked,

Brad shrugged, "I don't know."

Alexa puffed and sat down on a rock. "I think we should all just cut the crap and admit our tour guide here doesn't know where the hell we are."

"Lay off." I made her scoot over and sat beside her. "It's not like Brad meant to get us so lost. This whole desert looks the same to me."

Parker ran his hands down his face and said, "All right, here's what we're going—"

"I'm hungry." Brad dropped to lie flat backed against the scorching desert sand.

"Gee, that's a surprise," Alexa muttered under her breath.

"Brad, are you sure you should be laying on that? Isn't it like, a hundred degrees or something?"

He shrugged. "Maybe it'll burn away my hunger."

I smiled.

"Too bad it can't burn away stupidity."

I said to Alexa, "If it could, all that hot air inside your head would have saved what little sense you have left."

Lila smiled weakly and dropped onto the stone beside me. She was covered in sweat, and even with the sun, her pale skin never looked so clammy. I reached over and felt her forehead; it was skillet hot. "Lila, when was the last time you had anything to drink?"

"Well." She strained, thinking. "When did we run out of water?"

"About an hour ago."

"Oh, then about four hours."

"What?" Going an hour out in this heat was dangerous, but going four? That was suicide.

"Yeah, there was a mouse a little ways back that was really thirsty. I tried to open my canteen to share with it, but I accidentally poured too much out." Her eyes began drooping as if she was falling asleep.

I looked at her worriedly and said, "Lila, that probably wasn't a good idea. Are you sure you're all right?"

She opened her mouth to say something, but Parker spoke over her. "I see something."

"Is it the last of our hope?" Alexa said dryly.

"No, seriously, there is something over there."

I shielded my eyes from the sunlight and tried to make out the approaching shape. Clouds of dust swirled around it as it sped toward us. It looked like a yellow tank, bouncing along the uneven desert, and as it got closer, I could hear the bump of rap music.

"Hey, I like this song." Brad picked his head up from the ground.

Parker stepped forward just as the vehicle slammed to a stop beside us. Everyone stared at the Hummer parked before us.

The door opened and a man stepped into view. He was tall and in his early twenties. His dark-brown hair was cut close to his head, revealing his strong facial features. His jaw was more pointed than square. His nose was sharp, and his lips held a tight smile that glowed against his dirty face. His eyes were what startled me though, because they were Parker's eyes.

"Jack." Parker stared, dumbfounded at him.

The man looked at Parker appraisingly and said, "Hey there, little brother."

Parker shook his head, unable to form words. "Jack—"

"I go by J.C. now."

Parker nodded, still in shock. "How are you here? I mean... how... what?"

J.C. laughed and said, "We've got a lot to catch up on. But if it's all right with you, I think we should get out of this desert first."

"Um, okay, yeah," Parker said, shaking his head.

A moment of awkward silence passed before J.C. spoke. "Well aren't you going to introduce me to your friends?"

"Oh, yeah, of course. This is Brad, but you already know him. And this is Alexa and Lila."

"Hi." Alexa smiled ruefully at him, her eyes running across his broad shoulders. God help him.

"What's wrong with the little one?" J.C. looked nervously at Lila, who was sitting on the rock, struggling to keep her eyes open.

"She needs water. We've been out here the whole day."

"Yeah, I know." J.C. opened the back door to the Hummer and motioned for Parker to set Lila inside. "We've been watching ya'll wander around since noon. We didn't want to risk coming to you before the sun started setting, though. Too risky."

I huffed. "Too risky for you, but not too risky for the twelve-year-old girl who probably has sun poisoning?"

J.C. raised his eyes as he saw me for the first time. He didn't freak out. He just smiled and said to Parker, "I don't believe you introduced this one."

"*This one* can hear you and is fully capable of introducing herself."

J.C. laughed. "All right, fair enough. May I ask your name?"

"Rose." I tucked my hair behind my ears. "My name is Rose."

"Interesting name for someone who looks as soft as you. Does that violet color in your eyes run in your family?"

I started walking toward the Hummer. "No, but I'm starting to think that impropriety runs in yours."

J.C. laughed and the rest of us filed into the huge vehicle. Brad and Alexa sat in the very back with Parker and me cradling Lila between us.

"Little brother, what have you done to the girl with the violet eyes to make her think our family is full of impropriators?" His eyes met mine in the rearview mirror.

I looked away quickly and found a broad grin on Parker's face. "I don't kiss and tell."

I hit him.

"So are you telling me that my little brother is in a relationship?"

Parker didn't seem dismayed as he smiled over at me. "Not yet, I'm not. I keep trying, and she just keeps saying no."

"What's the matter, Rose? Don't you want to have somebody to grow old with?" J.C. teased.

"It has nothing to do with what I want," I mumbled.

Lila stirred in my arms.

I looked back to J.C. "Do you not keep water in this thing?"

"Wait." He fiddled under his seat before pulling out a faded-blue canteen. "I think there's about half of this left." He tossed it into the backseat.

I unscrewed the cap and put it to her lips. She drank like a newborn pup.

"So where are you taking us?" Alexa asked.

J.C. smiled ruefully and said, "To the Circle, of course."

"The Circle?" I asked.

He gaped into the rearview mirror and said, "You don't know what the Circle is?"

We all shook our heads, and J.C. laughed.

He said, "I thought you'd have known about it since you were wandering on top of it for the past ten hours. Why else would you be in the desert?"

"Brad had a feeling," Alexa said flatly.

"Wait, you said we were walking on top of it?" Parker asked.

J.C. nodded, "Yeah, it's underground. It's about the only place that's safe for humans to live anymore."

"Humans to live?" I asked, my brows furrowing, "You mean people are living underground here?"

J.C. smiled. "You're dang right they are. The Circle is the last human resistance army, living right underneath us at this very moment."

Silence filled the car. I looked over at Parker incredulously. He voiced my concern. "J.C., how is that even possible?"

"You have a lot of questions, and I promise I'll explain it all once we're inside. We're about to be there, anyways."

Brad leaned forward. "Good, I'm—"

"If you say *hungry* I am going to make you swallow your tongue," Alexa threatened.

Brad sat back into his seat gloomily.

J.C. put the car in park by a cactus that had split in two. He said, "There's the entrance. Be right back," and stepped outside.

Once he closed the door, Alexa all but yelled, "This Circle better not be four middle-aged men playing rook behind a deformed cactus."

We watched J.C. pull a huge, tan tarp from the ground a few yards behind the plant. It had been hiding a tunnel sloping into the earth.

J.C. was breathing heavy when he climbed back inside and put the car into drive. "Once we're settled inside, the gate keepers will reset the tarp."

As we entered the tunnel my head felt as if it were hit by a nine pound hammer. I wasn't sure, but I think I might have groaned as I cradled my head within my hands.

"What's wrong with her?"

"Just. Drive." I bit the words through my clenched teeth and immediately regretted it.

The sound of my own voice hit the walls of my mind and shattered into thousands of razor-sharp shards, like chips of a broken glass.

"I'm not going anywhere until—" J.C. sounded far away.

"Get her inside, now!" Parker spit.

I leaned back against the seat and put pressure on my eyes. They felt as if I'd laid hot coals against my lids and was slowly letting them burn through. Blurry images flickered against the dark side of my eyelids. I opened them, trying to blink, and nearly screamed from the light that burned into my irises. I squeezed my eyes together, and tears escaped them.

There were so many faces. Human faces, old and scarred, young and vibrant. They sped past my vision, blurring together like some kind of distorted slideshow. With each face a whisper of a thought grazed my mind, and together all the sounds hit me like a freight train. There were too many voices in my head, too many consciousnesses near. There were so many people down here, they overwhelmed me.

The hum of their thoughts buzzed like a swarm of bees, growing louder and louder to where I thought my brain might bleed from my ears. I grabbed at my hair, pulling as the buzz climaxed higher and higher and then...stopped.

There was silence.

I opened my eyes to six people staring at me as if I had just grown a second head. It was dark, and I smelled the faint mustiness of dirt.

"So this is underground?" I was hoarse.

"What the hell just happened?"

"Umm..."

I glanced over to my group, who all shared the same look. Their eyes said it all—we couldn't tell him.

"I had a migraine."

"A migraine," J.C. said flatly.

"Yep." I pushed the door open and turned to get Lila.

Parker handed her to me and then climbed out, followed by Brad and Alexa.

"Ya'll wait right here. I will go see where the higher-ups want you."

J.C. didn't wait to hear our response before disappearing into the lightlessness of the tunnel.

"All right, what just happened?" Parker turned toward me.

"It's confusing. I saw...faces...lots and lots of faces. And minds...I felt *so* many people's subconscious just now that I think I short-circuited my brain... Does that make sense?"

Parker hesitated. "How many did you feel?"

"Three hundred, easy."

"We're outnumbered."

After Parker said it, no one moved. Silence overcame us. Brad's stomach growled.

"Really?" Alexa looked at him flatly, and he shrugged.

"Should we run?" My eyes glanced back to the exit. The light from outside barely peeked into the cavern.

"Where? We're in the middle of the desert, and Lila needs rest," Alexa said.

I wanted to kick something. We'd done something very stupid. We'd let ourselves be led to a place where the enemy knew all the answers, and we were blind.

"So, running isn't an option," I said.

Parker pinched the space between his brows. "I think we're safe here. Or…at least safer. Jack is here and I trust him. He said there's a human resistance. We at least have to check it out."

Brad said, "I didn't see anything bad happening to us today."

"Welcome children." A man in his thirties walked into the tunnel, his arms outstretched beside him in a welcoming gesture.

I furrowed my brows. "Who are you?"

He smiled and walked toward us in no hurry. I felt the slightest sense of unease as he neared. "Let me guess, you are the Cancer? Strong-willed, undoubtedly beautiful, a little reckless."

I hesitated, my eyes turning skeptically to Parker. He was the only one who'd ever referred to me by that.

"You look to the Leo for an answer? Not surprising if you two already have those budding feelings."

Parker stepped in front of me, annoyed, and said, "She asked you a question."

The man sighed and said, "I'm Rayon Fellwhether, founder of the Circle."

Rayon's eyes were greenish yellow and sharp like a hawk's. His skin and hair were both a sickly sand color.

Now that I was closer to him, the unease bubbling in my abdomen was stronger. I wasn't nauseous like with the bugs, but something didn't feel right.

"You called me 'Cancer,'" I said, lowering my eyes on him, "So that means you know who we are."

Rayon smiled and said, "Oh yes. We have been waiting for the Gifted's arrival for nearly twenty years now."

My eyes widened. Twenty years was even longer than I'd been alive.

Parker asked, "Who's this 'we' you're talking about?"

"The members of the Circle, obviously. I don't doubt your dear brother has told you what we are?"

I shook my head. "A human resistance army, yeah I heard that. But what I don't get is how? How can you form an army to attack those things when every human I've ever seen loses their mind when they get around one?"

Rayon said, "You will learn all of this in time, but for now, I'll explain it simply. Whether or not society wants to admit it, people are not, in fact, created as equals. Some people's minds are stronger than others, whether it be because of some genetic mutation or just an indomitable will. The fact still remains that some people's minds are superior to others making them able to resist. These people are the ones who make up the Circle."

"How did you find them?" I asked.

Rayon shook his head. "We will have more time for questions later, after we've taught you to fight."

Alexa snorted. "You teach us to fight? We're the ones who've been battling this out in the open while you're hiding underground."

Rayon *tsked*. "Yes, you're right, Scorpio. You all probably are excellent fighters, but that is all you are. You are like wild dogs, succumbing to your instincts and attacking whatever is nearest. You do not strategize, plan, or think before you act! These are the things that are vital if you plan on beating the Infestation. Raw power alone means nothing against an army of thousands. We can teach you this."

Alexa stepped back, scathed. I found myself staring at Rayon; something in his voice and the way he spoke perplexed me. I cast my mind out to see what he was thinking.

He turned, met my eyes, and smiled. *Hello, little dream wanderer, care to take a look around? I have no secrets.*

His thoughts sent chills up my spine, and even though he opened his mind to me, I could tell he was lying. I could *feel* the secrets in their cages of his subconscious. They were like ravaged animals, gnawing and lunging at the bars of their restraints, daring me to inspect close enough so that they could devour me whole. There was something raw in his head, something untamed.

"Maybe you're right." I turned and sent Parker a silent look of caution.

Rayon's smile loosened. "Let's pick up tomorrow after you've rested, yes? I'll have J.C. show you to your chambers."

He turned to walk away but stopped. "Oh, and Rose?"

"Yeah?"

"Welcome to the Circle."

"Yeah, Rayon is a little bizarre." J.C. smiled. He led us down a dimly lit walkway. "Most of us just put up with him because he's such a genius. I think he's one of those people that are so intelligent they're socially inept."

Parker laughed. "So he's that intense all the time?"

"Pretty much, though he was kind of laying it on thick today." J.C. turned to his right, leading us down a corridor that split off into many other walkways.

I had been trying to keep track of all the turns, but now I was lost.

Alexa mimicked Rayon. "You fight like wild dogs, attacking the first thing you see! Blah, blah, blah. I'd love to see a wolf take down four men with a single kick like I can."

Parker laughed again. He carried Lila sleeping in his arms. J.C. stopped at a circular area with three curtained doorways at the end of the hall.

"Those are the closest things we have to doors down here, but at least you'll have some privacy."

Alexa walked to the curtain farthest to the right. "I'm going to bed." She didn't wait to for a reply before disappearing behind the curtain.

J.C. laughed, "Is that one always so fiery?"

Brad looked at J.C. angrily. "Yes, she is, and she is spoken for." He followed Alexa into the room. A moment passed before he walked back out silently and went into the room on the far left. I laughed.

"I'll put Lila with Alexa." Parker disappeared into her room.

J.C. said, "There are two beds in there, so you may have to room with someone else."

Great. There were no more beds with the girls.

Parker came back out, and J.C. clapped him on the shoulder. "Well, I'm going to go hit the hay too. My room is at the end of the hall, and the bath house is just beyond that to the right. Feel free to come get me if you need me."

"All right, thanks." Parker smiled and watched his brother disappear down the hall.

Then we were alone.

"How are you feeling? Anything hurting?"

"That's a dumb question, and you know it." I smiled and looked up at his face. The faded bruise from a punch was stained on his jaw. "Your poor face is never going to heal if you keep getting hit like that."

"What? You think getting bruised up will make me less beautiful?"

"You're still beautiful. You just look like you can't fight."

He drew me into a hug, squeezing me. "Hey, don't think I won't fight you here and now."

"Go ahead. I'll add a mark to the other cheek so you can be balanced."

He laughed and leaned in to kiss my forehead. I pulled his face closer and made him kiss me for real. My whole body went warm from it.

He pulled back and whispered, "I'm glad it's one of those times you're letting me be with you."

"You are always with me, dummy." I smiled.

"No, all I have are these rare moments where I'm allowed to steal a kiss when no one's watching. I want more."

I lowered my brows and said, "I don't know what else I can give. What do you want from me?"

He grew frustrated. "I want you to tell me more about what's going on in that head of yours than just the bare minimum. I just want *you*, Rosie, all of you, every little piece, and you won't give it to me. I don't know where we even stand. One minute you won't let me hold you, the next you're kissing me. I want answers."

"I…" I hesitated.

"You what?"

I looked away and whispered, "I think it's time we both went to bed…separately."

"And there you go, shutting me out again." He went into Brad's room and left me alone in the hall.

My feet barely even made a *tap* against the stone floor as I walked. My eyes stung, and I swallowed down the lump in my throat. I walked away from the bedrooms, away from Parker.

"Where are you going?" J.C. said behind me.

I stopped, debating whether or not to run, and then turned to him. I knew my eyes were probably bloodshot, and I was still covered in dirt from the desert.

His expression softened as he looked at me. "Here, we'll go where we can talk."

He stepped from the room and jogged to catch up to me. We walked in silence as he led me through hallways. We entered a cavern five hundred feet tall. There was a chilling, yellow glow from hundreds of lanterns filling the place. Gray-brown stalactites hung from the ceiling, breaking up patches of grayish colored glass.

I stared up and asked, "What's that glass for?"

"They're windows. There're holes in the desert floor, and we funnel sunlight through them to light the Circle in the daytime."

I nodded and noticed him looking at me out of the corner of his eye. His eyes were normal, not dilated. "My face doesn't make you go crazy?"

He chuckled. "Nah, I can control it. One of the gifts of having a 'superior mind' according to Rayon. I dunno how it all works, but it takes practice to perfect it."

"You have to practice it?"

"Yeah, it's not easy. It takes a lot of concentration."

"Are you struggling right now?"

"Not terribly. I mean, if you want me to be brutally honest, I'll tell you that thoughts that would make me blush to say aloud ravage my mind whenever you walk up, and they stay there for a few seconds before I squelch them. After I've wrangled them in, it's *almost* like speaking to someone normal."

I flinched. He motioned to the wall and sat down, leaning against it. I sat beside him. I pulled my knees to my chest and wrapped my arms around them.

"Why do you sit like that?"

"I don't know. Why do you sit like you do?"

He laughed. "I just asked because my mom used to sit like that. She said it made her feel like she wasn't falling apart."

I looked away and swallowed. "Oh. Yeah, I guess that's appropriate."

J.C. leaned his head back. He closed his eyes and spoke. "Right after Parker and I were separated, I slept cradling my knees to my chest. It was the only way I could fall asleep without thinking I would wake up with my insides laying on the sheets under me. It always felt like that, like I was on the verge of falling apart."

"How were y'all separated?"

"Our parents were killed by a drunk driver when we were pretty young. Parker was only about four, but I was six. Foster services stepped in, and somehow Parker ended up at a monastery, and I was placed in a boy's home. We didn't see each other again until years later."

"He never mentioned you."

He chuckled. "I don't doubt it. We'd bumped into one another at a diner in Birmingham after he found Brad. He tried to convince me to come out into the wilderness with him and help him find these kids he called the Gifted. I thought he was nuts."

"So you didn't go."

"Nope. I left him there. I even told the waitress to give him my tab." He laughed bitterly. "I was really confused back then. There was so much I just didn't understand. There's not a day I don't wish I could go back and make another choice. I'll never get back those years we spent apart."

I nodded, even though his eyes were closed and he couldn't see. He asked, "Do you have any siblings?"

I looked away. "No, not anymore."

He whispered, "I'm sorry."

I rested my chin on my knees. "It's okay. I just don't want to talk about that."

He nodded. "Why don't you talk about what's got you roaming the halls this late instead?"

"I don't know. I guess I'm just tired of ruining things."

"What things?"

"Anything. Everything. Take your pick."

"You know, a lot of the time, people think they've ruined something that can't be ruined."

"Everything can be ruined."

"No, a lot of things can't."

"Relationships can," I said.

He shrugged, "Depends on the people. Not you and my brother. He wants y'all to be together too much to let y'all fall apart."

"Well, that's stupid." I said, bitterly.

"Nothing you want for the right reasons is stupid, Rose."

I rolled my eyes. "Do you know how many bugs fly into bright lights everyday and are killed by them? They love the light. They *want* the light. They think it's beautiful, but it kills them. Every time. Rarely what we want is what's best for us."

J.C. was quiet for what seemed like a long time. The cavern was cool, and I could hear the faint sounds of people coughing and drops of water hitting puddles.

Finally, he spoke. "People aren't like bugs in a lot of things, Rose. People can love and make choices. Those bugs that fly into the lamps have no choice. They see the light, and instinct forces them to move. People are different. We choose who we get close to, who we allow ourselves to fall vulnerable to. If we get burned, it's because somewhere, deep within us, we wanted it or at least were prepared for it.

"Everyone knows that when they fall in love they can get incredibly hurt, but they do it anyway, because it's worth it. Those bugs have no regrets when they go toward the light, because even the smallest creatures know that even just a split second of pure, unimaginable beauty is worth every ounce of ugly it brings. It *does* matter what he wants. It's all that matters."

I sat for a moment, unable to reply.

I sighed and laid my head back. "I think I'm ready to go back now."

"I won't try to stop you. I'm pretty beat myself."

We walked back through the cavern, making our way back to his room. I told him goodnight and thanked him for staying up with me. I walked back to my hall and hesitated. The center room had no one in it, but Parker was in the other one, and J.C.'s words were still fresh on my mind. I sighed, disappointed with my cowardliness, and stepped into the center room. Parker had left me one of his oversized white t-shirts folded on the edge of the bed to sleep in.

I stepped out of my boots and shimmied out of my clothes. I sat on the edge of the lumpy mattress and pulled Parker's t-shirt over my head. It smelled like him, both woodsy and clean. I laid back and closed my eyes.

I couldn't get J.C.'s words out of my head. They were replaying over and over in my thoughts. "It's worth it," he'd said.

I groaned and kicked the quilt from my body. I fumbled my way through the darkness into the cul-de-sac. I stopped before Brad and Parker's curtain and closed my eyes. I took a deep breath and pulled it open.

Their room was larger than mine. On the floor lay two mattresses with a single crate between them. I could barely make out Parker's tangled brown curls on the pillow of the mattress farthest to the back wall. I closed the curtain behind me and stumbled my way over to him.

He opened his eyes, startled, and tried to say something.

I clamped my hand across his mouth and said, "Shh!"

I wormed in beside him under the covers. His body was hot against mine; he was not wearing a shirt. I was thankful for the darkness, because he couldn't see me blushing. I pulled the blankets back over us and finally looked at him. He was smiling stupidly.

"Shut up."

He laughed and pulled me closer. I rested my head against his bare chest. He kissed my forehead. "Goodnight, Rosie," he whispered and then closed his eyes.

I sighed, smiling despite myself, and then allowed myself to finally close my eyes. I fell asleep without a moment's hesitation.

CHAPTER ELEVEN

The light from the hallway touched my face. I struggled to open my eyes. I could feel that I was alone in the room, just as I could feel Parker's lumpy mattress underneath me. No other consciences grazed mine.

I stretched and sat up, rubbing my face. I was still lying in Parker's bed, wearing his t-shirt. I was glad everyone else had already left; at least now I didn't have to deal with their stares when I walked from the room.

"Rose?" A girl in her early teens peeked through the black curtain. Her hair was fiery red, and her face was freckled. She had vibrant green eyes.

She stepped into the room, uncertain, and I squinted. "Yeah?"

"I'm Beth. Rayon appointed me to be your Circle guide."

I yawned, and she grimaced like I was going to eat her.

I laughed and said, "I'm not going to bite."

"Oh…I know, I just—" Her consciousness grazed mine, and I felt fear.

I sighed. "Beth, can you, uh, get me some pants or something out of Alexa's room? It's the one behind the striped curtain."

She nodded and then reappeared with a pair of shorts. "Here you go." She stretched her arm as far as it would reach. She was acting like touching me would make her erupt into flames.

I took the shorts and squirmed into them under Parker's quilt.

"I'm going to go back into my room and finish getting dressed. Where should I go after that?"

"I'll wait for you outside your room."

I nodded and climbed from the bed. I passed into my old room to get my boots and knives. I had to go into Alexa's room to get a new shirt.

I finally joined Beth in the hallway. She gave me the once over and then looked away. She took a couple deep breaths before she was able to meet my eyes. My smile faltered.

"I was chosen for this job because of my mental power, yet here I was having to pause to collect myself."

"Don't worry about it. You're already doing better than a lot of people I've met."

"It should be better here, though. Everyone has control."

"Yeah, J.C. was telling me that. It's going to be a welcomed change. I was getting kind of tired of crazies."

She hesitated and looked toward the end of the hall. "I should warn you, though. People know who you are. They'll recognize you."

"I figured as much."

"No, I mean, the Gifted are like royalty or something to a lot of the people here. You should still be on the lookout for crazies."

I snorted. "Royalty? Have you met all of us? We can't even pay for our meals at Waffle House."

She motioned for us to walk down the hall. She pointed out hallways, making comments as to where they led or who lived near the end of them. I only half paid attention, taking note of the trail leading to the cafeteria and the one that lead to the bathhouses. We were passing through small halls, and Beth would hesitate whenever she thought she heard someone.

"Beth, why are we avoiding people?"

She didn't turn back as she spoke. "We're not. There's just many different ways to get to the sparring grounds, and I thought this way would be the simplest."

I sighed. "I don't mean to make you uncomfortable, but I can tell you're lying to me. You don't think this is the simplest way to the sparring grounds, and I'm starting to believe you aren't even taking me there. Beth, I suggest you tell me the truth, or I will turn around and walk back until I find someone who will."

Her eyes widened. "Oh no, you can't say anything to anyone yet."

"Why not?"

She shifted her small feet uncomfortably and looked down at the stone ground. "We…we haven't announce your presence yet."

"I didn't exactly think you'd have to. I saw a group of like fifty people when we got here."

"They were the Elite. Sort of like the Circle's police force. They're sworn to secrecy. Right now, only they, Rayon, J.C., and I know you are here."

"I don't understand. I thought the Circle wanted the Gifted. Why keep us a secret?"

"Rayon has to tell you, not me. That's where we are going. Your friends are already with him."

My hand went instinctively to my knives. "What is all of this about?"

"I can't tell you, not yet. My orders were to just bring you to your friends, that's it. I don't know why."

"Why did they let you in on the secret? Rayon and the Elite, I get. J.C. found us, so it's not like he couldn't know, but where do you come into all of this? What makes a thirteen-year-old girl important enough to know some huge cover-up that we are turning out to be?"

"I'm fourteen, and I'm not just some girl. I'm part of the Elite."

"The rest of them were grown, old enough to be your parents even."

She looked down the hallway before meeting my eyes. "I'm the only person who ever survived becoming a host."

———※———

"It certainly took you long enough to wake up. Do the other's always allow you to do as you please because of your beauty, or was this a special occasion because you shared the bed of your leader?"

Rayon sat behind a dark mahogany desk. The cocky look in his eyes made anger jump in my stomach.

"Jealous because you never had a beautiful woman willing to share your bed?" I smirked and sat with the others in the seats opposite his desk.

We were in his office, but it looked more like an underground janitor's closet to me.

Like the rest of the Circle, the floors, walls, and ceiling were pure stone, but the furniture here was different than everywhere else. Where our bedrooms were full of makeshift furniture and worn fabrics, Rayon's office was decorated with stylized pieces.

"Witty and lethal," he said, nodding in satisfaction. "Impressive."

"Thanks, I've been pondering on how I would impress you all morning."

Parker's voice was in my head. *I'm sorry for what I said last night. I was glad you came back.*

It's in the past. Let's not talk about it anymore.

Rayon said, "Now that the entire group is here, I feel as if I must lay out the basic information. I take it you all realize your presence here has not yet been announced to the masses. Some of you were told that by me when you arrived here. But some of you"—his eyes focused on me—"wormed it out of your guides on the way here.

"Any matter, I first want to explain why your arrival has been such a secret. You see, the Gifted are a big deal to us. The biggest deal, in fact. As some of you have already noticed, the members of the Circle have a certain feeling to their mind, a certain *strength*, if you will. Out in the general population our people stick out like flashing lights to the Infesters. That's why they have come here, to be your army. They want to fight this thing with everything they have, but at the same time, this is their refuge. Many of them have no place else to go, so they take the Circle very seriously.

"I called you all here because I need to stress the importance of your behavior. Everyone here has been waiting for you since the day they arrived. For some of them, that has been nearly twenty years. You are everything to them—the key to their biggest dream becoming actualized. That means that you must behave as such. You will have people coming to you and asking for advice. That means it is *not* acceptable to snort some sarcastic remark and walk away like they don't exist. It is *not* okay to ignore them all completely or to give any one member more attention than another.

"You all are the public figures. Do you understand that? From this moment on, you eat, sleep, and breathe the cause of the Circle. If this wasn't what you were expecting, *tough*. These people depend on you for their lives, and any one of them is willing to give up theirs for you. Treat them with respect, teach them, and remember that in the end, they are the only thing that is remotely balancing the numbers between the Infesters and the five of you."

Parker said, "We understand that. I give you my word that my group and I will follow it to the best of our abilities. What I need to address now is what is expected of you all."

Rayon sat farther back into his seat, a smirk lurking in his expression. "And what is that?"

"Firstly, each of my members has certain needs that must be met. Brad is Gifted with premonitions. He will be in need of a number of blank books to record his sights. I know it may be hard to come by, but at this point I am not willing to let any detail of his warnings fall forgotten. Lila and Alexa both have specialties that require ample room free from onlookers who could get in the way of flying objects. If there is not a location that suits this, I must demand that there be an allotted time each day that only they have access to the sparring grounds. Is that understood?"

"Perfectly."

"Secondly, as you have already noticed, Rose has a certain appearance that may be hard for some to resist. Do I have your word that there will be no assaults on her while she stays here ?"

"I promise you, young Leo, that no one will overstep their boundaries with her."

A surge of anger rippled through my chest. "That's funny. I didn't remember leaving the room."

Be angry with me if you want to, but I won't apologize. I won't be able to get a single thing done if I'm continuously worried about you getting mobbed by a swarming group of admirers.

Whatever.

Parker sighed and stood up. "If that is all you wanted, I feel that it is time for my group and me to go to our common room you were telling me about earlier."

Rayon stood and motioned to the curtain that hung in the doorframe. "Yes, of course. Just don't forget that you will be announced today at supper, so you must all be there." He spoke directly to me.

What was that guy's problem? Did I have "juvenile delinquent" tattooed to my forehead?

I followed the others into the hallway. Parker stayed behind in the room with Rayon. I eavesdropped.

"And one last thing, Rayon, if you intend for us to take the responsibilities of leaders, I expect you to treat us as so. Don't make comments about any of our social lives in public. What Rose and I choose to do alone, in our own rooms, is none of your concern. You will not speak to her, or any of us, like you did today again. Have I made myself clear?"

Rayon must have nodded, because I didn't hear a response. Parker came out of the room and stood beside me. Beth lead us down the hall. I grabbed his hand and smiled.

What? he asked.

"Thank you."

He smiled and squeezed my hand. "You have nothing to thank me for. That jerk deserved it. I couldn't stand him talking to you like that."

"You shouldn't get so worked up, though. Men have said far more grotesque things to me."

"I don't want to think of things like that."

"Well, it still happens."

We stopped in front of a large room. The curtain was pulled back so we could see inside. There were two couches in the corner with a foot table between them. A bookshelf covered the back wall, and on the other side was a desk similar to Rayon's. A table with six chairs dominated the center of the room.

Beth said, "This is the office granted to you by the Circle. You'll find this whole wing is open for your use, including new bedrooms you will be able to access after tonight's dinner. You also have your own lavatories, kitchenette—though only snack food is kept in the private wing—and an arms room found at the end of this hall. You will be allowed to move into the rooms after your introduction tonight. I'm sorry it won't be sooner, but the risk of you being seen there now is too high."

Alexa said, "Why? Are people allowed to roam our wing? What's the point in giving it to us then?"

"Not once you move in, no. Then it will be guarded by the Elite. However, until then, it is always busy. People go in and out at all hours fixing bedding, bringing in fresh flowers. You know, things they would want you all to see when you made your first impressions of them."

Lila said, "It makes sense. I mean, if they think we're such a big deal, they're not going to want us to sleep in rooms that haven't been touched in twenty years."

I sat beside Lila on the couch. "Why are we given such a nice space when everyone else is sleeping in rooms like the ones we had last night? Are they not mad that we're getting fresh flowers and bookcases?"

Beth shook her head. "The Gifted are their only hope for a better life. They'd give you more if they had it."

Parker dropped onto the couch beside me and blew air from his mouth. "Wow, I hope we don't disappoint them."

Parker sent Beth away with a message for J.C. to meet us in the office as soon as it was convenient. Once she'd left the room, there was a collective sigh.

Alexa walked around the room, her fingers grazing the volumes of books on the shelves. "Is anyone else freaked out about this whole leadership thing? If they get too into this, I think we may have to split."

"I wonder if they'd let me wear a crown," Brad thought aloud.

Parker moved to the chair behind the desk and rested his elbows on the table. "Guys, I don't think we have the choice to leave."

Brad shrugged. "Of course we do. You and Rose will take all the men in the front, Alexa can have the ones attacking from the back, and Lila and I will chill in the center while ya'll fight us out."

I threw one of the pillows at his head. "Thanks for volunteering us."

I looked up to see the weariness in Parker's eyes. He looked years older. "No, I'm being serious. Do you see how they have us guarded? We aren't even allowed to walk out of this wing right now."

"It's because they don't want us to ruin the surprise of our arrival, right?" Lila fingered the fringe on the pillow in her lap. The bags under her eyes had faded some, but she still looked as if she could sleep a few more years.

"That's what they keep trying to sell us on, but I'm just not sure. Something doesn't feel right to me," Parker said.

I said, "That Rayon guy rubs me the wrong way. And our guide, Beth? She says she's the only human to survive being a host."

Alexa said, "That's impossible, right? I mean, once one of those things gets in your head, you're gone."

Parker bit his cheek. "That's what I always thought. Brad, have you seen anything odd about anyone here?"

"Nope. All my visions lately have been as clear as a muddy bowl of water. I can't explain it, but I haven't seen anything clear since before Nallah was killed."

A cold pain plunged into my stomach, and I looked away. I could feel Parker looking at me.

I swallowed and changed the subject. "Where did Rayon find three hundred people with minds this strong?"

Alexa shook her head and said, "There's too much that doesn't add up."

Parker stood and pulled a notebook from the bookshelf. "I think we can all agree on two things. First, we can't leave yet, because they probably won't let us and because there are three hundred more people willing to help us fight than we had before. Secondly, we have a lot of research to do on this place and some of the people in it before we get too open. Agreed?"

We nodded. Parker sat beside me on the couch, pulled a pen from his pocket, and started writing.

"I think it's obvious Rayon's name should be on here. Where did he find out about us and all these people?"

"Don't forget to add 'figure out why he is such a creeper,'" Alexa said, and Lila giggled.

I said, "Add Beth. I don't think she's really a danger, but there's more to that whole story than meets the eye."

Parker wrote her name down and then bit the tip of his pen. He flipped back a couple of pages and wrote, "Master Plan" across the top margin. "We'll think of more people as they come up. But here's another one of our worries. How in the hell are we going to defeat this Infestation?"

A chill swept across the group, and we exchanged worried glances.

"That is the million-dollar question, isn't it?" I said.

"We still don't know so much. How many are there? Do they have like a central area or something? I mean, how do they keep reproducing? There has to be some central ground where they are created...right?" Alexa said and then bit her thumbnail.

"My main thing is this: I can defeat one easily. I could defeat two easily. Hell, I could probably take out fifteen without one getting a mark on me. *But*, I have a feeling that we won't be going up against numbers in the double digits with how fast they've been spreading. I'm good, but even I doubt I could take on three hundred of those things at once," I said and watched as the others nodded.

"If we could just find out where they originate, we could take out the source. Once we do that, they're limited to how many they already have created. It'd only be a matter of taking out the ones left. We can't make a dent, though, unless we ensure that they aren't just going to make ten more for every one we defeat."

"And in order to do that, we have to find out where they are all coming from. We know. We're going in a circle," Alexa said and sighed.

I said, "If we could just capture one and get it to tal—"

J.C. peeked in through the curtain and said, "Knock knock! I was told I was summoned?" His expression darkened when he saw the looks in our eyes. He sat beside Parker on our couch. "What? Did I interrupt some Gifted pow-wow?"

"No, we wanted you to come. I was kind of hoping you could help us out with a few things." Parker nonchalantly shut the notebook and handed it to me. I slid it under the couch cushion.

J.C. said, "Well, I'm not real sure what I can do, but I'll give it a shot."

"First, how did you meet Rayon?" Parker asked.

"Rayon actually found me. I was about seventeen, enlisted in the marines 'cause I felt like I had to do something with my life, and he recruited me into the Circle."

I shook my head and asked, "How did he find you in the Marines?"

"He has his ways. That guy can be a major sleuth. But I think it had something to do with you being my brother. Maybe, I dunno. He just said he was traveling around, looking for people that had this certain gene and—"

"Gene?" Parker interrupted.

"Yeah, like DNA? He said that he was recruiting people with this gene that made their brains stronger than normal. He said it was an elite group and that I'd passed the physical."

"Wait, so was he a part of the Marines too?" Alexa asked.

"No, he was a fed. You know, like federal agent? When he first came to our base, my sergeant joked saying that if he picked you, you'd never be seen again. That hundreds of marines, foot soldiers, and even a few pilots had been recruited and then vanished."

"And he picked you," I said.

"Yeah, he did."

"And you didn't resist? Even knowing all that your sergeant told you about him?" Parker asked.

"You don't resist your higher ups, especially feds. And honestly, I didn't even want to. I had been looking for a purpose, and he gave it to me. He told me why we had been formed, and after a while, I believed him."

Lila asked, "You'd been formed to fight the Infestation?"

"He didn't exactly call it that. He showed us, me and a few of the others from my base that had been picked, a host body being torn apart as the bug inside her escaped. There was no doubting him then."

"Where did he find a host body?" Parker asked.

"I'm not sure. I guess he was supplied with them, him being with the government and all. I mean, how else was he supposed to convince us to join his cause? No one believes this until they see it happen."

I shook my head, feeling more uncomfortable with Rayon the more J.C. spoke. I said, "Tell me more about this gene. How did he find so many of you who had it?"

"Well most of us here were in some government position, like in the Marines, CIA, even a few senators. So our medical records were on file. I just assumed he searched the national database, and we were the positives."

"How did you develop the gene?" I asked.

"He said we didn't develop it. We were born with it. It's some kind of human evolution or something. It's like we're humans two-point-oh."

"But there's so few of you considering he did a national search. Only three hundred in the entire nation?" Alexa asked.

"Even less than that. People have gotten married and had children inside the Circle. When I got here we had less than two hundred."

"And these children," I interrupted, "do they have the gene too?"

"According to Rayon, they do. He said if both the parents held the gene, so would the kids. Imagine it. We are raising an entirely new species of people in here."

Goosebumps chilled my arms. "I don't think I share in your enthusiasm."

Parker asked, "How did Rayon come to find out about us?"

"You mean the Gifted? I don't know how he found out, but he had a chart with zodiac signs all over it. He showed it to me once."

Parker's face was white as a stone. "Have you seen this chart since?"

"Nah, I actually never saw it again after that one time."

Parker reached into his back pocket and pulled out the chart he'd shown me the day we met. He spread it across the coffee table and swallowed. "Is this the chart he showed you?"

J.C. leaned forward to look at it. "Wow, yeah it is. Look right there. It's Rayon's initials."

Sure enough, J.C. pointed right into the corner where someone had written RF in elegant cursive. My blood ran cold.

"Where did you find this thing, Parker?" I asked.

"I found it when I was eleven. It'd just appeared in my room after service one day. It was the reason I ran away from the monastery in the first place. It was why I found Brad."

"Someone is outside the curtain," I said, feeling another mind outside our room.

"How does she—" J.C. started to ask, but Parker silenced him by waving his hand.

A tense moment passed before someone knocked on the outside wall. Beth peeked inside, and everyone deflated.

"I'm sorry, did I interrupt something?"

Parker stood from the couch. "No, it's all right. We were done anyways."

Brad looked at Beth closely. She shifted uncomfortably and tucked some of her hair behind her ear.

Brad smiled and said, "Your eyes look like emeralds."

Beth blushed and said meekly, "Um, thanks."

I caught a glimpse of Alexa. Her eyes locked onto Beth's face like hooks. She stood up and wrapped her arms around Brad's waist, locking eyes with Beth territorially. Brad was completely oblivious, smiling like an idiot.

Alexa looked at Beth and said, "Is there a reason you're here, *kiddo,* or do you just enjoy our company?"

Beth looked down and swallowed. I had to admit I felt for the kid; she was only fourteen. She finally found her voice. "It's time for you to prepare for your introduction."

"I thought that was at dinner," Parker said what I was thinking.

"It is, but preparations must begin now."

"It's like three o'clock," I said.

She shifted her weight, and I felt her uneasiness. She said, "Rayon believes it will require a little more time than ordinary to prepare for dinner. He did mention the dirt um…*crusted* into your hair."

I tried to run my hands through my black curls and realized I couldn't. I hadn't seen a mirror in days. There was no telling what kind of mess, and probably creatures, were on me.

"Are you implying that we have poor hygiene?" Alexa stepped from behind Brad and folded her arms over her chest.

Beth backtracked, her stutters coming out in incoherent mumbles. "Oh, no, of course… I just meant…I…"

Lay off. The poor girl can't help if she has a crush on Brad. She's fourteen; she's not going to mount him when you're not looking.

I don't care if she wants him or not. He's not my property.

I snorted and lifted one of my eyebrows. *Well you sure had me fooled. You staked claim over him like a tiger and her kill.*

She smiled devilishly. *If you're implying that I'm a man-eater, I'd have to agree.*

I laughed aloud, and the others looked at us, confused.

J.C. looked at Brad, who just shrugged. "Women."

Beth swallowed the obvious lump in her throat and spoke again. "J.C., could you please lead Brad and Parker to the male's bathing quarters and then to their dressing suites afterward? I'm going to take the girls to theirs, and then we all are to meet Rayon in his office at six. He wants to speak to you all once before you see the masses."

"You mean we're splitting up?" I asked.

Beth said, "Well, of course. You can't exactly bathe together."

Lila, Alexa, and I moved toward the door with Beth.

I said, "I guess I'll see y'all later tonight, then."

My eyes locked with Parker, and I heard his voice in my head. *Be careful.*

CHAPTER TWELVE

I was glad for the darkness when I took off my clothes in front of Alexa and Lila. The three of us slid into the bathing pool that bubbled with heat from an underground spring. The water was murky, and the floor was raw. Some of the uneven edges were perfect stools for soaking, though.

I could see the outline of Alexa's face as she laid her head against the stony edge. She sighed and smiled with content. "It's been a long time since I've been this comfortable."

I lowered my shoulders under the water and said, "I could stay in here for days."

Lila spit water from her mouth and said, "I'm glad you guys like it. I have to sit on my knees just to stay where I can breathe."

Alexa grabbed a bottle Beth had left us and squeezed it into her hand. "I don't know about you guys, but I'm looking forward to being clean for once. Look, the little hooker even gave us razors."

"Don't call Beth a little hooker." I said, smiling. I stole the bottle and lathered my chest in it. It tingled and smelled like vanilla.

I squirted some more into my hand before passing the bottle to Lila. I lathered it into my hair then leaned back and closed my eyes. "It's going to be nice to smell like a girl again."

Alexa snorted. "It's a wonder we haven't sent Brad and Parker running with our stench."

I lowered my head under the water and heard the shampoo's bubbles as they rose to the surface. I let myself sink to the bottom of the pool and sat with the uneven stone against my thighs.

I'd forgotten how much I missed the water. I opened my eyes and felt weightless. I couldn't see past my own hands, but I didn't mind. It was just the feeling of being surrounded so completely that made it impossible for me not to smile. I sat there for a few moments and then came back to the surface.

Alexa grabbed me by the shoulders. "Geez, Rose. We thought you'd been sucked into some hole we couldn't see."

"Huh?"

"You were down there for almost six minutes. How did you do that?" Lila sat on the edge of the pool, wrapped in a towel.

I said lamely, "Oh, sorry. I forgot y'all didn't know I could do that. It's weird."

Alexa shook her head and climbed out of the pool. She wrapped herself in a towel and said, "Do you have gills somewhere on that perfect body of yours that we can't see?"

"I can't breathe under water, Alexa. I just don't have to breathe at all." I crawled out into the cold after her. The heat from the pool's water steamed atop my skin. I wrapped myself in the only towel left.

We walked toward the entrance to the bath house. Beth was seated on a stool just beyond the arch. She stood hastily when she saw us.

"Alright, now that that's done, I can take you all to your chambers."

"I thought we couldn't go in there until after dinner?" I asked.

"Things change," Beth said shortly and turned to walk away.

The tunnels were dimly lit, and the shadows in my peripheral made me look over my shoulder with unease. I couldn't place it, but something just wasn't right.

Beth stopped in front of our wing so suddenly that Alexa came crashing into my back.

"I'll leave you here now. I will be back in two hours to take you to Rayon."

"Where are you going?" I asked, turning toward her as she brushed past us.

"I'm going to get ready in my quarters while you all are busy here." She disappeared down the hall.

"Twenty bucks says the little hooch wears a micromini tonight." Alexa said bitterly, staring after her.

I rolled my eyes and pulled open the curtain to our dressing room. "Just because she blushed at Brad does *not* make her a hooch."

She followed me into the room. "Uh huh, you say that now, but I bet you'll be singing a different tune when she sets her little teenybopper sights on Parker."

"She wouldn't dare."

We walked into the room, and Lila and Alexa brushed past me to the closets opposite the door. I turned to close the curtain behind us but stopped when a shadow on the adjacent wall flickered out of existence.

I stuck my head into the hall but didn't see anyone. A cold chill on my spine told me someone had been there, though. This place gave me the creeps.

"Rose?" Alexa was standing so close behind me that I jumped. She stepped back with one eyebrow cocked. "What? You look like you just saw a ghost."

"Not unlikely with me."

Alexa leaned past me and pulled the curtain closed. "Okay… so what are you going to wear tonight?"

I walked over to the closet. "What do you mean? I'm going to wear what I wear everyday: a pair of shorts, a t-shirt, and my knife belt. Speaking of…do you know where they put it?"

Lila peeked out of the closet and said, "I saw it over there by one of the vanities."

"Oh, thanks," I said and walked over to the white mirror table.

My belt was folded neatly atop it, and it was cleaner than it had ever been since I owned it. The leather was soft under my fingertips, worn with years of heavy use. They had mended the sheaths with thread, and the silver buckle had been shined to the point of reflectivity. I held one of my knives in my palm and admired it.

The faded handle had been repainted black, and the sign of the Cancer had been added in red where the blade met the handle. The blade itself was shined and sharpened as if brand new. I looked down unsurely at the weapon and couldn't decide how I felt about it. My physical body couldn't show how ragged and worn I truly was, but my knives could. They showed my story in a way my physical appearance never could. And now they didn't.

Alexa looked over my shoulder and said, "Wow, they managed to make those things look nice. That's something that I didn't know these little desert people could do."

"What? Clean?"

She shrugged and walked back to the closet. "Rose, what do you think about this?"

I turned to see her holding a long maroon dress. I snorted, "Alexa. That's a dress."

"I'm very aware, manwoman," she said and walked over to the faded-red couch in the middle of the room.

She threw the dress over the back of it and then dropped her towel unashamed. I looked away, startled.

She slid the dress over her shoulders and then said, "Tada!"

I turned back and had to admit that she looked pretty. Her hair was drying in gentle waves, and the silk of the dress shone wonderfully against her caramel skin.

She twirled and sighed happily. "I forgot how wonderful silk felt."

"Don't you think it's a little much?"

Lila stepped from the closet holding a short, pink dress. "I dunno, Rose. They did say we were being *presented*. That sounds fancy to me."

"Oh, not you too," I said and groaned. I plopped down on the couch, grabbing my towel, and said, "We're not royalty or anything. This is dumb."

Alexa walked over to the middle vanity and began trifling through the drawers. "Well, I'm not about to go out waving a scepter, but given the opportunity, any woman should want to be a princess."

"I guess I'm not a woman then," I said and walked past Lila as she buttoned the front of her dress.

"I've always had my doubts." Alexa grinned, and then she screamed.

"What? What happened?" My heart was in my throat.

"They have MAC makeup! The desert people have MAC makeup!" She squealed and dumped a bag of cosmetics onto the table.

"I could beat you." I shook my head and went back into the closet.

Lila and Alexa fiddled with their hair, while I scrounged through the closet for something to wear. There were sequins and feathers and long dresses made of silk, but all I wanted was a pair of shorts. I smiled triumphantly when I found a single rack in the very back of plain clothes. I found a pair of tan hiker's shorts and a plain white t-shirt.

I hesitated and called to Alexa, "Where did you find underwear?"

"Underwear?"

I closed my eyes. Lila giggled and then called, "Look in that silver crate near the back of the closet. It's kinda hidden by a bunch of frilly dresses."

I followed her directions and found the crate exactly where she'd explained. I dug through the multitude of unopened bags of underwear in all sizes. I finally found my size and ripped into the plastic bags with my teeth. I slipped on my dry clothes and stepped from the closet.

Alexa sighed. "Rose, could you at least try to dress up?"

"I washed my hair," I said and sat down on the couch. I slid my foot into my boot and started lacing it up.

"It is unfair that so much beauty is wasted on someone who doesn't even care for it."

"Do you think this is too much?" Lila asked and turned from the table to look back at me.

I smiled. The pink of the dress brought out the rosiness of her cheeks, and her slate-grey eyes sparkled brightly.

"No, Lila, you look beautiful. You're going to be a knockout one day." I walked over so I stood behind her.

She looked at the mirror, disappointed, and said, "Not with this Infestation. I'll be lucky to ever kiss a boy."

"Don't say stuff like that, Lila. You still have plenty of time to kiss as many boys as you want," Alexa said while painting her eyelids in makeup.

"How old were you?" Lila asked her.

Alexa paused for a moment and thought. "I was eleven, and his name was Matthew Grayson. We'd been sitting on a slide at the playground when he leaned in. I was so nervous I leaned *away* from him and ended up tumbling down the slide. I was so embarrassed, but he ended up kissing me anyways... You'll see that boys are like that, Lila. Once they have their mind set about doing something with a girl, it takes a lot to convince them otherwise."

"Lila, don't let her convince you that only applies to boys. Alexa is way more determined than any guy I've met," I teased.

"Yeah, whatever," Alexa said.

"What about you, Rose? I bet you've kissed lots of guys." Lila watched as I buckled my knife belt over my pants.

"Actually, Parker was my first kiss."

Alexa looked at me incredulously and said, "What?"

I shrugged. "Well, yeah. I mean, I've lived on my own since I was, like, twelve."

"So, Alexa had her first kiss when she was eleven."

"I don't know... I guess I never wanted to. When you grow up with everyone falling in love with you, falling in love yourself doesn't seem so great."

"Well, if Rose didn't have her first kiss until she was sixteen, then maybe there's some hope for me."

Alexa shook her head and said, "I just can't get over the fact that Parker was your first kiss. I mean…*Parker*."

"What? He counts."

"Yeah, it's just weird to think that the first guy you kissed was the guy who actually fell in love with you," Alexa said.

"Parker doesn't love me."

Alexa snorted. "Yeah, and I'm actually a nice person."

Beth peeked through the curtain and said, "Ladies? It's time to go. The boys are already with Rayon." I stood up, and Beth eyed me disapprovingly. "Did nothing nicer fit?"

I looked down at my shorts and said, "Look, I don't do dresses, and I don't do heels. I bathed. That's about as much as you're going to get from me."

"Alright then." Beth nodded and walked out of the room. She wore a simple black dress with a string of pearls that made her look much older.

The sound of her heels echoed as she walked. Lila, Alexa, and I hurried to keep pace with her.

We turned the corner and bumped into Brad and Parker. A fury of butterflies in my stomach unleashed when I saw Parker. He was dressed in an old fashion, jet-black tuxedo.

Brad turned, dressed identical to Parker, and whined. "How come she didn't have to dress up?"

Beth mumbled something about finding Rayon and left. Parker wrapped his hands around my waist, and I turned into him, his clean, woodsy scent filling my lungs. His brown hair had been trimmed, and he'd finally shaved away the stubble on his jaw.

He smiled and said, "I should have known you'd find some way out of dressing up."

"I don't do glamour."

"Children, children." Rayon stepped through a wooden door at the end of the hall, wearing a faded-gray suit that was more than a little disappointing compared to Parker and Brad.

"Um, I'm nineteen?" Brad said, looking down at Rayon.

Rayon's smile sent chills up my back. "When you get as old as me, then you may call me the child. I'm about to go out and introduce you. Are there any questions?"

Alexa asked, "What do you expect us to do out there? Are we making speeches? Smiling and looking pretty? What?"

Rayon locked eyes with Parker. "You will probably have to say a few words, nothing too elaborate."

Parker nodded like he'd expected as much, but I let out a sigh of relief, glad I wasn't the one who would have to talk.

"As for the rest of you, expect to shake a lot of hands and smile so much your mouth goes numb." Rayon started to walk back out the door but stopped before me. "Oh, and you. You will probably have to dance with every young man in the room."

"Excuse me?" Parker and I said simultaneously.

"She's not dancing with *any* young man in that room," Parker said.

I turned, stunned, and glared at him.

Rayon hesitated, looking between Parker and me. "I'll call you out to the stage after a brief introduction. Just come up, smile and wave, and stand until Parker's delivered his speech. Once that's done, you'll be escorted to a table in the front of the hall where you will eat, followed by time for the people to come and address you, and in some of your cases, where they may ask you to dance."

"Let's do this." Brad bounced on the balls of his feet.

Alexa stared at him and mumbled something about intolerable stupidity.

Rayon opened the door, and a wave of noise flooded into the hall. Light from the dining area filled the small space we were waiting in. The room quieted as he spoke, his voice carrying into the hall where the five of us stood silent as statues, listening to his every word.

"Welcome, brothers and sisters, and good evening!"

A wave of applause erupted so loudly that I jumped from surprise.

Rayon waited a moment for the claps to die down. "As we all know, tonight is a joyous occasion for the entire human race, a celebration of one of our biggest milestones coming full circle. Tonight, we rejoice in the arrival of our newest comrades against the Infestation, the newest weapons we have in the fight for humanity. Tonight, we welcome the last piece of the puzzle that will ensure our victory as a people and give us the promise of a life where we no longer have to live every day in fear, hidden underground! Please help me, friends, in welcoming the Gifted!"

CHAPTER THIRTEEN

The moment I stepped into the cavern, I felt like my mind was going to explode. Hundreds of minds assaulted me; I wasn't even sure which thoughts were my own. I hesitated and tried to cover my eyes. Everything was scrambled in a tangled mess.

Alexa grabbed me by the wrist and jerked me beside her. I shook my head, shrugging her off.

I said through gritted teeth, "I'm fine. Just give me a second."

Parker cleared his throat. I looked up and saw him standing behind the wooden podium, all eyes on him.

"Brothers and sisters of the Circle, my name is Parker Howell, and I come to you as the representative for these people standing behind me."

"The man on the end is my very good friend and the Capricorn, Brad Langston. The beautiful young lady to his right is our very own Libra, Miss Lila Meriwether."

Lila smiled charmingly and waved as an "awe" spread through the audience.

Parker continued, "Next to her is another one of my good friends, the Scorpio known as Miss Alexa McFolly. And finally, someone very special to me, who refuses to wear a dress even to important events, is the Cancer, Miss Rose Hawthorne."

He smiled at me, and I awkwardly waved. The crowd cheered and whistled, and I felt my face turning red. Parker winked and then turned back to the masses.

He said, "I know that we are young, and in comparison to some of you, we are green in the ways of combat. I know these facts to be true but also that they must be accepted and then overcome, for all our fates depend upon one another. If any member of the human race loses the battle against this Infestation, then we all lose. Because for each man or woman we lose to those creatures, they gain another ally. Knowing this, I must ask of you all a favor that is great but that is required if we must succeed, because yes, success is our only option. The other is too terrible to consider.

"I must ask of you, members of the Circle, to make a pact with the members of my group. I ask that you help us overcome our youth and inexperience by sharing your knowledge and wisdom with us in hopes that we may learn from you as you learned from living. In return, I ask that you all accept what we have to teach, for we have much to tell, in hopes that together we will form an impregnable force that the enemy cannot overcome. United, I know that there is no force we cannot defeat. Together, we can show these invaders just how powerful the human race *really* is."

A cheer exploded through the crowd. Parker smiled and then stepped away from the podium to stand beside me. He beamed.

I can't believe they liked it.

I smiled and squeezed his hand.

Rayon stepped to the podium and said, "Wonderful! Wonderful! The Gifted have arrived. Now, let us feast!"

Rayon turned to us and spoke quietly, "Make your way down the steps to your left and sit at the head table. After dinner is served, there will be music. You are required to stay until the last person leaves. Is that understood?"

We nodded and followed Brad down the stairs to a large table. It was at the head of the room in front of a massive, open space. Two buffet-style tables ran up the length of the walls, and people crowded around them, filling their plates and watching us.

Music began playing soft and slow from a small group in the corner using rag-tag instruments. The sound was pleasant, though.

Parker gently touched my knee, and I looked up at him. He was beautiful with his clean curls and freshly shaven face. A plump man wearing a white apron gave me a hearty helping of grilled chicken, peas, and some delicious-looking rolls from the trays in his hand, and I thanked him. I noticed passively that he was filling some of our cups with beer, though I'd received water.

I started cutting into my chicken but stopped when I realized everyone in the dining hall was staring at us. I looked down the row to see what everyone else was doing.

Parker spoke in my head, *They expect each of us to take the first bite, but then they will eat. They'll probably stop staring like zombies after that.*

Oh, so you noticed that too, I thought back.

Rayon tapped his glass, and everyone turned to face him. "Friends, may our guests dine."

I cut a small bite from the chicken and stuck it into my mouth. The lemon flavoring took me pleasantly by surprise. It'd been years since I had a professionally cooked meal; I didn't count Waffle House. A cheer bellowed from the masses when I cut my second bite, and just as Parker promised, the majority of the group dispersed to the tables.

Parker said, "That wasn't so bad, was it?"

"It wasn't as bad as, say, walking halfway across the country with no sleep."

Parker smiled and took a sip of his drink. "You still haven't forgiven me for that."

"You were forgiven for the no sleeping thing, but I'm still angry about my pants that you ripped."

"They must have been pretty special pants."

"The best."

He smiled and looked over at me. "Can I ask you a question?"

"You just did."

He rolled his eyes. "Why didn't you dress up? I was kind of hoping I'd get to see you all fixed up."

I snorted. "That's a hope that you will probably never see fulfilled."

"Why not?"

I finished my chicken with a very unladylike bite and said, "Because I'm secretly a man, and it's painfully obvious when I wear dresses. My shoulders are too broad, ruins the whole illusion."

"A man, huh? That explains the boots."

"Shut up," I said with a smile.

"Rose?" A boy of about sixteen stood across from me at the table. He had messy blond hair and soft-green eyes. He was wearing a weathered suit that looked as if it had once belonged to someone older, like a father.

I looked up and couldn't feel his thoughts; he was strong enough to hide them from me. I took a sip of my water and then said, "Yes?"

"I couldn't help but notice that you finished eating…and, well, I was hoping you would have a dance with me."

Parker's hand on my knee went stiff.

I looked at the boy anxiously and fumbled with my words. "But the music stopped."

As if on cue from some terribly directed comedy, the band began again with a sleepy number. I looked down at my plate, sighed, and then apologetically met Parker's blue eyes.

"Yeah, okay." I walked around the table to where the boy was standing.

A small group of people were already on the floor, but they made room for us.

He waited for some cue in the music I didn't recognize before resting his hand upon my waist. He took my hand in his and smiled.

My face reddened, and I whispered, "I don't know how to dance."

"It's all right. You're the girl. All you have to do is follow my lead." He smiled warmly and moved us in rhythm.

I stepped on his foot, and he laughed.

"If you knew me, you'd realize how unlikely that is."

He spun me in a tight circle and brought me back to him. He smiled easily and not one of his thoughts leaked from his mind.

"What's your name, kid?"

"Wes Deluka, but I'm not a kid. I'm older than you are."

I looked over my shoulder to see if I could see Parker, but a group of dancers blocked the way. I turned back to Wes and said, "Doubtful. How old are you anyways? Fifteen? Sixteen?"

He dipped me slowly, his arm withstanding my entire weight. "Seventeen, actually, and if the rumors are true, that makes me an entire year older than you."

"That depends on whether or not you think only years determine age."

"Do they not?"

"Not to me. There are other things that factor in."

"Like?"

The song began to slow, signaling its finale. "Like experience."

"What kind of experience?"

The final cord sounded, but his hand remained on my hip.

"Like having enough experience to know that if you don't take your hand from a girl's hip when the song ends, it means you have to dance with her again."

He smiled as the opening note for a more upbeat song began. "Who says I didn't know that?"

I smiled but faltered when I thought of Parker sitting all alone back at the table. I hesitated and looked back over my shoulder.

"He knows where to find you if he wants to cut in," Wes said softly.

"I know... It's just—"

"Think of it this way: you can walk back to that table now only to see your boyfriend for maybe three seconds before another guy comes up and whisks you away. That other guy may or may not be as easy to talk to, and I guarantee he won't be as good looking. Or you can stay over here and dance with me all night until your boyfriend comes out here to get you himself."

I bit my lip. He was right. If I wasn't dancing with him, I'd most likely have to dance with someone who would let their thoughts slip from their head like sand.

I turned back to him, took his other hand, and rested it on my hip. "Well, Mr. Deluka, I think you just charmed your way into another dance."

He grinned. "I guess I'll suffer through it."

"You better, or I might just have to go get Rayon to replace you."

Wes laughed with an open, broad smile that was contagious. "I find it funny that your first thought of who you replace me with is Rayon."

"It's not like I know too many other men in the Circle."

"Well, there is your boyfriend."

I sighed and instinctively looked back to the table. He wasn't there. "He's not exactly my boyfriend."

"Brother?"

I laughed. "No, not a brother either. Parker and I are just…"

He wiggled his eyebrows and said, "Friends with benefits?"

"I'm not sure how to describe us. We just…are."

"Is that his doing or your own?"

"You sure ask a lot of questions, Mr. Deluka."

He shrugged and said, "Just trying to figure you out, Miss Hawthorne."

"Well, when you do, could you tell me what you found out? Because I've been with me for sixteen years, and I still can't tell you why I am the way I am."

We danced through so many songs, my head was spinning. Wes was startlingly easy to talk to. He understood the art of conversation—when to talk and when to listen. It wasn't forced, like I felt like I had to make a reply to everything. Plus, he kept the right amount of distance.

At the end of a particularly fast-paced song, I was breathing hard and laughing. Wes led me off the dance floor toward the table with all the glasses of water. The room had mostly emptied, but there were still a few sparse groups talking in the corners. Wes handed me a glass of water, and I drank from it eagerly.

"That last one about killed me."

"Enjoying yourself?" Parker's breath filled the air around my face, and the overwhelming stench of beer hit my nostrils. I turned, shocked, and saw Parker's brown curls in sweaty disarray and his tie hanging from his neck like a limp sash.

"Are you *drunk?*"

"What else was I supposed to do while I watched my girlfriend get felt up all night by some other guy?"

"Hey, man, we were just dancing." Wes stepped between Parker and me, his broad chest blocking my view.

"Did anyone ask you your opinion, *boy*? Why don't you run along now and go screw somebody else's girlfriend. Mine's done for the night."

"Parker." I could sense other conversations quieting as people noticed us.

"I think it might be time for you to turn in, brother. You don't know what you're saying." Wes turned to me and said, "I'd be more than happy to escort you back to your room since he's no longer able."

Parker said, "Excuse me? I think you meant escort her back to her room so you could climb in the bed with her and make it a night, right? Well, I've got something to tell you, son. She is mine. She shares the bed with *me*. Not you. So I think you better find someone who isn't already claimed."

I slapped him. The hall fell quiet. Even the band stopped playing. I was struggling to control my breathing, my chest rising and falling quickly. I stared into his glazed-over eyes and gritted my teeth. *I am not your property. I am not yours to claim. I am leaving you here, and if you follow me, you will wake up less of a man than you did this morning.*

I held his gaze for a second longer to make sure he'd understood what I said. When his eyes flared, I pushed past him and left the cavern. I stormed into the Gifted's wing so quickly that Brad and Alexa jumped. They were sitting at the kitchen table holding hands, and Lila was asleep on the couch.

I went into the first room I saw and closed the curtain behind me. I paced and then kicked the wood frame of the bed. I sat on the edge of the mattress and buried my face in my hands.

What's going on? Alexa's voice was in my head.

I think I just broke up with Parker. He's down in the cavern. You need to send Brad to go get him. He's too drunk to walk back by himself.

There was a momentary pause, and then her voice was back, fiercer. *What did he do to you?*

Nothing. Just make sure he gets back here safely. That includes making sure he doesn't come into this room, because if I see him again tonight, he will be anything but safe.

Alright, do you want to talk about it?

No. I'm going to bed. I closed my mind to everything and lay back against the pillow. I pulled my knees to my chest and wrapped my arms around them. A single tear slid from my eye, but I wiped it away. I let myself sleep.

CHAPTER FOURTEEN

"Rose? Rose, come on. You have to wake up. We are supposed to be downstairs in fifteen minutes."

I groaned and pushed Alexa's hand from my shoulder. I pulled the white comforter over my head, hiding. She sighed and yanked it completely off the bed, exposing me to the cold. I jerked up and then looked around me, disoriented. I'd been so angry last night that I hadn't even noticed the room I was in.

The bed was large and imposing with tall, white posts and frilly sheets. There was a dresser against the wall opposite me with fresh-picked tulips in a hand-painted vase, and beside it was a golden basin of water. The room was small but very nicely decorated.

"This place is a whole lot nicer than it was when I fell asleep last night."

"Most things do seem better in the morning." Alexa shrugged and then turned to leave. She stopped by the door and said, "This is probably pointless, but have you considered opening your thoughts yet? I know that I, for one, don't appreciate getting a mental answering machine."

I rubbed my eyes and sighed. I would have to open my thoughts again sometime, but when I did, it really *would* be like listening to an answering machine. I'd have to hear every thought I'd blocked before I could welcome more.

I lay back against the pillow and groaned. I hated Parker for putting me through this. I hated myself for letting him. I took a deep breath and reluctantly pulled the wall back from my thoughts. The delayed messages began to poor through the barrier.

Don't you walk away from me!

Where'd you go? His room?

Your other boyfriend is lookin' for you.
I grimaced.
Don't worry about him, Rose. I got him. He'll be sobered up by tomorrow. I was relieved to hear Brad's clear thoughts.
Rose. Rose, I'm so sorry. Please talk to me. Parker's voice was clear. I could feel his regret.
I can't believe what I did last night. I can't believe I put you through that. I'm so sorry. Rose, please listen to me.
Rosie?
Rose, I know I deserve this, but I need you to listen to me. I need you to tell me I didn't just ruin this. If I did...I don't know what... just please respond.
Rosie. Please.
Rose.
I know you're blocking everyone's thoughts, because you can't just block mine, but I have to tell you this anyways. I was jealous. I'm sorry I'm that way. I guess it's just that I've never had anyone be so good for me, and I'm scared to lose that. It's not an excuse, but it's the truth. I promise I'll work on it. I'm hoping that in time you will forgive me, even though I know I don't deserve it. I'm sorry, Rose. I really, really am.

I let out a breath I didn't know I'd been holding and rubbed my eyes. Everything was muddy and dirty and confusing.

I sat up and swung my legs over the side of the bed. I was still wearing my boots...and my knives...and everything I'd worn to the dinner. I sleepily stumbled to the dresser and changed clothes. I didn't even really notice what I put on.

I dipped my hands into the basin of water and tried to wipe away the fatigue from my face. It was pointless, though. It wasn't like anyone I met wouldn't know I had been upset last night. I was sure the group of people who'd witnessed me slapping Parker had already spread it throughout the cavern. If I'd thought the looks had been overwhelming yesterday; today might possibly kill me.

"Rose?" Lila stood cautiously near the entrance to my room. Her blonde curls were pulled back from her face in a braid, and all the glamour from the night before had been washed away.

I hated the look that she gave me. Today was seriously going to suck if it was filled with as many "I'm sorry" glances as this morning was starting to suggest.

"Everyone else already left, but I volunteered to stay with you."

"You didn't have to do that, Lila. Rayon's probably already pissed at me about what went down last night. There's no reason to drag you into this by being late to whatever he has planned."

"I don't know about the him-being-pissed part, but I know what he has planned for today."

I raised my brows questioningly. She grinned and said, "Combat training."

I smiled broadly. "Maybe today won't be so bad after all."

We navigated our way through the tunnels, passing few people but nodding cordially at those we did. It was unnerving knowing that at any given moment there could be someone coming toward us from around the corner. I'd gone my whole life avoiding people, and it was hard for me to adjust to the fact that now I was supposed to welcome them all as allies. We stepped into a large cavern, smaller than the one last night but still massive in its own right. The stench of sweat and sawdust filled my nostrils. I inhaled deeply and smiled over to Lila.

A tension crept over my muscles as I saw him. Parker stood four feet from me, separated by Alexa and Brad, yet he never seemed so close. His brown curls were untamed as if he'd crawled out of bed and come directly here. His eyes were bloodshot. He turned toward me, and our eyes locked. A look of pure despair rang out in his expression, and I felt every ounce of his sadness, regret, and anguish. I bit my bottom lip and forced myself to look away from him.

"All right, so here's how it works." I looked up to see J.C. standing in a pair of gym shorts and sneakers with sweat dripping down his chest.

"I'm in charge of the sparring grounds, so what I say goes. I know that some of you have a little issue taking orders, but in here that could get you, or more likely someone else, killed. I don't know how you've trained before, but I can promise it's nothing like in here. You will do single combat training against one or more opponents every morning from eight until ten. There will be no tardiness. From ten to noon there will be an intergroup combat match where two of you will be put against one another and will be expected to fight as if you were enemies.

"At noon we will break for lunch. After lunch you will do doubles or entire group combat training until four. At four you will be sent to the showers, and at five you are expected to be in the board room in your wing. From five to seven you will take any guest from the Circle that seeks your attention, and you will work on devising strategies that could prove beneficial in the days ahead. Dinner is at seven, which is mandatory attendance, but after that the rest of the day is your own."

Alexa snorted. "You mean all two hours of it?"

J.C. stepped in front of her and said, "Ah, Miss McFolly. It seems that you are with me for the first half of today."

Alexa's dark eyes rose, and she said, "Well, aren't you lucky?"

A half smile broke his expression. He turned to everyone else and said, "As for the rest of you, one of the guys in the back is assigned to each you for the first part of today. They'll take you to where you need to go."

Only when J.C. said that did I realize that it wasn't just our group standing before him. There were average members of the Circle congregated around us, looking on eagerly and whispering amongst themselves. These were the warriors, the ones prized for their strength both physically and mentally, so of course I couldn't feel their thoughts. Parker was next to me, so close that my shoulder touched the middle of his chest. He whispered, "Rose, can we talk?"

I turned toward him ready to be angry, but it dissipated when I met his eyes. He had too much control over me; my emotions weren't my own when he looked at me that way. His expression was so sad and broken it made my chest hurt.

My voice was quieter than I'd intended when I said, "Parker, this isn't fair. Let me be mad."

"You have every right to be angry. I was a jerk, worse than that even. I just want you to know how sorry I am. I'll do anything."

"Hey, Rose! Guess who's leading your session this morning?" Wes came strutting over with a bright smile. It faded when he saw the intimate and incredibly tense conversation he'd interrupted.

I swallowed and pulled myself away from Parker. I felt colder as I walked away from him, ignoring Wes's hard eyes on me.

"So you went back to him, just like that?"

"It's not that simple, Wes."

"It seems that way to me. He got drunk, said some things I can't even repeat in front of a woman, and then you took him back as simple as pie."

"He's not ever like that. It was just the alcohol."

"A drunken man's words are a sober man's thoughts."

I laughed. I couldn't very well tell Wes that I had been in Parker's head, and his thoughts were nothing like that. "If it makes you feel any better, I haven't taken him back yet. What you saw was him trying to apologize again."

We stopped before an open space twenty feet wide. There was a large circle painted in white on the red dirt of the cavern floor.

Wes said, "You said yet. That means you plan on taking him back eventually."

I shrugged. "I don't know what I plan on doing today, let alone eventually. You'll learn that most of the time I just take life as it comes. It's when you start to make plans that everything falls apart."

"Has anyone ever told you that you don't talk like a sixteen-year-old?"

"Has anyone ever told you that you *look* like a six-year-old?"

He smiled and said, "You're going to pay for that in about four seconds."

I felt bad for him. I saw his punch coming before he even finished the sentence. I caught his fist and hit him in his exposed rib.

He doubled over. "You're fast."

I grinned and took a few steps back, giving him the room to make another attack. He took a deep breath, cracking his knuckles, and then threw a hit at my shoulder. I blocked and faked right. He fell for it, and I punched right above his kidney. He recovered quickly, and we exchanged hits. I let him get a few on me, enough to learn how he moved. He was a good fighter, skilled enough to know how to block and when to throw the punch, but he was slow.

"Don't compromise your safety for what you see as a good hit," I said.

I hit him in the rib cage after he'd overextended. His fists dropped to shield his abdomen.

"Second, learn how to compartmentalize. Letting the pain get to you during a fight can mean the difference between living and dying."

I kicked into his left knee. He collapsed and struggled to grab some part of me in an attempt to salvage the fight.

"Third, know when it's best to run."

I grabbed him by the arm he had on my knee and twisted it. He groaned but couldn't fight back. If he moved, his arm would go out of socket.

"I yield."

I smiled and let go of him. I helped him stand up, and he rolled his shoulders.

He shook his head and said, "I thought I'd at least last ten minutes."

"Well, four is a start."

We fought like that for the next two hours. Sweat beat down Wes's face, and he collected bruise after bruise. Had he been a lesser person, he probably would have given up after the third loss, but Wes was more open than I'd even hoped. He asked questions about what he did wrong, and we went over the correct ways to do things rather than how he'd been doing them.

When ten o'clock finally came, I had to laugh at the relief on Wes's face. I could already see the growing bruises coloring his skin.

J.C. stopped before him with a crooked smile and said, "Did you get in a little over your head there, Wes?"

"Let's see you fight her for two hours and see if you come out any better."

J.C. laughed and said, "No, thanks. I don't doubt you came out better than I would. I tried to fight Parker once and nearly came out in a coma."

Wes wiped at his mouth and said, "I doubt he's a good as her. Twenty-six. That's how many times she pinned me. And look at her, not even a hair out of place."

J.C. looked at me skeptically. He paused then smiled. He turned to address the whole cavern. "All right, everyone, time for the first Gifted match up. Today it's Rose and Parker. Both of ya'll to the center."

I froze. Wes grabbed my upper arm and whispered into my ear, "You can do this. Just don't think about him as being Parker. Think of him as someone else."

I nodded and rolled my shoulders. I stepped into the chalked circle of the sparring arena. Parker stood opposite me, his hair stuck around his face from sweat and his shirt removed. *My God, he's beautiful.*

"Look at her face. She's heartbroken." It was whispered, but with my hearing it might as well been yelled.

I turned directly toward the man who'd said it. He was short with thinning brown hair, but he didn't seem to notice me staring at him. He blended in well with the growing mass of fighters who'd dropped their weapons to come watch the fight.

The blond man he'd been addressing shook his head softly and said, "Poor girl."

I looked down at my feet with a rage building in my chest. I'd *never* been the "poor girl." Never in my life. Before Parker started messing with my emotions, I was strong and would have never had to have people like Wes giving me a pep talk. I most *certainly* never had complete strangers feeling sorry for me. This wasn't me.

I looked up and met Parker's gaze. I could see that he saw the shift in my emotion. His brows furrowed, and then he set his shoulders. He looked at me head on, his expression unreadable.

J.C. stepped between us, addressing the growing crowd more than Parker and me. "Here are the rules. There are none, other than if you step out of the circle, you forfeit. Winning is when the other person yields or passes out, and if any blood is drawn, well, then that's your own personal problem that can be dealt with later. Understood?"

Parker and I nodded. The anticipation building in my arms was getting to the point of maddening, making my muscles tighten, ready for action. J.C. stepped from the circle, and the crowd began to cheer. My mind blocked it all except for the deep, ragged breathing in my chest and my heartbeat.

I saw the ripple of his muscle before he actually made the charge. It wasn't like with Wes where I could just step to the side and be done with it. Parker was equal to me in speed and in strength.

He was at me in an instant. He threw a sharp right hook to my side, but I spun and kicked. He caught my leg and spun me. I hit the ground, and the crowd cheered. I spit and made myself stand back up. He smiled. I went at him, throwing punches so fast our hands blurred. He blocked one, missed one, threw one, and missed one. It was a dance. I finally got him hard on the jaw. He spit, and his blood was red on the ground.

He faked a hit and then surprised me with a roundhouse kick to my chest. It met my ribs with a crack. Red haze clouded my vision. I gasped and dropped to my knees, clutching my side. I looked down at my hands and saw the sticky red wetness on my hands. Parker's steel toe had pierced my skin.

He rushed to me, his hand on my back. "Rose, oh my God. You're really bleeding."

I shook my head, grimacing through the sickening nausea that meant the bones were mending. It itched, but the pain ended soon. Parker didn't know that though; he was still behind me, looking down at me protectively.

I took advantage of that. I threw my elbow into his abdomen, hearing the air leave his lungs. I rolled forward, unsheathing my Kukri knives in the motion. The crowd went wild.

Parker smirked at me, shaking his head. He scanned the area, looking for a weapon. I wasn't going to give him that chance. I charged at him, my knives drawn, but he vanished right before I was on him. He appeared on the other side of the circle, pulling a man's sword from his belt. People laughed and cheered, stomping and banging their weapons to their shields. This was what they'd been waiting for—the time when the Gifts came out.

I shook my head and said, *Cute magic trick, Houdini, but when you're ready to fight, I'm over here.*

He grinned lopsidedly. *What can I say? The people love a good show.*

He disappeared and then was at me with his sword. I caught it between my two curved knives, and sparks flickered from our blades as they scraped one another. My whole body absorbed the vibration of our blades meeting.

He vanished and then appeared behind me. I was barely able to block his attack. He knew it and smiled. He vanished again, and I was forced on the defensive. We fought like that for several minutes. We were moving so fast that I wasn't sure anyone could even see us. My own blade looked like a blur to me.

Parker finally made a mistake. He lunged too far and knew it the minute I smiled. I leaned into him, grabbing his blade with the grip of mine, and spun it from his hand. His sword hit the ground, ringing as a cheer broke from the crowd—the fight was mine.

Or so I thought. I saw the madness of his grin before I understood it. He turned, disappearing, and then an invisible avalanche crashed into my body. My knives dropped from my hands as I tried to catch myself. It was futile, though. He was on me. I felt the cold steel of my spare dagger pulled from my waist before it was pressed my neck. He used my own blade against me. Parker reappeared, his body pinning mine effortlessly beneath him. If I wiggled an inch to free myself, I'd cut my own throat.

His face hung over mine as he smiled at me. His breath was hot against my face, and his long brown curls tickled my cheeks. He said breathlessly, "I win."

My heart pounded in my ears. A million thoughts registered at once. Parker's bare chest leaned against my body so close that I could feel his racing heart. My eyes flashed down to his lips. I lifted my head far enough for our lips to meet.

Everything in my world went quiet. He hesitated for a terrifying moment and then responded eagerly. He dropped the dagger to the ground and used his hand to lift my head.

He was so distracted that he never noticed my hand slipping into his waistband and slowly drawing out the dagger I knew he kept there. Once he finally felt the cold steel pressed against his abdomen, it was too late. I had him pinned.

He looked down at the blade, shocked, and then back at me.

I laughed and whispered, "What can I say? The people love a good show."

He laughed and shook his head. He raised his hands in surrender and announced for the whole crowd to hear, "I yield."

The swarm of people erupted into mass hysteria. Cheers and whistles rang out, echoing against the walls of the cavern.

I laughed and stood up, dusting the red dirt from my clothes. Parker smiled at me, and I laughed, shaking my head.

J.C. came bouncing over to us, his face alight with excitement. "Brother, I cannot say I have seen a more respectable defeat in my life."

Parker shrugged, still smiling, and picked his dagger up from the floor. "I shouldn't have put it past her to try something like that."

"Hey now, I won fair and square."

Parker opened his mouth to reply, but a disapproving voice interrupted him.

"Do you plan on kissing all the opponents you'll fight if you get stuck in a battle?"

I turned to Rayon, smiling dryly, and said, "Well, maybe if they're all as beautiful as you."

J.C. snorted, but Rayon's dismal expression never faltered. Instead he sighed and said, "Cute. However, I need to speak with you and Mr. Howell in private."

"We've only been here two days, and we're already being called to the principal's office? That has to be a new record," I said, and Parker laughed.

We followed Rayon out of the cavern, grinning and waving wildly at the crowd as we stepped through them.

Rayon moved quickly, so Parker and I ended up rushing just to keep up. He stopped abruptly at his entrance and held the curtain for us to go inside.

I sat beside Parker in the armchairs directly in front of Rayon's desk. Rayon sat down, and his beady, washed-out eyes bore into Parker and me.

He spoke without kindness. "Last night was unacceptable. I thought I made it very clear that you were to behave as respectable public figures, *not* get completely intoxicated and put on a scene before everyone present. Some things should be handled in private, like when Miss Hawthorne here decided she was going to make things physical. I don't think—"

I sighed, feeling the little patience I had for the man dwindling into nothing.

He raised an eyebrow at me. "I'm sorry, am I boring you?"

"I'm sorry, but this crap has to stop."

"Excuse me?"

"Look, I get that we're important and that people look up to us or whatever, but I'm sick of you thinking that we have some obligation to follow your rules."

"I am in charge of the Circle."

"Good for you. I'm sure your mother's proud."

"Do you realize what I could do to you as punishment for your insolence right now, little girl?"

I leaned forward, resting my elbows against Rayon's desk. I locked eyes with him and said, "Honestly? Nothing. There's nothing you can do to me, because you have no authority over me."

"I already told you. I'm the—"

"The leader of the Circle. Yeah, I got that. But if you haven't noticed, none of my group is technically a part of your Circle. We came here to help in the fight against the Infestation, not to take part in some screwed up political hierarchy, and definitely not to be berated like children every time we make a choice that you don't agree with. You're not my dad, so don't think I'm going to do what you ask just because you ask it. I don't owe you anything."

Rayon and I locked eyes. I wanted him to say something else, to tell me that I was wrong, but he didn't. He just held my gaze. Parker cleared his throat and stood, motioning with his eyes for me to follow.

"We'll see you at dinner, I guess," Parker said, escorting me into the hall.

We walked a few steps before he looked at me. We couldn't hold it then. We broke into a hysterical fit of laughter so strong that I could barely walk. I turned away with my hand over my mouth. He was hunched over, his hands on his knees, with tears going down his face. I started hiccupping, which only made him laugh harder. He came over and held me in his arms. I laughed into his chest. It was a long five minutes before we stopped.

His body was warm against mine. He looked down at me, smiling, and gently brushed a stand of hair from my face. He whispered, "About last night—"

"You've already been forgiven. I guess I shouldn't be surprised that I can't stay angry at you for as long as I would like to think."

"Why would you like to think you could be mad at me?"

"Because that's who I am. I get mad at people and stay that way until I punch them. It's kind of just how I function."

He chuckled and said, "But you did punch me, a few times actually. Unlike you, though, I'm going to have the bruises to show for it."

I smiled and looked down at my chest. My shirt was covered in dried blood, and for a moment I thought it was Parker's.

He followed my gaze and said quietly, "You were bleeding so much from that kick. I dunno, I guess I thought you'd have blocked it."

I snorted. "Yeah, but I didn't. You cracked a few ribs, you know." I lifted my shirt to show the place where he'd hit me. Not even a bruise remained.

Parker's warm hand rested against the skin of my abdomen, and he shook his head. "I thought… When I saw all that blood, I thought I'd finally done it."

"Done what?"

"Ruined this. Pushed away everything I ever wanted."

I leaned into him and I felt safe. I closed my eyes, and his chin rested upon my head. We stood like that for a moment, neither of us willing to move, until I felt the itchy feeling in my head that meant people were about to turn onto our hall. Parker sensed my change and pulled back.

I smiled a half smile. "We should probably go to lunch before we get caught out here. We wouldn't want Rayon to have another scandal to deal with."

CHAPTER FIFTEEN

We were met with a cheering crowd when we entered the dining hall. Apparently our fight had spread further than just the men who'd watched us in the arena. It felt strange having people's adoration because of something I'd actually done rather than just because I existed.

"I think I'm going to throw up," I said through closed teeth.

Parker laughed. "Don't be embarrassed. They love you for what you did."

"But why?" I waved awkwardly.

We passed between two tables to get to the serving line.

"Because, for one, it was freaking genius. No one expected it. And two, I'd like to think it's because it shows that we're still people. I keep getting this feeling that Rayon has tried to make these people think we're so above them, above doing silly things like kissing to get the upper hand in a fight. I think they like it because it humanized us a little bit, made us a little more relatable... And then there's the fact that they love us together."

A woman stepped into my path. She was small and in her early sixties. Her eyes were deep brown and aged, but deep within them I could see that she was strong.

Her mind was blocked from mine tightly, but I could feel the...the *anger* pulsing through her. I half expected her to hit me, but instead she spat at my feet. The room grew quiet. I looked down at her saliva on my boots.

The woman shook her head and spoke loudly, despite how silent the hall had become. "You should be ashamed, disgraced even. You made a mockery of the practice that is supposed to prepare us for the fight of our lives. *Kissing* to win? Our girls watch you, especially, hoping to figure out how they should be in the days ahead. What did you show them today? That using their bodies is more important than learning to fight fairly? I'm ashamed to have my life in the hands of a girl like you."

There was a moment where I thought I might actually cry in front of all those people—a split second where I felt the lump in my throat get so large that it probably could have burst through my skin. I inhaled to steady myself. I wouldn't let this woman know she hurt me. I wouldn't give her the satisfaction.

I controlled my voice, surprised at how even I sounded, and said, "I'm sorry I disappointed you, ma'am."

I stepped past her, pulling Parker with me. The hall remained silent. I didn't look over my shoulder to see if the woman left or sat back down, though I hoped it was the first. Parker stood behind me while we got our food, protectively blocking me from everyone's eyes. For once I let him stand between me and all the looks without objection. For once, I didn't think I could handle feeling all those eyes locked on me. For once, I wasn't sure I was strong enough.

I saw Alexa, Lila, and Brad sitting at a table near the back of the hall. When Parker and I finally sat down, the voices in the hall slowly rose to a murmur. I had no doubt what their conversations were about.

Alexa gripped a butter knife in her hand so hard that her knuckles were white. "I can't believe that hag said that to you."

I shrugged and spun my fork through the pasta on my plate. "I think we should just drop it. It's not worth the energy."

Brad choked on the food in his mouth. "Did Rose just say something reasonable?"

I dropped my fork, giving up the pretense that I felt like eating, and said, "Funny. But I'm serious. I mean, she was kind of right. I wasn't taking that seriously when it's their lives on the line."

Alexa pointed her knife at me and said, "No. No freaking way you're letting that old bag of wrinkles get to you. You rocked today. Seriously, I thought it was brilliant. That woman can just go die if she has a problem with it."

I smiled.

Parker said through a mouthful of bread, "If we're going to keep talking about this, can I just ask if I was the only one surprised that Rose didn't punch her?"

I laughed. "Parker. Even I'm above punching some old woman just because she said something I didn't like."

"I'm not," Alexa said.

"That's a shocker." I said, smiling.

Alexa smirked and took a sip of her water.

J.C. came up to our table and sat at the end. "Hey, I heard what happened. Don't listen to Sunny. She's kind of our resident buzz kill."

Alexa snorted. "Her name is Sunny? I bet it's because of her warm personality."

J.C. ignored her and said, "She just takes things really seriously because her daughter was taken about a year ago."

"Taken?" I asked.

"Are you going to finish that?" Brad pointed at my plate, and I pushed it to him. He smiled and began to dig into the alfredo.

J.C. said, "Her daughter, Virginia, was only sixteen but was seriously one of the best fighters we had. She got ambushed in a K-mart though, and the bugs dragged her away. Never saw her again."

"Did that happen a lot? The bugs taking them rather than just killing them right when they caught them, I mean," I asked.

J.C. shrugged. "Sometimes, but not a lot. It's kind of why Sunny is as bitter as she is. I think she secretly thinks Virginia fought her way out of it and is coming back. I dunno. Whatever goes through her head is a mystery to me."

I folded my arms and said, "It makes sense, though. Who wouldn't get all serious about defeating the Infestation if they thought someone they loved was still alive, caught up in it?"

Alexa shook her head and said, "Not me. If they took one of y'all, I wouldn't hide out underground like that old hag. I'd go and personally kill every single one of them until they gave you back."

"Easy for you to say. You actually have a pretty good chance of taking those things down. But for the rest of us mere mortals, it's considered a big deal to kill even one. Going rogue is like suicide."

Brad looked up and asked, "J.C., what does J.C. stand for?"

J.C. looked at him strangely, but Parker shook his head.

J.C. answered, "Uh, it's for Jackson Cole. We figured out real quick that my name was a lot to yell when you needed my attention in a fight. So they shortened it to J.C."

I asked, "But Parker called you Jack. Why not just shorten it to that?"

"Because he was the only one I ever let call me that."

"You two complement each other well," I said, ignoring Parker's embarrassment.

"I could say the same about you two." J.C. grinned lopsidedly at me, making me think of the resemblance the two brothers shared. When they smiled like that, they were borderline identical.

You should eat. We have to go back to the arena after this, Parker thought to me.

I faked a smile.

Don't worry about it, slick. I'm not all that hungry anyways.

I'm sorry about what Sunny said to you. I hope you know she was completely wrong about you. You're nothing like she was insinuating.

He didn't have to mention what exactly that was. The woman had only been a breath away from saying I slept around to get what I wanted.

Aren't I, though? Think about it. I don't sleep with people to get what I want, but how many times have I used these stupid Gifts for my advantage? The train station, all those people in the fast food place... Parker, I use the way I look to manipulate people all the time. Is that so different from what Sunny was saying?

Parker's voice was adamant in my head. *It's not even in the same category. Rose, we're given our Gifts because they are meant to help us survive. We hold more of a burden than most people. We were given these Gifts to save humanity. But I believe God wouldn't have given us these burdens to bear if He didn't think it was all right for us to use them to save ourselves too. You especially.*

The rest of us can mask our Gifts and live amongst normal people if we want, but you don't even have that. You chose to live in seclusion, only using your Gift once a year out of necessity when you could have gone out in the world and gotten anything. You didn't, though. That's what makes you different than what Sunny was saying. You don't extort people with your Gifts, Rose. You use them to help others and rarely to help yourself. She just doesn't know you like I do.

I laid my hand against his knee and turned to him, our eyes meeting. *Why are you so good to me, huh?*

Because you deserve it. He smiled.

"Err...guys?" J.C. said, staring at us.

Everyone had stood from the table and was looking at us strangely. Lila, Brad, and Alexa were smug, knowing we had been having a conversation no one else could hear, but J.C. just looked confused.

"I feel like I just broke up some intimate eye sex," J.C. said, and I laughed.

"Don't worry about it." Parker stood and took my hand.

J.C. looked at us skeptically and said, "Okay...well, it's almost one, so we should get back to the grounds. It's time for doubles."

"What's doubles again?" I asked.

"It's when you are broken into a group of two and a group of three and pit against a group of regular people. It's the closest we can come to simulating what would happen if the group were broken up in the middle of a fight."

"Oh, that sounds cool. Who am I with?"

J.C. grinned back at me and said, "Today? You're with Alexa."

CHAPTER SIXTEEN

I turned, and a blade grazed the side of my face, drawing a trickle of blood from my cheek. Alexa gripped the forearm of the man who'd cut me, knocking his blade from its intended target. For a split second I was stunned. Had this been a real fight, she would have just saved my life.

Alexa incapacitated the man effortlessly, kneeing him in his groin and then breaking his nose. Only a single drop of blood escaped my cut before it healed. I wiped the trickle of red from my face and spit.

Alexa's voice was in my head as she said, *I'm sick of this no weapons crap. Are you thinking what I'm thinking?*

I grinned and was thankful she could be just as reckless as me. We lunged forward, faking an attack, and the circle of attackers fumbled. I laughed and took my chance. I threw a quick punch to the balding man before me, feeling his nose collapse under my fist.

By reflex, he tried to grab at his face, only he had a sword in his hand. I grabbed at the weapon, spinning his wrist, and pulled it from him. I pushed him to the ground and stepped back toward Alexa. She'd done the same thing and was now holding a sword.

We fought the remaining men. They were good, better than I had expected. Even as Alexa and I did complex maneuvers, spinning around one another and swinging, we only took out one. Four still kept coming.

We need a plan. They're too organized for us to beat like this, I thought to her.

A second passed before Alexa thought of a plan and shared it with me. I laughed aloud. It was so wild; only we would be crazy enough to try it.

I turned, and she stepped into a cradle in my hands. I threw her up, sending her flipping over the circle of opponents' heads. I back flipped in the opposite direction over the attackers. Our faces were only inches above theirs, our eyes locking. We grazed the shoulder muscles of the men beneath us with our swords as we skidded over them. We landed, and two of the men dropped to the ground with bloody shoulder wounds.

It was the two of us against the two of them that were left, and this time we'd pinned them back-to-back. I locked eyes with Alexa, and she nodded. We ran at the men as if we were going to each hit the man directly in front of us. At the last minute, though, we turned and took air. I threw my punch into the man closest to Alexa just as she threw hers into the one closest to me. They never saw it coming. Just as my feet hit the ground, my legs crouching and my hair wild around my face, the two guys hit the ground.

Claps sounded, and reality came back. Twenty-five wounded men lay groaning around me, but I couldn't wipe the smile from my face. Looking at Alexa, I saw that neither could she. People were standing and cheering for us. It was the second time that day people applauded me for something I deserved.

Alexa laughed and wiped the sweat from her forehead. I walked over to her and laughed as she drew me into a hug.

She said, "So I pretty much just wanted to say that we are the two sexiest ninjas who ever lived."

J.C. walked over to us and exclaimed, "I-I-I can't even believe that just happened."

I grinned and said, "Honestly? Me neither. I didn't think that would actually work."

"Only you two would think to pull something like that." Parker was suddenly beside me, his face alight with a new set of bruises and cuts. A nasty cut, dried with blood, broke through his eyebrow.

"That's pretty much why it's brilliant." Alexa said.

Brad walked up with half his face swollen and beginning to purple. He had a nasty gash that was sure to leave a scar going from his left eyebrow to the corner of his mouth. I thought Alexa's eyes were going to explode from her head.

"Brad...what happened to your face?" She rushed to him, her hands wrapping around his cheeks, and tilted his head.

His expression changed to happiness as she coddled him. "Beth. She's got big power for such a little woman."

"She's good?" I asked.

"She's better than good. She's almost at our level," Parker said.

I wondered if Beth's abilities had anything to do with her surviving becoming a host. Could it be possible that she'd somehow managed to retain some of their inhuman strength?

"I'm going to kill her." Alexa was completely serious. She searched the people around us.

"I'm not so hurt, Lex," Brad said, but Alexa was too angry to pay him any attention.

Messing up Brad's face was kind of like taking a key to the paint job on Alexa's car. There was no way that Beth was going to get away with that.

Parker added, "Yeah, as soon as the swelling goes down—"

"She'll be in a coma," Alexa finished. She finally caught her sights on the girl. She stalked off toward her, a dagger from her back pocket in her hand.

"Ah, hell," Parker said, running after her.

Brad hesitated and then followed.

I sighed and turned to follow them but stopped when a warm hand clamped over my shoulder. I turned, half expecting another attacker, but it was only Wes. He was looking at me with a cross expression, but I smiled regardless.

"Hey, I would stay and talk, but Alexa's about to commit homicide so—"

"I think your friends have it under control." He pointed, and I turned to look.

Alexa was standing chest-to-chest, yelling with Parker, as Brad tried to sneak the dagger out of her hand from behind her.

I snorted. "She's a little bit of a hot head, but she's the only one of her we have."

"Yeah, she's something." Wes grinned with his commercial-ready smile.

"Whadya need, Wes?"

"I was just wondering if I could walk you back to your room?"

I hesitated, looking back at my group. They seemed to be more than busy, what with keeping Alexa from murdering someone, so I was going to have to go back to my room alone anyways. I looked back at Wes. His emotions were inside of him, not even a single hint of them oozing out, so I wasn't quite sure what to make of the look in his eyes. Maybe he was just tired? Was this what fatigue looked like in normal boys?

"Um…yeah. All right." I smiled, pushing my dark hair back from my face.

His eyes widened with excitement. "Really? I mean, okay, sounds good. You ready to go now?"

I laughed at his sudden awkwardness. What was up with this kid? "Yeah, I don't think Parker and them will be coming any time soon."

We started walking back to my room. He wasn't as chatty as he usually was; instead he kept his hands plunged deep in his pockets and his expression hard.

He finally said, "So you took him back already?"

I shrugged "It's hard for me to stay mad at him."

"Of course it is, when you're not trying."

"Why should I *try* to be mad at him?"

"Because he's a jerk? Because he deserves it?"

I laughed and said, "Yeah, both of those things are probably true."

"So then why'd you take him back?" We stopped in front of my wing.

I stared at him, and my eyes raked over his hardened expression. I decided he needed to hear the truth. "Because I can't *not* take him back. He gets me, ya know, the whole crazy, irrational, psychopathic me that no one else does. I can't stay mad at him."

He nodded and leaned away from me, his body already turning to leave the hall.

I called after him, "Thanks for walking me back, Wes. Who knows where I would have ended up alone."

"Anytime, Rose girl, any time." I watched as he walked down the hall, disappearing into the shadows of the corner.

I leaned back against the wall and sighed. I survived my first full day in the Circle.

PART TWO

Strength does not come from physical capacity. It comes from an indomitable will.

—Mahatma Gandhi

CHAPTER SEVENTEEN

"**Y**ou don't understand. It was my soap. I spent my last ration this month on it, and he stole it!"

I sighed, staring at the man with the large nose and purple bruises on his jaw and had to fight the urge to add another one. This was a waste of my time, a waste of everyone's time, and we all knew it. Yet here we sat in our conference room, listening to the fourteen millionth stupid complaint that day.

Parker shook his head and said, "I understand that, Mr. Logan, I really do, but the problem is that you had no solid proof, and you attacked him anyway."

I snorted. Throwing his shoe at the other man was hardly an attack.

Parker shot me a look, telling me to be quiet.

I stared at him flatly until he turned back to Mr. Logan and said, "I'm afraid you owe Mr. Jones that bar of soap back and three days' rations as compensation for the attack."

Mr. Logan's brown eyes bulged. "Three day's rations? Are you trying to break me?"

I mumbled under my breath in disbelief. Logan was known for hoarding his rations. I knew that, he knew that, and so did Parker, which I knew was why he had assigned that punishment in the first place.

"Mr. Logan, I'm sorry if you feel the punishment is too severe, but I think it fits the crime," Parker said more patiently than I would have.

"The crime! What about his crime?" Logan pointed at the smug faced Mr. Jones in the corner. "He *stole* my soap first!"

"Oh my god, here!" Alexa yanked a bar of soap from her duffle bag by the table and chunked it at Logan's head. He ducked, then realized what she'd thrown, and picked it up eagerly. "Now, leave. Seriously."

Parker looked at her without humor, but I couldn't hide my smile. The two men left our chambers and went separate directions down the hall. Parker sighed and pinched the space between his eyebrows. "Beth, we're done for the day. Send whoever is left to Rayon."

"Oh yeah, like that'll do any good," I said dryly. "That man is only the leader in name. When's the last time he did anything?"

"Well he did calm down that fight in the cafeteria," Alexa teased.

"Nope, that was us," I said.

Lila asked, "Oh, well what about fixing all the records in the library that were four years off?"

I nodded. "Us too."

"And distributing the rations after half the east wing's magically disappeared?"

"Us, once again," I answered.

Alexa leaned back in her chair, shaking her head, and said, "The man is useless. What does he do all day besides hide behind corners and disappear for hours on end? The only times I ever see him, he acts like I've caught him doing something illegal and then slinks away like a freaking snake. He's just plain creepy."

Parker sat back up and said, "Well, obviously he doesn't listen to the people's problems like we do. That was the fourth pointless argument we've had today. We've got more important stuff to do than this."

"What do you suggest we do, then?" Alexa asked. "He's got us training these imbecilic cave people all morning, doing these stupid court meetings all afternoon, and then spending half the night arguing over how we're going to defeat that little thing called the Infestation. Where do you see the time to go find him and tell him we need a new schedule?"

"Finding him would take all day," I said.

Brad said, "Where do you think he goes?"

"I dunno." Parker ran his hands through his curls and said, "All I do know is that we've been here two months, and I feel like we haven't even changed anything. Sure the people fight better, and yes, according to J.C., they're more organized than they've ever been, but we're not any closer to figuring out how to stop this thing than we were in the beginning. I feel like we're stuck."

No one said anything. We looked around the table, solemn faced and tight lipped. This is where the conversation always died. None of us had the answers.

"Hey Parker?" J.C. poked his head in through the doorway, and we all jumped. He looked at us skeptically, but continued. "I was supposed to close up the sparring grounds tonight, but there's a situation in the west wing that I need to take care of. Can you close it for me?"

"Situation?" Alexa asked.

J.C. waved his hand dismissively. "It's nothing big. Someone misplaced a couple bags of grain, and they think they found it over there. They just need help carrying it to the kitchens."

"How many bags?" Brad asked.

"I think about thirty," J.C. said.

I laughed. "How do you misplace thirty bags of grain?"

J.C. shrugged. "It happens. But anyway, do you think you could help me out?"

"Why don't Parker and Brad go with you to carry the grain, and I'll go close the grounds? I've done it before," I offered.

Parker's brows raised in surprise. "You're offering help?"

"Yes, hell hath frozen over. Now are you going to take me up on it, or not?"

Parker laughed, standing from the table. "Sure. Alexa, are you and Lila coming with?"

Alexa snorted. "No, I have a date with the bathhouse."

Lila shook her head and said, "No, I'm going to go check out some stuff."

I shot her a sideways glance. "Like what?"

"Nothing," she said evasively, scooting past me toward the door. "Just some stuff I'm looking into."

I watched her go, skeptically, but didn't say anything. Lila was weird; nothing new there.

"Well alright, see you later," Parker said. I heard his voice in my head, though. *Cavern later?*

Of course. I smiled. That was when Parker and I got our alone time. Late at night, after everyone else was asleep, we'd sneak away to the cavern to talk. It was what helped me keep the little bit of sanity I had when everything else was so insane.

Parker and the others left, and I set off toward the sparring grounds, thinking of my few short minutes of freedom I'd get when the chores were over.

———◦◦◦———

Wes smiled as he walked up. He nudged me on the shoulder, and said, "Hey there, Rosegirl. Whatcha doin?"

I motioned to all the swords and daggers laid out before me. "Just packing up the rest of the weapons. J.C. had something to do, so I told him I'd close up for today."

"Here, I'll help."

We worked in silence, gathering all the swords and arrows and placing them in their containers. Soon all that was left was the forty-pound bag of arrows on my back.

"Ugh." I groaned and accidentally dropped it.

"Here, I'll get it."

Wes reached to get the bag, but I reached for it too, and our hands met. A swirl of emotions bombarded my mind, the most obvious being adoration. I drew my hand back from his like it was a hot coal. Lately, he'd been letting his emotions slip out too easily. "Wes," I scorned.

He groaned, "I'm sorry. You felt it again, didn't you?"

I crossed my hands awkwardly across my chest. "Yeah. Just remember what I said. Focus on keeping your mental defenses strong, and the feeling will pass."

"I still don't believe that. How are you so certain that it's your Gift that makes me feel like that?"

I sighed and looked up at him.

"We've talked about it, Wes. You agreed I was right, remember? You can't understand it, because your emotions are involved. But I promise you, whatever your feeling for me is completely physical. It'll pass."

He looked as if he was going to say something more, but he closed his mouth without saying a word and stuck his hands in his pockets. "Yeah, you're probably right."

I exhaled, relieved, and patted him on the back. "Hey, don't worry about it. I won't use this against you tomorrow when I whoop your butt."

"Oh, I'm so glad. I can already feel the bruises setting in."

"You'll be fine. You'll see that you'll eventually get better than me."

That made him laugh. "I don't think so. Two months of this training, and you're still beating me."

I smirked and said, "Yeah, I am pretty good, aren't I?"

He laughed, and his messy hair fell into his eyes.

"Rose, I'm lonely. Come to the bathhouse and gossip with me," Alexa called, standing with her arms crossed at the entrance to the arena.

"I thought you wanted to relax and be by yourself," I teased.

"Yeah, but that was before I smelled you all the way from our wing. Come on, you look like the Lock Ness monster."

I laughed and turned back to Wes.

He smiled and said, "Go ahead. I can put the rest of this up."

"Thank you! I owe you one." I turned to walk away, but he called after me.

"But, hey! Just for the record, she's crazy if she thinks you're anything less than beautiful." I gave him a hard stare that only made him laugh and then jogged to Alexa.

"What'd Wonder Boy want?" she asked.

"Why do you call him that?"

She rolled her eyes like it was obvious. "Duh. He's like normal boy perfection."

I snorted and said, "Normal boy? As opposed to the kind with three eyes?"

"No, as opposed to the ones that go invisible."

"He's not perfect, Alexa."

"As if. He's got the whole *Leave It to Beaver* charm going on. Have you seen those dimples? Gawd, they're enough to make my temperature raise a couple hundred degrees."

I laughed, shaking my head, and said, "You're impossible."

"Yeah, I keep hearing that, but you still didn't tell me what he wanted," she said.

"If I tell you, do you promise not to tell Parker?"

We turned the corner toward our bathing rooms.

Alexa raised an eyebrow and said, "Keeping secrets already? It's like you two are married."

"Shut up and promise me."

"Okay, fine, I promise. Now what's the big secret? Were you and Wonder Boy planning some secret meet up later to take off each other's clothes?"

"No, it's nothing like that."

"Well then, what? Spill."

I pulled the curtain shut to the bathing room. The humidity was almost palpable. I winced as I eased into the hot water. It felt good against my grimy skin, though, even if it was nearly scalding.

"Wes's crush on me isn't fading…like at all."

"And?"

I tried not to sound as annoyed as I was. "And that's a problem, don't you think? I mean, how am I supposed to train him if I feel how much he likes me?"

"Why are you training him anyways? Isn't that like a conflict of interest or something?"

I ran my hands through the water and scrubbed my legs. "I dunno. J.C. said something about how he shows more promise than other fighters, so he requires more one-on-one time with me. I mean, he takes what I teach him and teaches it to everyone else. I'm happy for that. With how it's working now, Wes is the only person I have to actually deal with. Can you imagine how much it would suck if we had to teach *everyone* everyday?"

"I don't know. I get the feeling we only train one person, though, because Rayon wants to limit how many people have direct contact with us."

"I hadn't thought about that." I bit the inside of my cheek.

"Brad wouldn't let me hit Beth today after she bumped into me. I think he's in love with her."

"That's ridiculous, Alexa. Brad is crazy about you."

"Is he, though? Whenever he's not with me, he's with her... And you should hear him talk about her, Rose. It's like she's the queen of freaking Ireland or something."

"Alexa, the queen of Ireland?"

"Shut up. I don't know." She buried her face in her hair and groaned again.

"You really do like him, don't you?"

There was a tense moment before she answered, "Yeah, I do. I guess I always have. Before, back when you were just some girl he saw in his head, I liked to pretend I didn't. I'd fawn all over Parker and watch Brad's adoration grow, and I'd secretly love every minute of him loving me... It was so easy to make him want me.

"The more I played uninterested, the harder he would try. Being here, being near Beth who's *so* interesting and *so* strong, has finally made me see that I could lose him, ya know? Maybe I played too hard to get for too long, and now he's found someone who actually gives him the time of day. Maybe I've lost him for good."

"Alexa, I've been in Brad's head. I know that he's crazy about you."

"He thinks about me?"

"Of course he does." I paused and then said, "And even if I couldn't hear his thoughts, I'd still be able to tell how much he likes you. He looks at you like you hung the moon."

She nodded and collected herself. She ran her hands through her hair and then cleared her throat. "You're a good friend, Rose. And as pathetic as it is to admit, you're actually the best one I've ever had."

"Actually, I can think of something more pathetic. You are the *only* friend I've ever had," I said, and Alexa snorted.

After we were out of the water toweling off, I thought to ask Alexa, "Have you heard anything from Lila? She's been gone a while."

She shrugged and said, "Nope. You know how she's been lately. Remember last week when she was talking to herself and got all clammed up when she realized we were listening? I don't know what she was saying, but all I heard was Rayon's name."

I laughed. "She wasn't talking to herself, Alexa. She was thinking aloud while she was writing. We all do it."

"Yeah, well, it was creepy. And she's been going off on her own so much lately. I kind of want to ask her what she's 'investigating', but then I'm not sure I really want to know."

"Yeah, but isn't her going off on her own this much a little strange, you know, even for her?" I held back the curtain for us to leave the room.

"If there's one thing I've learned about living with Lila, it's that it's easier not to question what she does too much. I love her, don't get me wrong, but she's completely insane. That year that she spent comatose makes her do these things."

"What do you mean?"

"She spent a year in a virtual coma, Rose. Her mind didn't die though. She didn't even have to relearn a thing. What do you think her mind was doing for that long? Playing solitaire?"

I scoffed. "Well, of course not, but I didn't think anything unusual. I mean, lots of kids go mute after seeing a tragedy like she did."

"They go mute, not catatonic. She told me once that it was like being in a never-ending vision she couldn't escape from."

"A vision? What'd she see?" We stopped in front of Alexa's bedroom.

She shrugged and said, "You tell me. All I know is that whatever she saw makes her do crap that looks senseless to everyone else, but in the end you figure out she was doing what was best."

"That's so weird."

"Yeah, tell me about it," Alexa said, uninterested. She turned and dropped her towel, and I looked away quickly.

"Alexa, seriously. Could you warn me before you drop trou, please?" I asked, looking away, but she only laughed. "Look, I'll meet you outside in a minute," I said and walked from the room, gripping my towel a little tighter.

I walked back to my room and wormed into fresh clothes, buckling my knife belt back around my waist. As heavy as it was, it made me breathe a little lighter.

I was lacing up my boots when Alexa leaned into the room and said, "Come on. Everybody is waiting on us in the conference room."

I sighed, lacing the last boot hastily, and said, "Can we ever be early for something?"

"Not likely," she said.

I scooted past her and into the hall. We half ran to the other side of our wing where the conference room was.

I heard Parker's voice before we actually entered the room. "Like I was saying earlier—"

"Hey, sorry we're late." Alexa interrupted him.

We walked in and joined everyone around the table that dominated the room.

My eyes gravitated to Lila's dirty face. She looked like the only one of us who hadn't bathed. "Lila—"

She cut me off, sounding tired, and said, "Before you ask, I haven't had a chance to bathe yet because I had to talk to Rayon. Don't worry. I'll get to it later. Now, Parker, what were you saying?"

Parker said, "Brad was trying to tell us some news of what he did today. Brad?"

Brad beamed and announced, "I had a successful scry today."

Alexa laughed and hugged him. "Really? What'd you see?"

Brad's smile dropped, and he fidgeted. "Well, um, I saw two things."

"And?" Parker asked.

"I think I might have seen the end of all this. Like... two separate possibilities of it."

I lowered my brows and said, "Why are you being so cryptic?"

Brad said, "Well, the first one was good. I saw you and Parker, only you were older. You two were just sitting at a table on some porch in the middle of nowhere, and you were laughing. There was no pain, no fear. It was all over."

"And the other one?" Parker asked, addressing the question I was afraid to ask myself.

Brad swallowed and then said, "Not so good... There was a lot of blood. I saw... I saw my body and Parker's and Alexa's. We were strewn across the marbled floors of this building, and we were just dead. Bugs were feeding off our corpses."

I felt Brad's subconscious, and I knew he was trying to keep something important from me. I asked, "Where were Lila and I?"

"I didn't see Lila."

My face was as still as stone as I asked, "And what about me, Brad?"

"You were alive. You...you were standing, watching us get eaten, but you didn't do anything. You weren't yourself, though. Your eyes were glassy, and you seemed different. There was someone with you, a guy. I feel like he was in your mind."

"Who was he?" Alexa asked.

Brad said, "I don't know. I couldn't see his face. I just *knew* he was there."

I sat back in my chair, biting my bottom lip. That second vision, how could that happen? How could anything change so much in the future that I'd stand and watch my friends get eaten without stepping in?

"We need to be proactive to make sure this second prophesy isn't the one that comes true," Parker said.

"Like what?" I asked.

Parker answered, "We need to get inside information about where the bugs meet. Start there."

"We could probably capture one and get it to talk," Lila said.

I shook my head and said, "Those things don't talk. They click and make siren noises. Last time I checked, none of us spoke that."

"Their lips can form words when they're hosts," Parker said.

"So we need to talk to someone who is or has been a host," I said.

Alexa said, "In other words, we need Beth."

Parker nodded. "She's our best shot. I mean, we could hope to find someone who's currently a host, but we can't tell they've even been infected until their skin starts peeling back."

"But don't you think if she knew anything she'd have told somebody already?" I asked.

"Maybe she just wasn't asked the right questions?" Parker shrugged.

I said, "Then what are the right questions? Look at your face. You don't even know. And besides, how are we supposed to get her to talk to us, anyways? She's scared to death of me, and Alexa makes an attempt at her life every other day. It's not like she's all that inclined to give us what we want."

"Maybe not you two, but I bet she'd talk to Brad," Lila said, and I looked at her.

I noticed the dark bags under her eyes for the first time. Her skin was a sickly, pallid color, and her forehead was covered in a thin layer of sweat. She looked awful.

I will physically maim Beth if she's alone with Brad, Alexa said to me.

Stop it. You will not.

Try me.

I could feel her mind, and I didn't catch the slightest hint of humor. As best as I could tell, she was serious. *Fine, I'll fix this. But just so you know, threatening someone for talking to your boyfriend is, like, stage five crazy.*

I said, "I think it's best if she answered questions in front of all of us."

"Why? I'm sure Brad is more than capable of telling us whatever she says," Parker said.

I said, "I know, but I think it's better if I hear too. Maybe she'd let something slip out subconsciously, and I could pick up on it. Plus, I'd be able to tell if she was lying."

Parker nodded and said, "So it's decided, Brad and Rose will ask Beth—"

"We won't ask Beth anything, because we still don't know what to ask her."

Parker shook his head and said, "Well, I think we should probably start with whether or not she knows where they congregate or, even better, if she has any idea where the mother hive is located."

Alexa rolled her eyes and said, "Don't you think if she knew that, this place would be all kinds of attacking it?"

I shook my head and said, "Think about Rayon. Does he seem like a real go-getter to you?"

Alexa snorted, and Parker pinched the skin between his eyebrows.

He said, "Look, it's worth a try. If she doesn't remember anything, then she doesn't remember anything. The only thing that could go wrong is if we don't ask and then find out later that she knew something that could have helped us."

Brad leaned back in his chair and stretched. He said, "So, Rose and I will try to speak with her after dinner. I don't know about you guys, but I—"

Alexa rolled her eyes and said, "Let me guess. You're hungry."

Parker stood and said, "Now that that's settled, I guess we can all go to dinner."

We started filing out the door but stopped when Lila said, "You guys can go ahead. I'm going to go get cleaned up and then probably go to bed. I didn't know how much today took out of me until just now."

I looked over at her and gasped. The back of her light yellow t-shirt was covered in a pool of blood from a deep slash down the back of her neck.

"Oh, I got that today sparring. I thought it would have closed up already," she said, unworried.

Instinct took over, and I reached out and pressed my hand against it. My fingers tingled like they were full of hot sand. I felt a rush of warmth, like everything good was flowing through my fingertips, and I felt it enter Lila. She gasped. The cut slowly closed, leaving perfectly smooth skin. I pulled back and looked at what I'd just done, too stunned for words.

"Did she just—" Alexa pointed at Lila's neck.

"She did," Parker said, nodding.

"I'm sorry." It was the first thing I thought to say.

Lila laughed and hugged me, her frail arms wrapping around me. Suddenly full of energy, she said, "Sorry? You just saved me days of keeping that thing clean."

"How in the world did you do that, Rose?" Alexa asked.

"I don't really know. I just touched her."

"It kind of itches," Lila said, scratching at her neck.

"Yeah, that's how it feels to me whenever I heal."

"Do you think you could heal Brad's face? I get it's rude to ask someone else to use their Gift or whatever, but look at that thing. It's grotesque."

I laughed. Alexa was right. Brad had cleaned the large gash on his cheek, but he was wrong if he thought it looked any better. It was puffy and raw, and I knew it had to be painful. "I can try."

I walked over and rested my hands on his cheeks. I thought about the feeling I got when I'd healed Lila. I thought about the warmth that had traveled through my fingers, and for a frightening moment nothing happened. I furrowed my eyes and thought harder, thinking about how badly I wanted to do something good for once. My fingers started tingling with the hot sand. I smiled as the liquid, warm feeling rose from my chest and out through my fingers. I watched as Brad's skin knitted itself back together. I pulled back my hands and laughed.

Brad rubbed his hand over his skin and said, "It felt like little spiders were crawling on my jaw."

Parker looked at both sides of Brad's face and shook his head. "She even got rid of some of your old scars. That's incredible."

A low rumble escaped my stomach, and everyone turned to look at me.

I laughed and said, "I guess healing makes me hungry."

Alexa said, "Oh, lord. We made another Brad."

Parker slung his arm over my shoulder and said, "Nahh, I bet even Rosie can't eat as much as that garbage disposal."

"Garbage disposal would imply that I eat anything. I'm actually very picky about my food."

Alexa snorted. "Brad, you ate a lint ball once because you thought it might have been an old raisin."

Brad shrugged and said, "Raisins taste good, though."

Parker shook his head, and I just laughed.

"Can we just go to dinner already? I'm famished," I said.

CHAPTER EIGHTEEN

We were greeted with little fanfare when we walked into the cafeteria. A few people looked up, a few more nodded, but the vast majority hardly spared us a glance.

"You know, we became old news fast," Alexa said as we passed between the tables to the serving line.

I smiled over my shoulder and said, "I know. I like it."

I was behind Brad in line. He'd run to be first, as usual. I watched as he piled his plate high with food, and I laughed.

"Hungry, Rose?" Parker teased.

I looked down at my plate and shut my mouth. I had as much, if not more, food as Brad.

I slid into the wooden table near the back. "When you start sewing up people's skin with your mind, then you can pick at my appetite."

He laughed and slid in beside me. Alexa and Brad sat across from us.

J.C. slid in next to Parker and said, "Geez. The kitchen's going to be out of commission if you guys keep eating that much."

I pointed at him with my fork and said, "Hey, you're lucky I got to the cafeteria before I had to result to cannibalism."

"I would've been too chewy anyways," J.C. said, flexing his arm muscles.

I snorted, ignoring him. I saw Beth standing at the trash line, her plate picked clean, but I waved to get her attention anyways. She looked over to me, her eyes widening with surprise, then looked warily back at the line. She sighed and walked over to us.

I gave Alexa an apologetic smile when Brad pulled the chair beside him out for Beth. She sat down and blushed when Brad grinned at her.

"Sorry, I would have waited to eat if I thought you guys wanted to talk."

I swallowed a mouthful of food and smiled as sweetly as I could force. "Ehh, don't worry about it. You can't expect any of us to wait on a meal, so we generally don't expect it of anyone else."

She smiled lightly, her expression weary. I read her face. She was wondering how long she had to stay in order to seem cordial.

I gave Brad a desperate look and said to him, *Say something to her.*

He nodded with a serious look in his eyes. *Don't worry. I got this.* "Hey, Beth, did you see the magical voodoo healing Rose did to my face?"

"She did what?" Beth exclaimed.

I slapped my palm to my forehead.

"Way to go, Brad," Parker said.

J.C. looked completely confused, and for a hopeful second, I thought he might not have heard what was said.

"What? I'm not supposed to tell that Rose evolved to healing other people?" Brad asked, looking around.

If my hand weren't already against my forehead, I would have slapped it again.

J.C.'s eyes widened, and he exclaimed, "Oh, I see it now! Look, his cut is gone."

"Great. Wonderful. Why don't we just tell the world?" I said. I pushed my plate away suddenly not as hungry as I'd been.

"Why not?" J.C. asked.

Beth answered for me, saying, "Because it takes energy to do things like that. Healing every person in the Circle who ever hurt themselves could kill her."

"Well then why not just offer to heal the ones who really need it?" J.C. asked.

I said, "Who is to decide who really needs it? I'm not going to tell one person they deserve to be healed and another person they don't."

Rose! Lila's scream broke through all my mental barriers like a drill.

I felt her mind next to mine, so full of terror that it was debilitating. I tried to speak back to her, but an ice-cold presence shut me out. I winced as the subconscious scraped against my mind. It felt like a rusty blade was digging through my thoughts. The connection broke. I couldn't feel her.

"Rose, what is it?" Parker.

I stood up and said, "Lila needs us. Right now."

"What? Where is she?" Alexa stood up.

"Outside her bedroom. Our wing."

I turned to run out of the cafeteria but hesitated. I turned to Beth and grabbed her by the forearm, yanking her to her feet. "Get up. You're coming."

She stumbled to catch her footing, but it didn't matter. I was moving so quickly, she wouldn't have been able to keep up had I let go of her.

An overwhelming roll of nausea hit me when we neared our wing. I pushed past Alexa and Brad. My whole body went cold.

Lila was lying in Parker's arms. Her pale face was nearly translucent and covered in a layer of sweat. My heart was beating in my throat. I looked down at her, her frail chest shaking as she struggled for air. The rims of her slate-grey eyes were sickly and yellow. The life in her face quivered as if it was fighting to stay present. My eyes burned.

Beth said quietly, "She's been taken. She's a host."

I looked at Beth and said, "How did they save you?"

"They pulled it out through its incision, the incision on the back of my neck."

Ice flowed through my veins. I turned to Lila, filled with regret. I looked down at her shaking body and whispered, "The incision I healed."

Alexa was hysterical, pushing past Brad toward me. She wailed, "Cut it back open. Get it out of her!"

Beth's face darkened, and she said, "You can't. If it's been closed then it's too late. It's in too deep."

"Screw you." Alexa pulled the dagger out of her back pocket, tears running down her face, and dropped down to Lila. I could see the desperation in her eyes, but she had to do something.

Brad grabbed Alexa and restrained her. She fought against him, kicking and screaming. He held her back, silent, as tears rolled down his face.

"I-I-I can fix this. Just…just let me touch her." I dropped to my knees beside Parker. Clear trails of water slid down his cheeks as he cradled her body against him. I laid my hands against her forehead, her pallid skin clammy to the touch. My hands shook so badly I almost couldn't keep a grip on her face. I thought of the warmth in my hands, the feeling of saving someone, but nothing happened. The feeling wouldn't come.

"You can't save her. It's not a wound, Rose. There's nothing to heal. It's taken her mind." Beth's voice was so soft I barely heard it above Alexa's wailing.

"You're wrong." I lashed out at Beth, making her take a step back.

Tears were falling from my eyes. I turned back to Lila and pushed the hair out of her face. I whispered, my voice unsteady and quivering, "Lila? Lila, baby, please hear me. I need to you be okay."

A distant look overcame her face, and she smiled. She said, "It's not your fault, Rose. It was never was."

I wiped her face and patted her cheek when her eyes began to close. I begged, "Lila, please. Please don't let it have you."

She smiled, looking directly at me, and said, "I won't." Her eyes closed, and she gasped. A stream of dark maroon blood trickled from her nose. Her body went slack beneath me. I couldn't feel her pulse.

"She shredded her own mind so it wouldn't take control," Beth said. Her voice was the only sound in the room.

I stared down at Lila's face, pale and smeared with her own blood, and felt an overwhelming sense of emptiness. I was so cold. I was detached, as if none of it was really happening. Alexa screamed into Brad's shoulder. Parker cried as he rocked Lila's body.

It all seemed far away, like it was happening to someone else. I couldn't feel my fingers or even the tears falling from my eyes. It didn't feel like it was my body that stumbled into the wall and slid to the floor. It didn't feel like it was my scream that burned at my lungs. It didn't feel like it could have possibly been my chest filling with a cold, stinging emptiness.

But it was.

Lila was dead.

CHAPTER NINETEEN

I didn't go with everyone to the service they were having for Lila. I couldn't be there with all the grieving faces and accusing looks from the people who had barely even known her. The whole Circle knew what I'd done. I killed her, sealing her fate when I healed the incision on her neck. It was my fault she was dead.

Beth stood in the doorway, her eyes about as lifeless as my own. She said, "Hey."

"Why aren't you at the funeral?"

"I could ask you the same question." She sat beside me on the couch and pulled her knees under her chin.

I said, "I couldn't be around all those people."

Beth nodded and then looked down at her toes. A moment of silence passed. Her voice sounded strangely loud when she spoke again. "So did you figure it out? Who implanted her, I mean."

I nodded. "It was Rayon. She'd been suspecting him for weeks now, but she never told us. I guess she got too close."

"You're sure it was him? Positive?" Beth asked, shocked.

I nodded. "According to Lila's journals, he'd been working against the Circle for a while. He was a host. This whole time, he had one of those things inside of him."

"Why did no one know?"

"Lila wrote that he had wanted to be implanted. He'd wanted one of those things inside him because he was sick, and it would have healed him. She thought because he'd willingly changed that it made it easier for him to control. He could hide his true nature from us."

Beth shook her head, her voice small, "He raised me. He... he was like a father."

I shrugged, numb to emotions, and said, "Yeah, well, he's gone now. Cleared out his office and ran."

Beth was silent.

"I wish she would have told someone. If we had known, we could have helped her," I said, shaking my head bitterly.

Beth wiped a tear from her cheek and asked, "Why didn't she?"

"She had this unwavering belief that our fates are predestined. She wouldn't have tried to intervene and change anything."

"Yeah, but even after he implanted her? Why not say something then?"

"She thought I'd healed her when I closed that incision. All I really did was put the nail in her coffin, though." It burned like fire to say it, but I did regardless.

"You didn't know, Rose. There's no way you could have saved her. None of us knew until it was too late."

I nodded, wrapping my arms around my torso a little tighter. Beth turned toward me and asked, "So what are you going to do now?"

"I don't really know. Before she…died we had been talking about finding a host that could still talk. We wanted to ask it about the mother hive."

"What would you do if you found one who could tell you?"

"We'd go to the source and take it out."

"Could you do that? I mean, really do it?"

I met her eyes and said, "These things have taken too much from me. It's the only thing I could do."

She sighed and then looked back at me. "I can get you what you want."

"What?"

"I can get you what you want. I just need a few hours. Do you trust me?"

I hesitated before answering. What did I honestly have to lose now? "Yes."

She stood and then said, "Then I'll be back. And I'll bring what you need."

I'd always been able to tell when the sun went down, even when I wasn't outside. Now was no different. I felt my internal clock shift to nightfall while I lay like a zombie on my bed. I wasn't under the sheets, and I wasn't even the slightest bit sleepy.

Everything flashed behind my eyes when I shut them, like images illuminated by lightning strikes. I saw everyone—Nallah, the woman from the van, my parents. I saw them the most. They were there every time I closed my eyes, looking at me with accusing glares. I could feel their anger, the resentment they held. Now Lila's face joined them. Her slate-grey eyes were there, lowering on me hard and unforgiving. The wound on the back of her neck still bled as she glared at me. It seeped down her torso, staining the white dress she wore to the funeral. I was drowning in it.

"Rose."

My eyes shot open. It took me a minute to register reality. Parker stood at the foot of my bed, wearing a black button-up and slacks. The dark color was haunting against his face. Dark bags hung from under his eyes, and I could see the red rim of his lids where he'd been crying. I was ashamed to be in front of him. I was behind his hurt. I'd killed one of his family. How could he look at me?

I sat up and avoided his eyes. I inhaled shakily and stepped from my bed. I turned away from him, crossing my arms on my chest, and stood, feeling exposed.

Parker said with a voice full of anguish, "I can't get her face out of my head. It's like every time I close my eyes, she's waiting for me."

I said without turning to look at him, "The same thing happens to me."

"I just...I feel like I should've saved her. I'm the leader, I'm supposed—"

I turned back and said, "No, don't do that. This didn't have anything to do with you. She knew you loved her and would have done anything for her. She never would have blamed you, so you shouldn't either."

I met his eyes and wanted to shatter. They were red and overflowing with tears. I never thought I'd see him cry. I looked away.

"Why won't you look at me?" He took a step toward me, and I stepped away.

I hated myself for it.

He fell silent. He stood motionless and then shook his head. His voice was hard when he said, "No, you don't get to do this. You don't get to shut me out. Not today."

He took a step toward me, trying to wrap me in his arms, but I stopped him. I could sense every emotion he had in him: fear, sadness, love. I couldn't ignore them when he looked at me the way he was. "I-I-I can't do this."

Parker took my wrist and stepped closer to me. I didn't step away. I squeezed my eyes shut and warm, salty tears seeped from them. I shook my head and whispered, "I told you I can't get close to people. I told you that loving me would get people killed."

He let go of my wrist and gently wiped the tears from my face. His hand rested against my cheek, and he said, "You didn't do this, Rosie. No one blames you."

I shook my head and pulled away from him. "You should. You *should* blame me. But-but this stupid face won't let you. I'm not healthy for you... I-I think it's better if we—"

"I'm not losing two people I love today," he said. His expression was so strong, so heartbreakingly sure, I wanted to cry even harder.

"Don't tell me that. Don't say you love me."

"I love you." He didn't falter.

I could see the truth in his eyes. He shouldn't love me, but he did. It was there right in front of me. I looked away from him, but he lifted my chin so I couldn't. He opened his mind to me and let me into his thoughts.

I saw myself through his eyes. I was smiling at him, but I was glowing. I didn't look scary or inhuman, just warm, like I was surrounded by sunlight. He thought I was amazing and good, and there in the front, shining and impossible to doubt, was his love for me. *Me*, not my face.

I closed my eyes, and another tear broke through. I was breaking. He loved me. He loved me, and it would kill him.

My jaw shook as I said, "I don't love you."

His hand cupped my cheek. He leaned into me and kissed me as if I was made of glass. I shook my head.

I said again, weaker and barely above a whisper, "I don't love you."

He kissed me again, though this time I couldn't hold back. I wrapped my arms around him and kissed him. I couldn't deny it. I wanted him. I wanted to feel that he was there, and he wasn't leaving me.

I fumbled with the buttons on his shirt, but he pulled back from me. His eyes searched mine. I pleaded he'd see how badly I needed him, now, how badly I wanted him. He hesitated but then kissed my forehead softly, picking me up in his arms. I closed my eyes and let him carry me to the bed.

He kissed my neck, his lips like warm rose petals, and I gave myself to him completely.

⸺⸻⸺

I lifted my head off Parker's chest and smiled. He looked like an angel. His eyes were closed without worry, and his lips rested in a faint smile.

I traced across his chest, my fingers barely touching his skin. He opened his eyes and smiled. "Waking up to your face is something I could get used to."

I grinned. I lay on my belly, propping myself on my elbows, and said, "You look so peaceful when you sleep."

"Really? You snore."

I shoved him.

He laughed and reached up to stroke my hair. "It's all right. I think it's cute."

I smiled and tilted my head to kiss his wrist. He pulled me into him so that his arm was around me.

I rested my chin on his chest and breathed in deeply. "Thank you."

"For?"

"For not letting me push you away."

"It was for selfish reasons. I don't think I could have survived if I lost you too."

There was a moment of silence. I let out a shaky breath and felt Parker's arms tighten around me. "I can't believe she's really gone. It doesn't seem real."

"I know what you mean. The whole time I was at the funeral—"

"Rose, Beth is—Oh my God. I...um... Sorry! I'm gonna... I'll be... Beth is waiting for you in the commons!" Alexa said, standing in the doorway with her hands covering her eyes.

I cowered under the covers, humiliated, and said to Parker, "Tell her I'll be out in a minute."

Parker smiled and shook his head. "She's already gone. She ran out with her hands over her eyes."

CHAPTER TWENTY

When Parker and I stepped from my room, I avoided Alexa's eyes like the plague. I hoped my cheeks weren't as red as I figured they were. I sat beside Parker on the couch in the main room but then stopped when I felt a conscience that was unfamiliar to me.

Beth had not come alone. Behind her was a man in his early twenties. He shared in her pale complexion, but his hair was more strawberry-blond than red. And his eyes were different somehow. They were green too, but they flickered with something else. Looking into them was like looking into an open flame. They shifted continuously with light and spilled out warmth. They were transfixed upon me like I was the only person in the room.

I waited for the madness, the eager praises and lunatic advances, but they didn't come. He mumbled something to Beth, and she nodded, stepping forward. She looked back at him, and I could sense her hesitation.

She said, "I need you to promise that you'll let me explain before you rush to conclusions. There's too much you don't know."

"I'll say," Parker said. He glared at the man, his whole body tense. I wasn't the only one who saw something strange in his eyes.

"This is my brother, Ben," Beth said, turning to him.

When I felt his subconscious open, it was normal for a moment, but then it changed into a cold, slippery mess that thought things foreign and unrecognizable. I did a double take, zeroing in on the foreign presence, but as soon as I did, it was gone. His mind was human again.

I lowered my eyes, perplexed. He met my stare, and I was sure he knew that I knew something was off. I stepped toward him and shrugged his sister out of the way. I stopped inches from him and examined his eyes. I watched intently as they shifted between the monster and the man. "There's one of them alive inside you."

"He's a host!" Parker yelled, yanking me back.

"No, he's not… not in the way we think. They're both active, the bug and him. I can feel them," I said and stepped back in front of Parker.

I squinted as I looked deeper into his eyes. They changed just like the feeling in his mind. I'd never seen anything like it.

"How is that possible?" Alexa asked.

"You have a lot of questions, that's obvious. I can answer them. *We* can," Beth said, looking anxiously between us.

"Can you help us find the mother hive?" Parker asked Ben directly. His expression was hard and uncaring.

Ben assessed him and then smirked. When he spoke, he spoke directly to me. "Yes."

Parker stepped in front of me, guarding me from him. "Then talk."

"How are you like this?" Alexa asked.

Beth and Ben sat down on the couch.

Beth said, "Well, it started with me. The epidroméas inside of him was the same one that took me when I was ten."

"Epidro-what?" Brad asked.

"Epidroméas. It's Greek for 'invader.' Supposedly the Greeks were the first ones who ever encountered them."

"How'd it get from you to him?" Parker motioned to Ben, who sat silently, his stare never leaving my face.

I shifted, uncomfortable under his gaze.

"My dad was a surgeon when all of this broke out. He, um, was a little unconventional when it came to the surgeries he practiced…"

I said, "He practiced in removing these things."

She nodded and said, "He was really good by the time I was infected. It'd barely even touched my nervous system."

"If your dad took it out, how is it in him?" Alexa asked.

"Ben was diagnosed with a stage four glioblastoma multiforme brain tumor about a month before I was infected. The survival rate for that...well, it wasn't good."

"So what? Your dad took the thing out of you and stuck it in him?" Alexa was only half joking, but the somber expression on Beth's face made it obvious that was exactly what her father had done.

"The epidroméas are the ultimate cure for anything, even brain cancer. When they enter the body, they purify it before taking control of the brain. That's why the person always looks like hell before their mind is taken. The epidroméas is forcing all the toxins out of their body through their skin."

"How did it never take his mind?" Parker asked.

Beth hesitated and then said, "Ben's mind was ready. My father prepared him rigorously before he was implanted. When it finally got to his brain, he fought it."

"You can do that?" I asked.

Beth nodded and said, "We practiced with him, made him try to focus on one thought for hours and not shift from it. It's harder than it sounds, but it made his concentration strong enough so that his willpower would never falter, and the epidroméas would never get control. So now they share his mind."

I met Ben's strange gaze and asked, "Can you understand its thoughts? I mean, do they make sense? Every time I've ever been near one of their subconsciouses, everything comes out jumbled, and it feels like metal slicing through my thoughts. Is it like that for you?"

He hesitated and then said deliberately, "It's different...being in the same mind. I can't hear as much as *feel* what its thinking. I know its intentions, and I can utilize certain aspects of its abilities, but I can't talk to it directly... It's hard to explain."

"What aspects can you utilize?" Parker asked.

"Some of the things remnant in Beth—the strength and speed. The ability to fortify my mind."

214 ANNA KATHRYN DAVIS

"I knew you were all super womanny because that thing had been in you," Brad said to Beth with an easy smile.

She blushed.

"What can you do that she can't?" Parker asked.

"I heal myself, like all the epidroméas hosts can do, and I manipulate the air around me. Make it do what I want."

"What do you mean?" Parker said, his brows lowering questioningly.

A gentle breeze grazed my cheeks. There shouldn't have been any wind. We were underground.

"How?" Parker was the only one besides Beth and Ben who kept his composure.

"All the epidroméas can manipulate an element while in a human body."

"You act like they have a choice to stay," I said, my suspicions rousing.

He smiled and said, "You already know this answer, don't you, misí pontikioú? I can see it in your eyes. But, yes, when and *if* they leave a host's body is up to them."

My brows lowered, bewildered at what he called me. The words tickled my brain like the sandy tingle I got when I healed.

"But don't they usually bust out? You know, get so large and… *buggy* that they rip through the human's skin?" Brad asked, making exploding gestures with his hands.

"They have to choose to start the physical transformation. From what I've gathered, it's a personal choice. If they stay in the human body, they have the ability to manipulate the elements, but they run the risk of the host rejecting them, like I did. Plus, they're also more easily killed in a fleshy human body than they are when they're in their hard exoskeletons. They enjoy the human body, though. It allows them to stay connected to the earth and feel things they can't feel on their own like the warmth of the sunlight and the steady thump of a heartbeat. Not to mention, they find our bodies attractive."

"You're the first person I've ever heard talk about them like they have any intelligence," Alexa said bluntly.

"I'm the first person to spend a great deal of time living in their heads." Ben smirked and then looked over at me. His expression seemed to see right through me. "Go ahead, little Cancer, and ask me what you're wondering."

"Earlier you called me something, something I didn't understand. What did it mean?"

"I called you *misí pontikioú*. It's Greek for 'half-ling'."

"Half of what?" Parker asked, but a cold rush in my stomach told me I already knew.

"It's what the epidroméas call the Gifted. It means half human, and half—"

"You're wrong." I shook my head. "None of us except for Lila have ever been infected."

Ben's eyes never left my face as he said, "Not like me, maybe, but you all are. You have epidroméas blood flowing through your veins as well as human."

I met his eyes, and said, "It's not possible. All of our parents were normal humans."

"Yet you all do things normal humans can't. It's their blood. It's why you can do the things you do. The mutation your leader, Rayon, spoke of? This is it. This generation is filled with humans who have the blood. These people in your Circle, the ones who can resist the allure of the Epidromeas? They have a little, but nothing in comparison to what the four of you have. You're the only ones with enough to be a different form of human, entirely."

"So that's why we're Gifted? Because we're like the bugs? I've never seen a bug that can go invisible and see the future. They can move things with their minds and shoot a target from three hundred yards away? They can hear thoughts and heal others?" Parker asked skeptically.

"Yes to all of that but the last ones. Those two abilities are exceedingly rare. Only the most powerful epidroméas can physically hear other's thoughts."

"What about planting thoughts? Like changing the way people see things just by saying it?" Alexa didn't have to mention the restaurant. It was already reeling in my head.

"I think it would take an exceedingly strong epidroméas to do mind control like that."

"I can do it," I said, ignoring Beth's round eyes staring at me in shock. She'd never known the extent of my Gifts.

"I know," Ben said.

"And I hear thoughts. I heal people with my hands, just like I heal myself without thinking about it. I evolve all the time, but no one else does."

"I know." Ben said again.

"Why? Why am I the only one that these things happen to?"

Ben smiled and said, "Because you're the one dancing with death, the most infected. Call it a Gift from fate that you turned out the way you did. At any given moment, you're a hair's breath away from turning."

"No," I said, shaking my head.

"Think rationally, Rose. They hear human thoughts. You hear everyone's. They heal themselves. You heal yourself and others. They desire the most beautiful human hosts. You're the most beautiful woman alive. If an epidroméas could design a human, you would be it. If I were to even guess, I'd say you show an affinity to an element as well. Probably water, considering your sign."

Alexa gasped and looked over at me. "You do! Rose, think about you in the pools. You can stay under for minutes, longer than anyone I've ever met."

I looked back to Ben and asked, "What does this mean? Why does it matter that we have their blood, me more than anyone?"

"You all are going to be the most hunted. Everyone is attracted to your blood. The epidroméas crave the human blood, and the humans crave the epidroméas."

Parker asked, "That's why they go crazy over Rose, isn't it? It's not just her face. It's the blood. We're immune to her, though, because we have some of their blood too."

Ben nodded. "Very good. Where as you all see Rose as beautiful, stunning even, you still see her just as human. Her high levels of epidroméas blood are neutralized by your own. The general population, however, has nothing, so she's overwhelming, like an open bottle of brandy wafted in the face of an alcoholic. They can't help but to become intoxicated by her."

"If the Circle members are the only ones who have some of this blood, too, that would mean they're also the only humans who can fight back," I thought aloud.

"Yes. That's why Rayon collected them all in one spot, so he could take them out, one by one. I never met him, but it makes the most sense."

"Wait, how did you never meet Rayon?" Brad asked.

Ben said, "I'm not a part of the Circle. I live in the city, Phoenix, actually. I put off the epidroméas aura because of the one in my head, so I've done well. I'm actually on pretty good terms with the local government, which is, of course, run by the epidroméas now. They all think I'm just one of them who has decided to stay in the human body. There are quite a few of them."

"What did you say about auras? Like auras as in energy-cirlcing-the-body-voodoo auras?" I asked.

Ben said, "It's not voodoo. But basically, yes. Every person puts off a veil of energy around them that the epidroméas are susceptible to seeing. They recognize each other by the orangey-yellow light epidroméas cast. Humans generally have auras that are red and blue, and you guys, well most of you, are a peachy-cream color. You might blend in their society, because it's just enough yellow, but you might raise a few questions."

I sighed and said, "You said *most* of us are creamy peach. What does that mean I am?"

He smiled and said, almost in awe, "Yours is magnificent. Pure white. The only one I've ever seen like it."

"What do the colors mean?" Parker asked.

"It's a scale to recognize the amount of power a person can wield. Red and blue usually means minimal activity. The closer you get to white, the more powerful the person is."

I said, "And being pure white means…"

"Unimaginable power," Ben said, eyeing my reaction.

I kept my expression flat, careful not to betray my own surprise.

"So what does this mean for us now that we know all of this? Where do we go?" I asked.

"Now we work on getting every one of the normal humans here healed and suited for combat."

"What combat? Where are we going?" Brad asked.

Ben's flickering eyes sparkled as he said, "I'm taking you to the mother hive."

CHAPTER TWENTY-ONE

E veryone separated to prepare for what had to be done. Brad went to the cafeteria to talk to the cook, and Alexa went to the armory to instruct the packing. Parker was with Beth and J.C., who'd taken control when Rayon left, planning out the mechanics of moving three hundred people out into the open where epidroméas were everywhere. That left me and Ben. Alone.

I'd been told to go the infirmary where all the men I'd helped cripple in the sparring sessions were healing. The only problem was that I had no idea where the infirmary was. It was the highest room in the cavern, the one closest to the surface, but other than that, I knew nothing. That was how I got stuck with Ben. His affinity for air allowed him to detect the differences in air flow. He was pretty much the only person we could spare that could get me there and back.

We walked in silence. People buzzed past us, nodding respectfully but continuing with their work. I could feel the anxious energy buzzing through the air as the preparations were being carried out.

"You didn't ask the question I'd been expecting," Ben said.

"Which is?"

"Of whether or not the epidroméas can ever take full control of me."

"If it could, you wouldn't be talking to me now."

"That's not necessarily true."

"So it can?"

He nodded and said, "When I sleep or if I'm taken by surprise."

"So how do you keep it from doing it?"

"I have it locked inside a box, if you will, in my head. I've made my mind a mine field, full of warning signs and triggers that wake me if the epidroméas leaves the box."

"How did you figure out how to wire your brain like an object?"

"My dad taught me. It's difficult at first, because you have to learn to never let a part of your concentration leave the traps you set. You don't know how hard it is to completely divide your focus into two separate thoughts. It was the hardest thing to learn, to never lose focus on a thought I was barely even thinking of. Even when I slept."

I looked at him then and saw the light behind them flare. I shook my head and said, "Your eyes. They don't stay still. How do you hide that from the other epidroméas you live around?"

He chuckled and said, "They don't notice it. In fact, most people don't. You see my eyes flickering unnaturally because you see the human and the demon. Most people don't see that. They just think I have jumpy eyes that take in a lot of things at once. Most of the epidroméas think it means I'm observant. They think it's a good thing."

"Do you know why I notice these things?" I asked.

The hall was starting to incline, meaning we were nearing the surface.

He shrugged and said, "I'd guess because of your levels of their blood. I wasn't kidding when I said you were on the brink."

"How much of me is them and how much is human?"

"You don't want me to answer that."

I stopped and took him by the wrist. He looked down at my hand and then at me. His expression was hard, but I glared back at him stubbornly.

He held my gaze but then faltered and said, "Rose, the answers I have are not ones you want to hear."

"But I need to hear them. Why am I different? Why is no one else like me?"

"Because you have more foreign blood," Ben said, evasively.

"But how much more?"

"Why is it so important to you how much it is? It changes nothing. It doesn't matter," he said.

I shook my head and said, "It matters to me."

"But why?"

I swallowed and admitted quietly, "Because I need a reason for why I'm like this. I need to know why; I need to know who I am."

Ben's hard expression faltered. He shook his head, wiping his hand down his face, and said, "I'd say you're about ninety-ten, not in your favor."

"Ninety," I said. It was like a weight had dropped down on my muscles, making them heavy like wet clay. I was ninety percent bug.

"They're not bugs," he said.

I jumped, staring at him, and he sighed.

"You're so used to having your mind open to read everyone else's thoughts that you're not accustomed to guarding your own. I don't even read minds, but I can hear yours. You're projecting them like a bullhorn. Anyone with a shred of telepathic ability could hear what you just thought."

I huffed, my pride hurt, but I swallowed it. "I'll... I'll try harder."

He nodded, and we started walking again.

My thoughts were racing, and I couldn't quiet them. I said, "Why do I have so much?"

He shrugged. "Why was I the sibling to get cancer? There's not an answer for you just like there're no answers for me."

A few moments of quiet passed before I asked, "So if I'm ninety percent of these things, what are the rest of the Gifted?"

"They're ninety-ten as well."

"You mean where I have ninety percent of this foreign blood, they only have ten?"

He nodded.

I shook my head and said, "Can I even call myself human, then? Ten percent is not a lot of my makeup."

He shook his head and said, "You're human, but you're not the same kind of human. Picture everyone else as they are, but you as something else, something greater."

"Oh stop."

"What? Do you not see the things you can do as great?"

"If you only knew the things I've done, you wouldn't ask me that question."

He smirked and said, "I wonder how it feels to live in the world as you see it. Only good and bad, light and dark—there are never any gray areas. It must be suffocating."

I turned my gaze back in front of us, the light from the infirmary now lighting the end of the hall. In a few steps, we'd be there.

I said, "I keep my sanity because I know that there is a good and bad and nothing in between. If I let myself believe that there are gray areas, then everything I know would change."

"You act as if that were a bad thing."

We stepped into the infirmary, and I immediately wanted to turn back around. The wave of thoughts hit me like a bulldozer. I had to close my eyes and rub my forehead. How was I supposed to do this?

Ben whispered to me, "Shut it out. Put it in a box and focus on what has to be done. Think of your friend that died. In order to stop more deaths like hers, you need these men to be well enough to fight."

I scowled, shaking him away, but I understood what he was saying. This was necessary. I had to do it. I wrestled with the overwhelming pain of the wounded people and shoved it into a box layered with needles into the back of my head. Ben shook his head, grinning, and said, "I should've known you'd master it the first try."

I stepped toward the woman standing behind a white cart at the front of the room. I said, "Um, Hi…I'm Rose. I don't know if you were told, but—"

She looked up and said with a warm smile, "Oh, yes, dear. J.C. said you'd be arriving. The beds are lined up in order of most critical. The worst on your left. I'm Jan, and I'll be up here if you need me."

I nodded and turned back toward the sick. I hesitated. There were over fifty beds here, and every one of them was filled with a body. How was I supposed to heal all of them? Healing Lila had seemed like a great feat, and she'd only had a cut. Some of these men had multiple broken bones. It'd be amazing if I could heal even one of them, let alone all fifty.

I took in a deep breath and willed myself to go to the first bed. A dark man lay on the bed, his head wrapped in gauze. He also wore two casts on both his legs. I didn't recognize him and breathed a little easier knowing it wasn't my fault he was there.

He was unconscious, so I positioned both my hands around his face. I pictured the warmth flowing from my fingers into his skin and healing his broken bones, starting with his skull and flowing to his legs. I felt the hot tingle as the energy left my body and entered his. I could feel it pulsating inside him. I pulled back and opened my eyes.

I watched the swelling recede from his face. When it stopped, I saw that he was actually rather handsome. I smiled, looking down at him as his eyes opened for the first time. He smiled back at me, laughing, and I stood from the bed with a warm sense of compassion swelling in my chest. I could help these people, really help them, and not be the reason they were hurting for once.

Ben rested his hand on my shoulder after I'd healed the last person, bringing me out of my thoughts. I shook my head and looked around me; all the beds were now empty.

I exhaled and said, "Wow. I really did it."

Ben smiled and said, "You did. How do you feel?"

"A little hungry but mainly exhausted," I said. Letting my mind wander had somehow disconnected me from reality. Now, however, I was aware how the healing had exhausted me. My whole body felt drained.

Ben chuckled, and I gave him a sidelong glance. "You act different around me," I said.

"How so?"

"You laugh and actually speak. You were so quiet earlier when we were all talking."

He walked toward me, shrugging, and said, "Maybe it's because I think you and me have more in common than the others."

"No offense, but I have a hard time seeing that."

He chuckled again, and I found I liked the sound. It seemed warm, like the fire in his eyes.

"Tell me, Rose, why do you treat me differently than everyone else?"

"I guess I just don't see the point. You're not going to hurt me, though I don't think you could. You're not dangerous."

"I have a demon inside me. I think that's pretty dangerous."

I snorted and said, "We all have demons. You've just got yours under control. You're probably more stable than I am."

He smiled. "How do you know that I'm not going to break any second? How do you know I won't give in and let it have me?"

He was close enough to me now that I could see directly into his eyes. They were unsettling, bright and shifting, yet there was warmth there.

"Because you're good. I can see it in your eyes."

"I knew you were different than the others," he said with a grin.

"No, I'm not. Not really." I sat down on one of the empty beds and sighed, feeling my muscles relax. It felt like I'd poured concrete into my legs. I was so tired.

"You're special, Rose. I don't understand why you want to change that," he said, sitting down beside me.

"Because being special all the time doesn't feel special. It just sucks." I shook my head and yawned. My lids were so heavy.

"You're tired."

I nearly laughed as I said, "What told you that?"

"Well, for one, you look half asleep even as we speak, and two, your aura is faded."

"No more Snow White?"

"No, still white, just low intensity. Come on, let's get you to bed," he said, offering me his hand.

"Bed," I repeated, taking his hand.

He lifted me to my feet, but my eyesight shook. The room spun, and I groaned.

He laughed and let go of my hand. I faltered and stumbled forward before he caught me. My body felt cold and dry, like I'd run too far without water.

I brought my hand to my eyes and said, "I don't think I can walk."

"No problem." Ben scooped me up in his arms as if I weighed nothing.

I wanted to protest, to tell him to put me down, but the exhaustion was too much to ignore. How could I have let myself get to this level? Lifting my eyelids seemed like too daunting of a task at the moment. I gave in and leaned my head against Ben's chest.

I closed my eyes and mumbled, "If you tell anyone you had to do this, I will break your face."

He laughed, his chest jumping under my head, but he nodded. He walked from the room, carrying me like a child. I didn't even make it past the doorway before I fell to sleep.

CHAPTER TWENTY-TWO

"I don't like this plan," Parker said, shaking his head.
I threw up my hands and sighed. This was the fourth plan he rejected.

Beth was giving Parker a tired look. "Parker, look, you don't seem to realize that any plan short of us running away is going to put Rose in danger. There's no other way."

"But that way just seems like we're asking for her to get hurt. I couldn't send anyone in my group into that place without backup, not just Rose. It's ridiculous," Parker said, shaking his head.

Alexa's face reddened. "Listen, meathead. We've already established that she won't be alone. Ben will be right beside her the whole time, and Beth and I will be in the building."

You're just upset because you won't be there. This is a good plan, Parker. Don't let your worry cloud your judgment, I said it softly, drawing his eyes to me.

He sighed and pinched the skin between his eyebrows. I knew his resolve was fading, and he didn't like it. "Run it by me again."

Everyone sighed, but Ben spoke anyways.

"Tonight we take everyone in the Circle to the fringes of the city and hide them in the subways. No one has used them since the Invasion began, so they'll be safe. Before the sun rises, Rose and I will sneak Beth and Alexa into the hotel. There they will stay hidden in our room and convey messages between you and us via the walkie-talkies. Rose and I will play politics the day prior to this month's gathering, which oddly enough is a ball, to secure our way inside. Once at the ball, we'll let in the army from underneath the building and ambush the epidroméas when they lease expect it, permanently taking out this order. We may not know where their capital is yet, but this is as good a place as any to mount the human resistance's first attack."

Ben finished, and everyone turned their attention back to Parker. I could see that he wanted to find something wrong with the plan but couldn't. It was killing him that he was going to have to split us up.

He shook his head and said, "I don't like it, but I don't see any other way."

"Finally," Alexa said.

Parker sighed and said, "We've got about four hours before the sun starts to set, so that should be enough time to get everyone packed and ready. They need to be told to bring only the essentials: two weapons and a pack for their canteen, blanket, and food. I don't want to see any suitcases or trunks. Alexa, would you and Brad mind going to the kitchen to help James finish packing the meals? Remember, two loaves and a canteen of water per man."

Alexa nodded and stood, smoothing her pants' legs. She waited for Brad to join her, giving him a strange look when he smiled at her excitedly. "What are you so excited about?"

"Kitchen means food," he said, grinning.

Parker continued after they left the room. "Beth, would you and Ben mind going to the armory to help with the weapon's assignment? We're settled as far as our group being armed, but the general population still needs some guidance."

"Yeah, no problem." Beth stood and walked to her brother. She reached her hand out to help him stand, but he ignored it.

He turned to me and said, "We will need to leave in an hour. We have things to do before we can get Beth and Alexa into the hotel, and they are things that cannot be done with them right behind us."

I furrowed my brows and said, "What? We can't sneak them in until after nightfall anyways."

"But you and I need to enter in daylight, make sure people know we are there. You will need to change too. Something better than that."

"What's wrong with this?" I looked down at my shorts and combat boots. They seemed perfectly fine for an enemy raid to me.

"You look dangerous in them," he said. He frowned when he realized I took it as a compliment. "You can't look dangerous. You need to look fragile, harmless. It'll be easier to plant ideas into their minds if they think you're not a threat."

"I don't think I even own anything that isn't a pair of shorts or a t-shirt."

"Here, I'll take her to Alexa's closet. I'm sure there's something there for her," Parker said, standing up.

I raised an eyebrow at him, but he shook his head dismissively.

Ben nodded and said, "I'll come find her in your wing in about an hour." He left with Beth, and then it was only Parker and I in the room.

He took my hand, and we walked to Alexa's room. I could feel the pulse in his palm against mine. I extended my thoughts to him, but I found a metal wall around his thoughts. I was confused, but I didn't want to pressure him into telling me why it was there.

We stopped at her walk-in closet. He started fumbling through her clothes. I was trying to help him look for something to wear, but he was so tense. I couldn't make myself pay attention to anything else. The muscles in his shoulders were taut, and he was rifling through the clothes so aggressively that one of the plastic hangers actually snapped in his hand, dropping the silk shirt that hung from it to the floor. Parker closed his eyes, his jaw clenched, and braced his hands before him on the wall, breathing out heavily.

I reached out and laid my palm against his shoulder. "Hey, tell me what's going on."

He hesitated, looking before him, and then he said, "I'm worried about you."

"You shouldn't be. I'll be fine," I said, stepping closer to him.

He shook his head and turned to me. There wasn't much room for us in the closet. He tucked my hair behind my ear and said, "I just don't like the idea of you being so far from me. If something goes wrong…"

"There was a time you believed that there were very few things that could hurt me before I hurt them," I said with a small smile, one he returned. It hurt me to know he was this upset when there were so many other things that needed his attention.

I laid my hand against his chest, our eyes meeting, and said, "Please don't worry about me. I know you think you always have to be there to protect me, but Parker, I promise you I can do this. It's only two days inside their world, and hardly that. I can handle it."

He let out a heavy breath and tried to smile. "Sometimes I forget how strong you are."

I smiled and leaned into his open hand on my cheek. "There's a difference in being stubborn and being strong."

"And you're both."

I hugged him, and a silent moment passed between us. I felt the apprehension in his mind even though he was trying to hide it from me. I could tell he really didn't want me to leave him and not because he didn't think I could handle the pressure of what I was getting into. He didn't want me to have to.

Parker ran his fingers through my hair and said softly, "Just think about it this way, Rose. After tomorrow, the first step at getting our world back will be over with. We'll be that much closer to being able to disappear from all of this mess and just be normal."

I closed my eyes and smiled against his chest. He rested his chin atop my head, and said, "I love you, Rosie. I really do."

"Yeah, I know," I whispered back. I let him hold me a minute but then pulled away. I looked at him and said, "So what is it we've decided I'm going to wear?"

"Oh," he said, remembering why we were in the closet in the first place.

He picked up a yellow sundress from the rack, and I grimaced.

I shook my head and said, "No. There is no way I am wearing a dress."

He laughed and held it in front of me, as if trying to size it up. "Oh come on. I think it'd look nice. I've never seen you in a dress."

"And you never will, if I have any say in it. Please just let me wear pants."

"Fine, manly woman." He shook his head and rummaged through the clothes. He pulled out a pair of dark denim blue jeans with holes up and down the legs. "Ah, here we go. You're supposed to look like some kind of heiress, right? Isn't that your cover story?"

I hesitated, fingering the fabric, and said, "Yeah, but I'm not sure if this is what Ben meant when he said that."

"Well, when I think of a pampered heiress, I see these jeans, a low-cut top, and some dramatic sunglasses. You know, that I-just-rolled-out-of-rehab fashion?"

I groaned and said, "I guess I prefer that instead of that dress. Hand those over and see if you can find a shirt while I wrestle them on."

Parker turned his back to me to look through the clothes while I changed. I took off my old shorts and then stood in my underwear, staring at the jeans. They looked a little small, even for me.

"Parker, are you sure these are my size?"

He didn't look back at me as he said over his shoulder, "Just try it on, and we'll see."

I sighed, and bent down, stepping into them. They were already clinging to my skin like rubber, and they were only at my ankles. Great.

I grimaced as I tried to pull them up, jumping up and down and wiggling to try to get them over my thighs.

"Are you all right?" Parker asked, pausing his search for a shirt to ask me.

"I'm… fine," I breathed out just as my hands slid from the fabric of the waistband and smacked me in the face. I groaned.

"Really? Because I think you just made a dying noise."

I scowled, huffing, and said, "These pants don't fit."

"Here, let me see," Parker started to turn around, and I panicked. I didn't have them on all the way, and rather than have Parker see me standing awkwardly in my underwear, I tried to jerk the pants up quickly. I misjudged my own speed, though, and fell backward, landing in a pile of clothes.

Parker started laughing so hard, tears fell from his eyes. I glared at him and said, "I'm glad you find this funny, but the minute I can move, I'm punching you."

Parker stretched his hand out to help me stand, still laughing. I took it, rising awkwardly, but realizing, triumphantly, that I had managed to get the jeans over my hips. "Ha!" I shouted at him after getting the pants to button. "I got them on!"

Parker wiped one of the tears from his face and handed me a golden chunk of fabric. "Here, put this on with it."

I looked down at the sequined material in my hand and hesitated. Parker turned his back to me so I could put it on. I slid it over my shoulders and then took the fur jacket, purse, and sunglasses Parker handed me.

I looked in the mirror and was shocked I *did* look just like some wild party princess. The fur coat was massive, but it made my frame in the little golden top look extra curvy. That, partnered with the skintight jeans and sunglasses, made me look like I'd rolled out of bed and gone to the nightclub.

I took the sunglasses off and stood, staring at my reflection, unsure. I bit my bottom lip and my brows furrowed.

Parker stepped up behind me in the mirror and said, "What's the matter?"

I shook my head, swallowing, and said, "I don't know. It's just different, I guess."

Parker laughed. "Yeah, you look like a girl for once."

"No, it's not that," I said, not bating his joke. "It's just… I've always tried to downplay my looks. My body already messes with people enough without all the fancy clothes, ya know? It feels wrong to dress like this when I know what it's going to do to whoever sees me. It just feels dirty."

Parker turned me toward him and tucked a strand of my hair behind my ear. He said, "Don't think of it like that, Rose. This is keeping you alive. If dressing like this makes people forget to think, then so be it, because it means they're not thinking of ways to kill you."

"You're right, I know," I said, unconvincingly.

Parker's face darkened, looking past me.

"Are you ready?" Ben said behind me.

I turned to see him standing at the entrance to the closet. He was wearing a pair of black slacks and matching leather jacket over a deep-red button-up.

I straightened my jacket uncomfortably and said, "Oh, um, yeah. Can we just have a second?"

"Make it quick. We need to be on the road before sunset."

I waited until he was far enough from earshot to turn back to Parker. The closed expression he'd worn earlier was back, and he crossed his arms across his chest.

I stepped toward him and rubbed my hand across his forearm. I said softly, "Hey, now, you knew we couldn't play dress up in here forever."

He didn't smile, so I sighed and moved his chin so he had to look at me. "If you don't hug me good-bye right now, I might just have to kill you."

He let out a heavy breath and drew me into him. His arms wrapped around me and I felt his lips on the top of my head as he whispered, "Come back to me, Rosie. Promise you'll come back."

I felt a lump rising in my throat, but I swallowed it. I looked into his eyes and couldn't believe the glossy tears threatening to break through. I nodded and said, "I promise."

He leaned in, and our foreheads pressed together. I closed my eyes and listened to his breathing.

His voice was in my head, saying, *Two days. Two days and we can be together again.*

I nodded and turned to leave him standing alone. What neither of us would say, neither of us *could* say, was that we would only be together if one of us didn't die in the fight.

CHAPTER TWENTY-THREE

"You look nice."

They were the first words Ben had spoken to me since we left Parker. We walked through the corridors past groups of people scurrying to pack, but they hardly noticed us. They only had three hours before they would leave their home for the last time; I couldn't blame them.

"Thanks," I said.

Ben looked at me from the corner of his eye and smiled. "It actually wasn't what I'd pictured when I said heiress, but this works better for you. I would have been crazy to try to make you look meek. The wild party girl persona will do just as well."

"What's the story as to why I'm with you then? Isn't it weird some average guy is coming to a function with a millionaire?" I asked.

We paused to let a particularly large group of people carrying boxes of weapons pass us.

"Not exactly. I'm kind of a big deal."

I snorted and said, "Yeah, I'm sure."

"No, I'm serious. I'm the CEO of Belltour and Associates. It's a multibillion dollar company."

I scoffed and said, "You're not a CEO. You're like twenty-one."

"Twenty-three, actually, and you'll learn that the epidroméas don't pay much attention to age. They're more concerned with abilities."

"So, I'm guessing that means you're able?" I said with a smirk.

"My aura seems to tell them so."

"What color is yours exactly? Is it yellow like the epidroméas or red like a human?"

"I'm kind of light orange. I've learned to manipulate the color by the amount of the energy I let the epidroméas inside me have."

"Light orange," I repeated. "Light meaning it's close to white. They think you're powerful?"

He nodded with a debonair smile. "Yes. Most of them think I am very powerful. It's why I have the elevated position that I have... I'm surprised you remembered that."

I shrugged and said dryly, "I don't tend to forget things that classify me as freakishly powerful, like ya' know, the fact that I have a pure-white bubble around me."

"It's not a bad thing, Rose."

"Yeah, says the guy who's never experienced it," I'd said under my breath.

His flat expression told me he'd heard it anyways.

We entered the cargo deck, and I had to squint in the dimness. It was poorly lit and warmer than the rest of the cavern because it had an opening to the outside. My boots crunched on the pebbles beneath me as we walked.

"Ah, here we are," Ben said, pulling a pair of keys from his pocket. He led us over to a shiny, black convertible. He laughed and motioned for me to get in.

"A Jaguar? Seriously?" I asked, sliding into the leather seat beside him.

He winked and put it in reverse. "Like I said, I'm kind of a big deal."

As he backed out, the lights on his car illuminated the Circle's parked Jeeps. Tonight they would all be filled with humans, some of whom would die. I lowered my eyes as we drove past them. We stopped only at the exit while two men I'd never met pulled the tarps back, exposing the cavern to sunlight.

Ben put on a pair of sunglasses and laid his foot to the gas. We stormed out of the Circle, flinging gravel behind us. The sun was close to setting, but I lowered my sunglasses anyway. I did it partially because the wind whipping my face made it hard to open my eyes but also because I didn't want Ben to see the water budding behind my lids at leaving.

"They'll be fine," Ben said.

I sighed and looked out over the vast, red expanse. "Would you be able to believe that there was a time I didn't care about anyone but myself? That something like this, leaving them behind, I mean, wouldn't have made me think twice?"

"Maybe," he said, grinning.

I gave him a look, and he laughed. "Okay, no, but I know it's true. The epidroméas have files on all of you. Yours says you're heartless."

"Well, that's accurate."

"Okay, maybe not in those words, but they do know you were rogue. Actually, I'm not sure if they ever found out that you finally joined the others."

"Wait, you mean they actually do have files? Like, on us? With pictures and everything?" If they had a picture of my face, there was no way I would be able to blend into them as one of their own.

He smiled and said, "They have pictures of everyone but you, ironically. There're rumors about what you'd look like, though."

"I bet those are interesting. Any of them come close?"

He turned and looked at me. He said with a dry smile, "Not one. Most of them believe you're a blonde."

I grimaced and said, "Why is it men go straight to blonde when they hear 'world's most beautiful woman'? It's so cliché."

We made a sharp turn from the dirt of the desert to a paved road. I looked in the rearview and knew it didn't matter if we left tracks. No one would be going back to the Circle's cavern after tonight.

"I disagree. When I picture a beautiful woman, I always think of dark hair."

"Oh, I'm sure that's completely coincidental," I said, tucking a strand of my hair behind my ear.

He smiled. "Don't worry. I'm not putting the moves on you. I'd be a little afraid of what Parker would do to me."

I snorted and said, "I'd be more afraid of what *I'd* do to you."

I could tell from the faint glow very far in the distance that we still had about thirty miles to go, but with Ben's driving we'd be there in only a few minutes.

I let my focus drift to Parker and the others. They would have to make this drive later tonight, but it'd be more dangerous. The sun would be down, and they'd have far more people with them, probably twenty Jeeps full, and that was on the off chance that they only had to make two trips to get everyone to safety in the subways. I selfishly wished Parker would let someone else lead the convoys, someone like J.C., but I knew he wouldn't. He'd be out in the open, risking his life as long as there was still someone who might need protection. He was too valiant for his own good sometimes—too valiant for my own peace of mind.

I sent up a silent prayer to whoever was listening and asked that my friends would get there safely. If they could make it to the subways, they'd have a fighting chance at survival. It was while their numbers were separated between convoys that they would be vulnerable.

The car slowed drastically as we neared Phoenix city limits. I could already feel the low hum of thoughts buzzing from the city, and a wave of dread flooded me. I was going to have to focus extremely hard at not only shutting them out but keeping myself in. For the first time I was going to be around creatures who could hear my thoughts as easily as I heard theirs.

Ben pulled the car into park on the side of the highway and pulled the keys out of the ignition. He turned to me, pulling off his sunglasses, and looked at me seriously. "Just so we're clear. Your name is Roselyn Kennedy—"

"You made me a Kennedy? Real life?"

He said, "Shut up. Yes, you are Roselyn Kennedy, heiress of your host father's oil business in Alaska. You plan on modeling throughout Europe, but you just recently turned eighteen and haven't decided to give up your partying ways yet. We met in the Jet nightclub in the Mirage Hotel in Vegas. That's where they think I've been this whole time.

"You opted to go for the wild party girl, so you're going to have to play the part—drink whatever is given to you and act drunk if needed. I'm almost positive the alcohol will have no effect on your immune system considering how fast you heal. Don't let anyone on to that, though. Act drunk. Be flirtatious and overly seductive. Just get their guards down enough that you can plant what we need you to in their heads. Understood?"

I nodded, and he sighed in relief. "Now I need you to remember this word: *katharóaimos*."

"What does it mean?"

"Pure bred. Basically the idea is that two epidroméas still in human bodies conceived a child that would be born epidroméas and not human. To them, it'll mean that you weren't implanted in a human. You were born into one... It's very, very rare among epidroméas. It will be the easiest way to explain your aura."

I asked skeptically, "How rare are these things?"

He shifted uneasily in his seat and said, "You'd be the first."

I shook my head and said, "No. That's only going to raise suspicion. I can't be something that doesn't exist."

"It doesn't exist, but they all think it does. I promise it's a good plan. Once we use your influence to make the lower-downs believe that you're a *katharóaimos*, we'll let the grapevine take the news to the big dogs and make them come to us. They're the ones you really need to talk to, and this way we get them to come to you and make it look like we never wanted to get their attention. It's the quickest way in."

I looked away hesitantly and said, "I dunno, Ben. What if they don't buy it?"

He grinned and started the car again. He said with certainty, "They will. You'll make them."

We didn't say another word until after we entered the city's limits. The buildings were tall and lit up brighter than the stars, and as we drove past them, I felt myself staring in disbelief. "I don't understand. How is this place thriving and then other places are falling apart?"

"The epidroméas like to be at the center of things. Big cities gave them a buzzing place to play human, so they came in and wiped out the little towns that couldn't offer them anything and then took over the big cities that could."

"That's terrible," I said, thinking of the small town by my old cabin that had been a virtual wasteland. It was nothing like this place. Here, everything was huge and buzzing with life. I had to struggle to remind myself that the people I saw walking the streets and driving the cars weren't people anymore. They were just *playing* people.

"How in the world is Parker going to sneak everyone in? This place is crawling with them."

"The subways have entrances farther out of town. Their chances of getting in undetected are high."

"What about Alexa and Beth? How are we getting them in?"

A smirk came across Ben's face, and he said, "You'll see. We'll be seeing them very soon, I suppose."

"You have this all figured out, don't you?"

"Wouldn't you like to know?" he said, giving me a devilish smile.

We were getting closer to a building that was livelier than the others. It was tall and sleek with tinted-glass windows that stretched into the night sky. There were palm trees lining the red brick drive. Women in long dresses walked arm in arm with men in expensive suits into the building.

"Are you ready to enter the lion's den, dear little Cancer?" Ben asked, smiling over at me.

My pulse quickened, and I swallowed hard. We pulled into the parking lot, and I could hear my heartbeat like a drum in my head. Standing on both sides of the entrance were two bugs.

They weren't hosts covered in the less scary, fleshy shield of a human body. They were exoskeletons and antennae.

I turned to Ben sharply, and he said to me, *Security.*

He pulled into the wrap-around drive, stopping when a man in a hotel uniform approached my door. He opened it for me. For a panicked half second, I thought he was going to attack me.

I braced myself for the punch, but Ben said coolly in my head, *Concierge.*

I shook my head, unnerved by my own stupidity. I rose from the seat, and the concierge stepped back, looking at me in awe. Ben threw the keys to him, and he snapped back to reality, catching them with expert reflexes. He looked between Ben and me and then cleared his throat. Ben smiled easily and crossed the distance in front of the car to me. His demeanor was cool as ice, which helped, considering I looked about as comfortable as a wet cat. Ben wrapped his hand around my hip, pulling me into him intimately, and smiled at the concierge.

Ben winked and said, "Just park it in the usual, Luke."

Ben led me to the lobby of the hotel. I held my breath when we passed the security bugs, but they didn't spare me a second glance.

The air conditioning slapped me in the face when we entered the lobby. There was classical music playing in the background and the hum of voices coming from a room somewhere close. A massive chandelier hung from the ceiling, and the ivory floors reflected the lights from outside like mirrors.

I was aware of several pairs of eyes on us as Ben led me to the imposing counter in the far corner of the room. He let go of my side, leaving me feeling strangely vulnerable, and rested his hands on the edge of the counter.

He smiled and said, "Good evening, Bridget. How are you doing today?"

The host sitting behind the desk had curly brown hair and pale-green eyes. She smiled back at him, and even I could feel the adoration flowing freely from her. She giggled girlishly, her hands resting on the keyboard beneath her, and said, "I'm doing much better now that you're back. How'd you fare in Vegas?"

"Ehh, I came back with a little more than I'd planned for." He grinned and motioned toward me.

A flare of jealousy heated the brunette's mind, but she concealed it quickly and plastered a toothy smile on her face. "Hi, sorry I didn't see you there. My name is Bridget."

I hesitated. How was I supposed to react?

I pushed my hair back with my sunglasses. "Hi, Bridget. My name is Roselyn Kennedy, and I have a hangover the size of Texas, so if you could please hurry up and get us a room, I'd be very thankful."

Bridget was taken aback, and then her expression wavered. She turned to Ben and failed miserably at speaking under her breath. "She's the most beautiful call girl I've ever seen."

Ben snorted, and I felt a pang of anger. I *told* them this dumb costume looked like a hooker. I stepped to Ben's side and looked down at her from the other side of the counter. Her eyes dilated when she saw me up close, and I said, my voice nearing ice, "I'm not a call girl, and you know I'm not a call girl. Your jealousy is ridiculous, and you realize that. So instead of sitting here, making stupid jabs at someone you don't even know, go ahead and get us into a room so I don't have to stand here, putting up with you for any longer than I have to."

As soon as I stopped talking, Bridget's eyes returned to normal, and she shook her head. She muttered something under her breath like she was disoriented, but then started clicking away at her keyboard. Ben squeezed hard at my waist in warning. *Whatever*, I thought. I was uncomfortable enough as is. I didn't need her making prostitute jokes on top of everything else.

Bridget handed Ben a golden card that he took with a thankful smile. He turned and, with his arm wrapped around my waist, started walking to the elevators. He hesitated at the doors.

He turned back to the desk and said, "Oh, one more thing, Bridget. I'm expecting a few suitcases to arrive within the hour. Would you mind sending them up to our room when they arrive? Miss Kennedy is waiting on her clothes."

"Oh, of course," she said.

He winked, and she nearly swooned. We got on an elevator made completely of mirrors. A man dressed in the hotel uniform asked Ben the number of our room.

"Penthouse. Top floor," Ben said, and the man nodded, pressing a button before him.

The doors closed, and it was just the three of us in the elevator.

Ben's voice was in my head, *Could you please try to look less like a spitting cobra?*

I made a face at him, one he was sure to see reflected off the stupid mirrored walls, and then closed my eyes. I took in a deep breath through my nose to steady myself. I could do this. I was fine.

We need to do something to make sure we're not bothered, something to make them not even consider coming into our rooms once we're in them.

Like what? I thought back. He shared his idea with me, and I almost choked. *Ben, there's no freaking way.*

Come on, he thought, *do you have any better ideas?*

No, but maybe if we—

No time! The elevator bell dinged, signaling we'd made it to our floor.

I barely managed to brace myself before Ben shoved his lips onto mine. He kissed me hard, wrapping his arms around me and carrying me from the elevator and down the hall to our room. My stomach was in my throat as he fumbled with the key card in the lock, all while still holding me up. The door finally fell open, and we crashed inside. I stood up and pushed Ben as hard as I could. He barely moved. I pointed at him, wiping my mouth with the other hand, and said, "You suck. You suck on so many levels, you know that?"

He shrugged, dismissing me, and straightening his tie. I peeled my jacket off and threw it over the grey-marbled counter of the kitchenette area. I sat on the edge of a boxy-looking couch and buried my face in my hands.

I groaned and said, "Parker is going to kill me."

Ben walked over to the kitchen and opened the refrigerator. He pulled out a water bottle and took a swig. He said, disinterested, "No, he won't. It had to be done."

"Was fooling that single guy in the elevator really that important?" I asked.

"No, but there are cameras in the elevator, and the ones watching those *are* the ones we need to fool. If they think that every time we come in this room we're ripping each other's clothes off, they won't come knocking. Ergo, they'd never find out Beth and Alexa are hiding in our room."

I fell back against the couch, lying stretched out with my arms above my head, and said, "But still, I don't think Parker's going to be too happy about this."

Ben sat beside me on the couch. He crossed his legs right beside my face. I knocked them away.

He said, "Well, no one said you have to tell him."

"See, when you're in this thing called a relationship, you tend to try to be honest with the other person."

Ben snorted and said, "You're sixteen, Rose. Why are you so ready to be tied down to someone?"

"Sorry I can't follow in your Casanova ways," I said. I rolled over to my belly and propped my head on my folded arms.

"I'm not a Casanova."

"Uh huh. Tell Bridget that."

He smirked and raised his water bottle to me. "Touché."

"That's what I thought. So don't judge me on my relationships. Besides, it's not like I planned for me and Parker to…you know, we just kind of did."

Ben smirked and said, "We're still talking about falling in love, aren't we?"

I threw one of the throw pillows at his head and said, "You're disgusting. Yes, I was talking about falling in love."

Ben took a sip of his water and slowly nodded. "So it's true then, you do love him?"

"Yeah, I guess I do."

Ben sighed impatiently. "How many boys have you slept with, Rose?"

"What?"

"No, better yet, how many boys have you even kissed, not counting me just then?"

"That's none of your business."

"Uh huh, yeah. My guess is it's probably just been Parker. Do you think he can say the same?"

"Go to hell," I said, sneering.

I stood up, but Ben caught my wrist. I turned back at him, ready to throw a punch, but the expression on his face had changed. It was softer.

"All I'm trying to point out is that love means different things to the two of you. He's had more experience with women, so when he says he loves you, it's comparative. You, on the other hand, have no experience, nothing to compare your feelings to. How do you know you love him?"

"Shut up," I said. I jerked my wrist from his grasp.

"How do you know, Rose?"

I opened my mouth to reply, but I faltered. I didn't know what to say. How could I not know what to say?

A sharp knock came at the door and stole our attention. Ben looked at the door and then started unbuttoning his shirt.

I stared dumbly down at his hands and said, "What are you doing?"

"Get out of eyeshot from the door." He dropped his shirt to the ground and started unbuckling his pants.

I turned from him and ran to hide behind the kitchen counter. From my perch I could see his khaki pants hit the floor. He touched the handle and then hesitated. He ran his hands through his hair wildly, making it look like he'd just wrestled a cougar. He opened the door to our suite in only his boxers.

"How can I help you?" he asked.

I couldn't see the host on the other side of the door, but I could hear him. "Um, yes sir, I have a few suitcases here that you said you needed brought up to your room."

Ben pretended to look behind him hesitantly. "Okay, yeah. Um, just set them inside here. And please, make this quick. You understand, right?"

He winked, and I heard the guy chuckle. Ben pulled the door farther open, and I heard the rustling of suitcases. A man in his thirties dragged in three of the largest suitcases I'd ever seen. I held my breath as he placed them directly on the other side of the counters I was hiding behind.

The man paused after he'd laid them down and looked around him. I blushed, realizing the scene Ben had set up. Ben patted his chest, his muscular torso freckled with chill bumps. "All right, thanks, man. I, uh, don't have my wallet on me…"

The host chuckled and shook his head. "Don't worry about it. This one's on the house."

Ben laughed, and they headed back to the door. The bellhop hesitated and whispered to Ben, "Do you mind if I ask you a question?"

Ben faltered slightly but kept his easy smile. "Sure, ask away."

The bellhop leaned in closer and asked, "That girl you're with, Miss Kennedy? Is she really a call girl from Vegas?"

Ben laughed genuinely and said, "No, she's not. Roselyn just turned eighteen and moved out of her father's place in Alaska. She's a model."

"Her father, eh? You mean her host's father?"

Ben's eyes sparkled, and he said, "No, I mean her father. Roselyn is a *katharóaimos*."

The bellhop's eyes widened to the size of moons, but Ben simply smiled and shut the door.

I popped up from behind the counter and said, "Oh my gosh, did you see his expression? I think he actually believed you."

Ben shrugged and said, "Lewis has never been that hard to fool. Once I convinced him that I was considering giving up my host body to become one of the bugs. He totally believed it."

"Is that so farfetched?" I asked. I walked from behind the counter over to the suitcases.

"For someone like me it is. Most of the ones you see in the exoskeletons were really weak hosts. They couldn't be successful in that aspect, so they became warriors. They're not pretty, and they don't exactly have a place within our society, but they're respected. I'm surprised Lewis never became one."

"Huh," I said, sitting down on one of the suitcases. It moved under me, and I jumped. "What the hell?" I reached for my knives and then cursed when I realized they'd been confiscated for the sake of looking harmless.

"Simmer down, little Cancer," Ben said, grinning.

He walked past me and unzipped the suitcase. Alexa collapsed against the carpeted floor and gasped. Her hair was unkempt, and her clothes were basically one big wrinkle, but I smiled at seeing her.

"Alexa!" I exclaimed, pulling her into a hug.

"Whoa there, party princess," she said. She pulled away from me and tucked her hair behind her ears. She gave Ben a dirty look and said, "Would it have killed you to pay for fragile care?"

"I did," he said, shrugging.

He started unzipping the other less-tall suitcase. Beth collapsed onto the carpeting almost as eagerly as Alexa did.

"Well then, you should sue," Alexa said.

Beth rolled her neck and said, "I swear someone was purposely kicking me in the elevator. The knocks were coming in tune to the crappy music."

"That was me," Alexa said, and Beth shot her an angry scowl.

I snorted and shook my head. I looked at the third suitcase and then said to Ben, "Wait, if Beth and Alexa were in those two, who's in that one?"

Ben said, "Not who. The correct question is what?"

"*What* is in it then?" Alexa said.

"Clothes. Some for me, but most for Rose. We have two big days ahead of us."

Alexa rolled her shoulders and said, "So while you two are out playing social elite, me and the cradle queen are stuck in this room all day."

Beth sighed and said, "Stop calling me that. You're only two years older than me."

"Yeah and that's six hundred and fifty more days of living than you have," Alexa bit back. She rolled her eyes and then noticed the room for the first time. She looked at me suspiciously and then raised an eyebrow.

I sighed, "Ben, please explain your nakedness."

He shrugged and said, "Rose attacked me in the elevator. She couldn't keep her hands off me."

My expression flattened. "Thank you, Ben, really."

Alexa looked between Ben and me and said, "So umm… what?"

Ben laughed and sat on the boxy, white couch. "We had to come up with something to make sure nobody would come snooping around the room and find you guys."

"You couldn't think of anything else?" Alexa asked.

I said, "Believe me, it wasn't my idea."

Ben waved his hand dismissively. "Whatever. We gave quite the convincing show."

"I'm sure Parker will think so," Beth said.

I turned sharply toward her, but Alexa was already scowling. She bit, "Listen, jailbait, if you breathe a word of this to Parker, I will personally rip every one of those freckles off your face."

Ben said, "All right, girls, how about everyone just go to bed? It's late, and Rose and I have to wake up early tomorrow."

Beth stood, trying to smooth out the untamable wrinkles from her jeans, and said, "Fine, but I'm not sleeping in the same room as her."

"Afraid you'd wake up to me holding a pillow over your face? Yeah, I'd be afraid too," Alexa said, smirking.

Ben ignored her and said, "Beth, there's three bedrooms. You can take the one back there, and, Alexa, you can have the one behind the kitchen." When no one moved, Ben nearly shouted, "Go!"

They both stalked off and left Ben and I alone in the living room. He was nearly naked, and I couldn't help but look at him. He really wasn't half bad.

His face turned up, and I knew I'd projected my thoughts. He smirked and said, "Like what you see, Little Cancer?"

"Get out of my head, Ben."

He laughed and said, "Like I said, I don't read minds. You're just screaming your thoughts at me."

I pinched the skin between my eyebrows, and said, "I keep forgetting that."

"You'll get better at it. Then again," he winked, "maybe you don't want to. Maybe you want me to hear how hot you think my body is."

I shook my head, laughing, and said, "Good night, Ben. I'm going to bed. Alone."

He smiled and said, "Suit yourself. But my door is open."

I crept down the hall to the last room on the end.

I opened the door slowly and peeked my head in. I cursed the bright sliver of light that cut through the darkness of the room like a knife. I saw a large bed with a single mound laying on its far edge. I stood dumbly for a moment, chastising myself for not even considering the fact that she might have already been asleep. The mound shifted, and a sleepy face looked up at me, dazed.

"What the hell, Rose? Creeper much?" Alexa grumbled, and I snorted.

I stepped in and closed the door behind me, fumbling in the shadow. "There're no beds left. Looks like you drew the short straw and have to share with me."

My searching hands found the edge of the bed just as she replied, "Yeah, whatever. Better you than jailbait."

I bit my lip to keep from laughing and pulled off my clothes. I stood in my underwear in the darkness and then swore. "I didn't get any pajamas."

Alexa rolled away from me, laying her head on the pillow and closing her eyes, and said "Doesn't matter. Parker sent one of his t-shirts. It's on the end of the bed."

I smiled even though I knew she couldn't see me. I ran my fingers across the silky fabric of the comforter until I hit the cotton material of the shirt. I slid it on and stood for a moment, cherishing the smell. I squirmed under the covers and pulled them up to my chin, shivering. "Alexa?" I whispered at her still form. I was afraid she'd fallen asleep.

"Hmm?" She grunted.

"Do you know if Parker and everyone got to the subways all right?" I nervously pinched the fabric of the comforter when she hesitated.

"He's alive."

"And Brad? What about him?"

"They're both fine." She hesitated, and I got the feeling she was hiding something.

"Alexa, what aren't you saying?"

She sighed and said, "We made it to the subway, but we had a run-in on the second trip. We lost some people, Rose. Wes was one of them."

"Wes Deluka?" I asked, dumbfounded.

"Yeah, he was in the back with J.C. when a few of the bugs caught them off guard. J.C. managed to get away with only a scratch, but they got Wes."

I fell silent. Wes had been the closest thing to a normal friend that I'd had. He'd laughed at my jokes, and we'd had actual conversations. I taught him how to fight too. He was too good to die like that.

I swallowed and managed to say, "How quick did he go?"

"I'm not sure. Some of the bugs who got away took him," Alexa said sleepily.

I grimaced and felt even sicker. The bugs only took people captive for one reason: to eat them. I closed my eyes and tried to shake the image of him being snapped like a toothpick beneath their pinchers.

"Good people shouldn't die like that. Not like they're nothing but meat," I said.

"Yeah, but they do. Good night, Rose," Alexa said, yawning, and then closed her eyes.

"Yeah, good night," I mumbled distractedly and then turned my back to her.

I cradled my pillow to my chest. I couldn't believe Wes was gone. Selfishly, I realized that a small piece of me was relieved that it hadn't been Parker or Brad, though. A small piece of me was glad that it had been Wes and not them.

I hated that piece.

I sighed and tried to shut my eyes, praying that Wes's bloody body wouldn't haunt me in my sleep.

CHAPTER TWENTY-FOUR

I didn't sleep much, but it wasn't because I wasn't tired. I was, both emotionally and physically, but I couldn't fall asleep. Every time I closed my eyes, the shadows behind my lids morphed into my deepest fears. I pictured failing at controlling all the bugs' minds and getting Ben killed, and then I saw what the world would turn to if I did. Everything relied on me getting what I needed out of the *things* today, but I was worried that I couldn't. I was terrified that I'd let everyone down.

When I saw the faintest glimmer of light peek under the curtains, I decided it was finally acceptable to get out of bed. I pulled the covers back and slid out of the bed as quietly as I could. I crept into the hall, shutting the door behind me. I turned and jumped when I saw Ben standing right behind me.

"What the heck? Were you just standing outside my bedroom?"

"No, but I heard the door open and wanted to see who was up." He turned from me and walked to the kitchen.

I followed him and watched as he opened the refrigerator.

He took a swig of orange juice straight from the jug, and asked, "So why *are* you up?"

I stood awkwardly by the cabinets, painfully aware that I was wearing nothing but Parker's white t-shirt, and watched him wipe his mouth and put the jug back. "I couldn't sleep. You?"

"I don't really sleep much. Two hours and I'm usually good," he said, shrugging his shoulders. He pulled out a carton of eggs and a gallon of milk.

"Two hours? I thought I was doing good to be able to operate on four."

"Well, technically, I'd say you don't even need that."

"Yeah, I do. I mean, I guess I don't *need* it, but it sure makes everything easier. My brain slows when I stay awake too long, and my reflexes aren't as sharp. It's not a good feeling either. I can do it, but I try not to. How does that explain you, though?"

"I have an energizer bunny in my head. You, on the other hand, are just superhuman," he said, stepping past me.

He pulled a small skillet from the cabinet under the sink. He cracked an egg onto it, and the egg sizzled loudly.

"You're making eggs? At five a.m.?"

He shrugged. "You want one?"

"Sure," I said, ignoring his laugh. I stepped around him and searched through the upper cabinets for the plates. I pulled two down and put them on the counter beside him.

Ben said, "I like coffee with my eggs. How about you?"

"Nah, I've never liked coffee. The caffeine has no effect on me, and the taste kind of reminds me of dirt."

He laughed, shaking his head, and said, "Alright, would you mind putting just enough water in the machine for me, then?"

I pulled the nozzle from the sink's faucet and sprayed water into the machine. I watched as the plastic meter rose until reaching capacity. I glanced at the coffee pot. It was streaked with previous use. I grimaced and ran it under the water, scrubbing at the stains.

"Have you ever tried to manipulate it?"

I jumped and nearly dropped the glass pot. "What? Coffee?"

"No, the water."

"Don't be dumb. I can't."

"Have you tried?" he said with a smile. He turned back to the skillet and cracked another egg.

"Well, no."

"You're never going to know if you don't try," he said with a smile.

"What if I don't want to? What if I've had enough abnormal Gifts for a lifetime?"

"Well, I'd say that's dumb. You're special. Why not embrace it?"

"Because being special all the time loses its appeal, Ben."

"You're acting like it's a bad thing. It's not. Elemental manipulation is one of the most human things the epidroméas do. It's why so many of them choose to stay weak in the human body, just so they can manipulate one of the elements."

"But how? How does staying in a human body make them able to do things that even humans can't do?"

Ben waved his hand dismissively as he said, "Humans would have been able to do it eventually, I guess, had their brains been given enough time to evolve. In every human mind there's a connection to the earth, one that's so abstract most people don't have control over it enough to be able to activate it. But the epidroméas have control over every part of the human brain, every single crevice. That is including the part that lets them manipulate their connection to the earth."

I asked, "Does every epidroméas have control over something? Should I be worried that when the others storm the function, monsoons and fires will break out?"

"Nah, not here. The strength of their ability over an element is directly attached to their auras. Besides you, I've got the clearest aura around here, and I struggle with winds lasting longer than a few seconds. I don't think we have to worry about elemental warfare yet."

I furrowed my brows. "Yet? Does that mean that we might have to eventually?"

"Possibly. Right now we're just dealing with minor leaders, but once we get to the really big guys, then we may have to worry about it. By then, hopefully, you'll be strong enough to combat them. We're lucky you're water."

"But I'm not water. I'm nothing."

"You of all people should know that just saying something doesn't make it true, little Cancer."

He turned the stovetop off and handed me a plate. I took it quietly and went to sit at the table in the corner. Ben joined me once he'd poured himself a cup of coffee.

I took a bite of eggs and said while chewing, "Why would me being a water-manipulator-person-thing be lucky?"

He smiled and said, "Because water is the strongest element. It's the most versatile. Think about it. Water can be all three states of matter. It can put out fires, erode any piece of earth, and act as a barrier against any assault of the air. Water is the strongest but the hardest to wield, too."

"Why?"

"Most element users only have to learn one state of matter to control. For instance, fire users don't have to worry about their fires suddenly becoming liquids just like earth users never worry about their stones suddenly turning to gas. Water users do. Water is a fickle element, full of power and a lot of potential, but water is also free. It goes where it wants, not paying attention to any premade barriers, and it takes whatever shape or form it pleases. If you ask me, I think it's only fitting you got the element that breaks all the rules."

I said, "Hypothetically speaking, how does one control their element? Like…how do you make a breeze whenever you want it?"

He shrugged. "It's different from user to user, I guess. What works for me probably wouldn't work for you. You just have to… *feel* your element. Let it become of piece of you, like an extra arm or something. Don't try to control it, just let it be. It'll happen. I mean, hypothetically and all," he added with a grin.

I stood and placed my emptied plate in the sink. I wiped my mouth on my sleeve and said, "I should probably get in the shower. I look like a hot mess."

He took a sip of his coffee and said dismissively, "Good. I wasn't going to say anything, but you smell like fermenting garbage."

"Charming, Benjamin. Really," I said and walked to the bathroom.

I shut the door behind me and immediately peeled off Parker's shirt. I placed it on the towel rack by the door and then kicked off my underwear. The tile of the shower stall was cold against my bare feet, so I turned the faucet's knob to the highest temperature.

I sighed when the streams of warm, clean water poured over my body. It was like the minute the water touched my skin, I could breathe. I stood under the shower head and lathered my hair in shampoo.

I looked to the bottom of the shower and watched as the soap mixed with the water cascading off my body and then swirled into the drain. Ben's words passed through my mind. He said just to *feel* the element, but how did someone not feel water? Was how water made me feel unusual from how everyone else felt it? If so, I'd been *feeling* my element my whole life.

I looked down at the current and wondered if it would be okay to try to manipulate it. It couldn't hurt anything, right? I concentrated on the hypnotic swirl of the water around the drain and then hesitated. I shook my head and made myself focus. I could do this. It was just water.

I focused on the water falling from the nozzle and then thought the simplest command I could: stop.

Nothing happened.

The water kept moving all around me, spinning down the drain and falling from the showerhead. I exhaled with relief and laughed. I leaned my head back against the tile, smiling, and looked up. My heart stopped. The shower's steam no longer swirled above me. It hung motionless in the air.

I stared at it in disbelief. Each individual droplet was visible, shaking as if filled with tension. I reached up and combed my fingers through the densest part of the steam. My hand left a gap that the water vapor didn't refill. I leaned back against the shower wall and closed my eyes.

Why couldn't I just be normal for once? Was it so hard to ask that I *wouldn't* wake up one day to find out I had some new superpower or that maybe the fate of the world *didn't* depend on me? Hadn't I already been Gifted with enough?

I rubbed my hand against my forehead and sighed. I peeked through my fingers and saw that the mist was still there, unmoving. I said, exasperated, "I guess I have to tell you to stop, don't I? Well, um…release."

I watched as the vapor panicked wildly for a few seconds and then settled back into its natural churning.

I turned the water off and stepped from the stall. The cold air met my bare skin and raised chill bumps down my back. I shivered and grabbed two towels from the back of the commode. I wrapped one around my hair and then the other around my body. I took in a deep breath, but it came out shakily. I leaned against the door and then slid down it to sit on the floor. I buried my face in my hands.

What would this mean for me? Would everyone expect me to manipulate water to wipe out every host that came at me? I imagined myself sending a tidal wave over a room full of hosts and watching them drown, slowly sinking beneath the current as the life was pulled from them. I was nauseas.

I could kill a thousand hosts with my bare hands if I wanted, and I probably wouldn't regret a thing, but something about using my element to do the same task made me sick. I couldn't explain it, not in words, but somehow I knew that what I could do shouldn't be used to harm people, not unless it was a last-ditch effort to save my own life. The water didn't just feel like a liquid to me, not like a tool. It felt alive, like a living, breathing part of me.

"Rose? Are you okay? You're casting out all kinds of confusion right now," Ben said on the other side of the door.

"Just peachy," I mumbled.

I pulled myself up and opened the door. A river of steam flowed over my head and into the hallway.

"What were your thoughts so confused about?"

"My life," I said plainly, but shook my head when he looked confused. "Yeah, don't worry about it."

"Okay... I got the clothes you'll need for today if you want to put them on now."

"Is it decent?"

"Yes. Although I'm saving a negligee for tonight."

I snorted and reached for the stack of folded clothes he handed to me through the small opening in the bathroom door. "Thanks, I'll be out in a minute."

He nodded and turned away. I wormed into them and then marched, uncomfortably, to the small living room.

Ben sat on the couch, reading a magazine. He looked up when I came in and grinned. "You look almost presentable for once."

I grumbled unhappily and tried to sit beside him on the couch. The skirt wouldn't let me; it was too tight. I swore. "Oh come on. Is this real life? Did you really get me a skirt I can't even sit down in?"

He said, "If it's any consolation, your butt looks amazing in it."

"If you think I won't risk ripping this fancy material just to hurt you, you're sadly mistaken."

He shrugged and said, "Ehh, I had to risk it. Someone had to tell you."

I smiled, shaking my head, and squirmed into a sitting position. It was uncomfortable, and I couldn't breathe in deeply, but at least it was an improvement from having to stand constantly.

Alexa came walking in sleepily from her bedroom. She wiped her eyes and said, "It's, like, seven o'clock. Why are you guys up? And what the hell are you wearing?"

I sighed and gave Ben an I-told-you-so look. "Ben thinks this is the perfect blend of professional business woman and sex goddess. Apparently the fact that I can't, ya know, move isn't a problem."

Alexa shrugged and sat beside me on the couch. "So what's the plan for today?" I asked.

"I'd rather wait until Beth woke to—"

"Save it. I heard Alexa's voice the minute she started talking," Beth said sleepily from behind him.

We turned to see the younger redhead standing in the doorway of her bedroom, her hair in two messy braids.

Alexa sneered and said, "Kind of like waking up to angels, isn't it?"

Ben shook his head and said, "It's too early for this. Beth, just sit down and don't say anything back to her."

Beth glared at Alexa, but she just smiled. Beth sat across from the couch.

Ben looked at her and then said, "Well, now that she's up, I guess we should talk about what's going to happen today. Rose and I will spend the better half of the day in the lobby and parlor. There we will focus on attracting the lower levels into our snare and getting them to believe our story. We will be in the parlor however long it takes to get the attention of the big guys. Once we have their eyes on us, Rose and I will see to it that we have a private meeting with them tonight. The goal of today is to get our foot inside the door with the big players, understood?"

I nodded, but Alexa seemed disinterested. "So what is it me and the pre-k princess are going to do while y'all are doing all of this?"

Ben sighed and said, "Did you remember to bring the walkie-talkies I left for you?"

Alexa nodded and said, "Yup. Mine's in my room, but I don't know about hers."

"I have mine." Beth snipped bitterly.

"You're going to be conveying messages between us and Parker. Set your radios to channel eight," Ben directed.

"And you're sure they'll get reception in the subway tunnel?" I asked.

"Yes, trust me. Now just do it."

Beth and Alexa disappeared to their own rooms and returned with two yellow walkie-talkies. Alexa's beeped noisily as she turned it on, and she settled back beside me on the couch.

"Now test it. The code word is violet rose," Ben said, avoiding my eyes.

The code was the color of my eyes and then my name. I doubted it was a coincidence.

Alexa looked at him skeptically and then pinched the button down on the side of her walkie-talkie. "Um hello…can anyone hear me?"

"Code word?" I recognized Brad's voice almost immediately and felt my heart jump with excitement. If he was speaking to us, he was alive.

Alexa said, "Brad. It's me."

"I don't care, Alexa. What's the code word?"

I snorted, and Alexa sighed.

She said, "The code word is violet rose, you moron."

"Yep, that's it. We're good to go. How are you, Lex?" Ben asked.

She shot a demon look at Beth and said, "As well as I can be, you know, considering I'm with kinderqueen all the time."

Beth lowered her brows and pressed the button on her walkie-talkie. "Brad, could you please tell your evil girlfriend to stop calling me names?"

Brad said, "You tell her. I'm sure she can hear you."

Ben stole the walkie-talkie from his sister. He held down the button and said, "Brad, this is Ben."

There was a moment of silence before Brad said, "Oh hey, Ben. What's up?"

"Give me an update. How's everything looking?"

"It's all right, I guess. We made it here losing only three, which is a miracle if you ask me. Everyone's settled in for now. Most are still asleep. The last convoy only came in about two hours ago, so everyone's pretty tired. But they're holding on, and they'll be ready when they're needed."

Ben looked up at me and said, "What about Parker? How's he?"

"Are you asking for Rose or for yourself?" Brad asked.

Ben shrugged and said, "A little of both."

"Well, Parker's asleep right now. He was up until six this morning getting everyone in, but he's holding up. He was near where the bugs attacked last night, but there's not a scratch on him. Y'all have nothing to worry about."

"All right, thanks," Ben said. "I just wanted a quick status report. Rose and I are about to head out, so all the messages from now will be from Alexa and Beth."

Brad laughed and said, "I'm glad I'm as far away as I am, because I have a funny feeling those two are going to start a blood bath in that hotel room. My money's on Alexa."

Beth said into the walkie-talkie Ben was holding, "Brad, we can hear you. We're in the room."

A moment passed before he said, "Oh."

Alexa smirked and said into her walkie-talkie, "Don't worry, babe. You're right. I'll be the one who comes out on top."

"You know a lot about being on top, don't you Alexa?" Beth said, and an icy look crept over Alexa's face.

I stepped between them and said, "Wait until Ben and I are gone for this stupidity. I don't want a headache before I have to go into a room and control a couple hundred minds. Alexa, tell Brad you'll check on him in a few hours."

"I heard you. Someone's holding their button down," Brad said.

Beth looked down at her hands and back at me apologetically.

"Okay, whatever. They'll talk to you in an hour or so. Over and out," I called back to Beth's walkie-talkie.

Brad laughed and said, "Yeah, over and out. Alexa, be good."

Ben sighed and looked between his sister and Alexa. "If you two can't act professionally toward one another, the whole plan needs to be scrubbed. I can't have Rose diverting some of her energy to sending you messages if I can't trust that you're going to relay the important things to Brad and Parker."

Alexa looked away, scathed. I knew it was the biggest hurt of all for her to think that someone might not be able to trust her in the fight. "Don't worry. I promise you that we won't ruin this."

"Beth?" Ben said, looking at his younger sister.

She sighed and said, "Yeah, I promise too."

"All right, that's settled," he said, standing.

He walked over to the table in the corner and picked up a pair of spiked heels. He grinned at me knowingly and asked, "Ever worn heels?"

"Ever had a stiletto shoved into your eye?"

Alexa laughed, and Ben's expression flattened. He walked over to me and held the shoes out for me to take.

I just looked at them.

He sighed and said, "Come on, Rose. They make the persona. We need to be believable."

I shook my head and said, "Then you wear them. How do you expect me to roundhouse kick someone in the temple if I can barely walk."

"You'll be able to walk."

"How would you know? You've never seen me wear heels."

"Rose, people have seen you do a back flip over a grown man's head while still cutting into his shoulder. A pair of four-inch heels is not going to kill you."

I took them angrily and slid them onto my feet. I teetered for a frightening second and wondered if I fell backward how badly the stupid skirt would rip.

"Look at that, you can move," Ben said.

"I am going to shove this spiked heel so far down your throat you will start to digest it," I threatened.

He laughed, raising his hands in surrender, the sparkling in his eyes betraying his lack of sincerity.

I walked over to him and asked impatiently, "Well, are we going to do this or not?"

"Everyone knows the plan?" He looked around and received nods from Beth, Alexa, and me. He nodded and then clapped once. "We'll see you all tonight, then. Be safe."

He led me over to the door and placed his hand on the knob. He hesitated, smiling over at me, and said, "Well, little Cancer, ready or not, here we come."

CHAPTER TWENTY-FIVE

The bellhop gave us knowing glances when we stepped onto the elevator. His smug smirk made me blush. Ben coolly asked him to take us to the parlor. The lights above the doors flashed painfully slow as the elevator lowered. After what seemed like ages, the light finally rested on number three.

The bellhop smiled and said, "Here we are, the Parlor."

The mirrored doors opened, and the buzz of activity made my head vibrate. Nausea rolled into me like a tidal wave, and I nearly staggered back. Ben squeezed my hand. My legs felt like they were made of sand—terribly heavy and as if with the smallest movement they would disintegrate into a pile on the floor. Ben gently pulled me out of the safety of the elevator and into the busy parlor.

I'd assumed that the parlor was just an area with one or two couches, maybe a piano on the side with some mediocre pianist trying to earn a few tips. What I hadn't anticipated was an upscale club *named* the Parlor. It was an ocean of rich mahogany with red and brown fabrics and low lighting. There were booths along the walls where hosts in both business attire and evening wear ate and drank out of glasses that were full of a dark-red liquid. I half wondered if it was something other than wine.

Golden chandeliers hung over an open space where a few couples danced closely together. A jazz band played low music on the small stage at the head of the room.

Ben leaned into me with an effortless smile on his cheeks. He whispered, "Stop looking so frightened. You're a billionaire party princess, remember?"

I pretended to giggle, ignoring the shaking in my knees, and nodded. He let go of my hand to wrap his arm around my waist.

He guided me over to the podium where a host with white hair greeted Ben with a bored expression. When he saw me, though, he blinked and then stood straighter, adjusting the tie at his neck. I shifted uncomfortably under his gaze, pulling at the hem of my skirt.

Ben pulled me closer to him. "We would like a booth."

He looked at Ben's hand around my waist and said, "I'm sorry. We have a strict reservation-only policy."

Ben nudged me forward, and I almost stumbled. The man's expression slackened as he took in my appearance from so close. I gritted my teeth, trying not to squirm under his eyes. I swallowed and said, "Look at me in the eyes."

The man's eyes snapped back to my face, and he stared at me, blank faced. I said, "Please give us a table near the back."

I looked away, giving him his thoughts back.

"Right this way," he said, fumbling with two menus.

He turned and led Ben and me through the rows of tables. Every couple we passed became uncomfortably silent as we went by. I could feel them watching me.

"That was wonderful," Ben whispered into my ear as we walked.

I shook my head. "That was wrong."

The waiter stopped at a small, two-person booth in the back. It was hidden behind a wall of roses and lit with a single, red candle. A beautiful oil painting of a man and woman embraced barefoot on the streets of Venice hung on the wall above the table. It grabbed my attention the moment I saw it.

I looked up at the painting and asked, "Do you think I'll ever be able to do that? To be able to just stand barefoot in a foreign city and *not* have to think about anything else?"

"What?"

I looked away from the painting to him. "I just look at things like that and I wonder if my life will ever be like that, you know? Will I ever be as careless as the people in this painting?"

"It's just a painting, Rose."

"Never mind," I said. I sighed and looked sidelong at the painting again. It was beautiful.

"We don't need to lose focus now," he said, not unkindly. He scanned the crowd lazily, like there was nothing special about what he was doing. It was pretty convincing.

"It's ten a.m. What are all these people doing down here?" I asked, looking about the room less nonchalantly than he did.

He didn't look back at me as he said, "Time is a different thing for them. When you don't have to sleep so much, it becomes irrelevant. If the sun is up, it's daytime. If it's down, it's night. The rest is unimportant."

I nodded and let out a shaky breath. My nerves were on end. There were so many minds buzzing, so many I could sense that I wished I couldn't. One stood out more sharply than the others. His mind was zeroed in on mine, minutely aware of me.

I looked up to Ben and said, "There's one over there—no, don't look—that's taken an interest in me."

Ben snorted and said, "They've all taken an interest in you."

"No, I mean he's noticed how I look, but he's more interested in my aura. He's been watching us since I came in."

"What exactly does he think about your aura? Can you get specifics?"

I closed my eyes and singled in on the host's mind, trying to follow the trace he left in the room. His mind was much brighter than most of the others, and it drew me into it. Just as I entered his head, it felt like a hundred metal knives stabbed into my mind. I pulled back instantly, wincing at the pain, and Ben instinctively grabbed my hand.

"Rose? What just happened?" he asked.

I shook my head and whispered, "His head hurts. His thoughts are like knives slicing in. I-I-I can't get in."

Ben said something under his breath and leaned back against the booth. His whole demeanor changed.

"What? Did I do something wrong?" I asked, confused.

"That host, the one you're trying to get the thoughts from? He's a telepath."

My whole body went cold. "You said there wouldn't be any around here. You said none would be strong enough to read my thoughts well. You said—"

"I know what I said. But now I'm unsaying it, because it's happening. I want to tell you something, but I don't want to frighten you."

"What?"

Ben hesitated and then said, "His aura…"

"What about it?" I asked, lowering my brows.

"It's like yours… It's white."

"What do you mean it's white? How did you not notice when we first came in? I thought I was the only white aura you'd ever seen?"

He quieted me, looking around, and then whispered, "Calm down and listen to me. You were the first white aura I'd ever seen, and now he is the second. No, I don't know what it means, so don't ask."

I inhaled through my nose and tried to steady myself. My feet were shaking under the table, and for the hundredth time, I cursed Ben for putting me in those shoes. I swallowed and asked, "So what do I do? This won't work if he can hear my thoughts."

"I don't think he can."

"How could he not? I don't even know how to hide them that well."

"You said his thoughts are like knives, right? I'm almost certain yours are the same to him. Call it a hunch."

"I'm not sure I'm comfortable with a hunch, Ben," I said.

Ben shifted in his seat and whispered, "You better get comfortable with it, because here he comes."

"What?" I turned sharply and was startled to see a body right in front of me. My eyes met the center of his red button-up and then slowly rose to his face. I gasped.

He was the most beautiful person I'd ever seen. He was literally stunning. He was tall, just over six foot two, and he was muscular. He was in his early twenties, but his demeanor screamed something more mature than that.

His skin was golden brown, lighter than Alexa's but darker than mine, and his hair was raven black. It hung to his shoulders in long, gentle waves. He had a very masculine face with strong cheekbones and a square jaw, but his eyes were what caught me. It was like looking into my eyes but more vibrant. His were royal purple, deep and regal, whereas mine were light like lavender. He looked back at me in awe. He was struck as dumb by me as I was of him.

He stood there, staring at me staring at him, until Ben coughed uncomfortably across from me. I remembered myself and what I was supposed to be doing.

I swallowed my fear and smiled up at him. "Hi."

His expression wavered, his eyes shooting over to Ben and then back to me with a smile.

"I wanted to know if I could ask you to dance," he said with a light accent, one I couldn't place. It sounded almost Italian but not quite.

"I, um—" I looked at Ben. He nudged with his head for me to go. I swallowed, looking back up at the man, and said, "I'd love to."

I stood and let him lead me to the dance floor.

He turned to me when we reached the floor and smiled. He reached up to take my waist but then hesitated and nodded to the guy on the piano. The band began playing a new song, slow and sultry. He turned back to me and then rested his hands on my waist. Warm sparks shot through my veins from where his hands were.

"Do you always get what you want?" I asked, motioning to the band.

We swayed in tune with the music, all eyes in the room on us.

He shrugged and said with a smile, "I'm never told no."

"That could be a problem then, because neither am I."

He smirked and said, "Tell me your name."

"And what will you give me for telling?"

"How about this, a name for a name?"

I smiled. "And then maybe a story for a story?"

"My name is Adrian. Adrian Coallati," he said. His name rolled off his tongue like water, the deepness of his accent permeating through the English he spoke. "And what about you, little flower? What is your name?"

"Roselyn Kennedy."

"You fascinate me, Roselyn."

"Maybe because you can't see what I'm thinking?"

He raised an eyebrow. "You'd only know that if you had tried to read my thoughts."

My face reddened, but I forced myself to remember the part I was playing. I looked back up in Adrian's eyes and said, "It's a drug, diving into the minds of others. You'll have to forgive me if I offended you by doing so. I just can't resist the power."

"Forgive you? Why? It's not every day I meet a woman who *knows* what she's thinking…and what everyone else is too."

I said, "So what's the story, Adrian? How come you're here?"

"What makes you ask?"

"Your aura. Why are you here in this little congregation when you could be somewhere with more powerful people like yourself?"

"Ah, you mean why am I not in Versailles, taking the capital by storm? I've found that the most interesting experiences happen outside the palace walls. I could ask you the same question, though, little flower. Your aura is too big for this place as well," he said.

Versailles, France was the capital. I stored that in my memory.

I shrugged, smiling lightly, and said, "Sometimes it's nice to be a big fish in a little pond."

His eyes drifted back to Ben, and he said, "But don't you miss the company of your equals?"

I took the final plunge and said, "I've always been around lower auras. I'm a *katharóaimos*."

He looked around and then leaned in closer to me. His whisper was hot against my ear as he said, "I shall let you in on a secret, little flower. You're not alone."

"You're one too?" I said in shock.

"The first, assuming you're under twenty?"

I swallowed hard, regaining my composure. "I just turned eighteen."

He smiled, spinning me out as the song ended. "I enjoyed our talk, my little flower. I do hope to see you again."

I nodded speechlessly and turned to go back to Ben. Adrian stopped me, reaching for my arm. A current of hot fire burned through the fabric of my sleeve into my skin. He grinned and said, "And when you're tired of playing with the boy, know that I'm always ready for an adventure."

He dropped my arm, and I turned back to Ben. I felt Adrian's purple eyes fixed on me as I walked away. I slid into the booth across from Ben, a cool smile plastered across my face to try to offset the utter fear in my chest.

"What did-"

"Versailles," I interrupted.

"Excuse me?"

"The capital, the place we have to take down to end all of this for good? It's in Versailles, France," I said, smiling, watching him sit back in shock.

"You're positive?" He asked.

I nodded. "After we take down this place tomorrow night during the ball, that's where we have to go."

He ran his hands through his hair with a slow whistle and then said, "You got that out of him in one dance?"

272 ANNA KATHRYN DAVIS

I took a sip of the water in front of me and leaned over the table. I took Ben's hand in my own for show. I said lowly, "One more thing, he's a *katharóaimos.*"

Ben's eyes widened to the size of my fist, but I stopped him with a shake of my head. Now was not the time to say anything.

He nodded and wiped his hands down his pants leg. I could tell he was having a hard time processing what I just said. He took a few sips of his water, shook his head, and said, "Tell our friends we're coming back to the room."

I nodded. I closed my eyes and thought of Alexa and felt her consciousness graze my own. Her mind was hot, almost uncomfortably so. She was angry. Great.

Alexa.

I felt her attention shift to what I was saying.

Change of plans. Ben and I are coming back to the room. You and Beth stay away from the doors so no one will see you when we enter. See you soon. Oh, and please have me a pair of pants or something when I get up there. I'm not wearing this skirt after that door closes.

I closed the connection and let out a deep breath I didn't know I'd been holding in. Ben looked at me, and I nodded, showing him the task was done. He wiped his mouth with the napkin, placed it on the table, and then stood up. He held his hand out to me as I stood too.

Ben and I walked past the quiet groups of hosts and then waited for the elevator doors to open. When it finally came, we stepped inside, and Ben told the bellhop where to take us. I looked forward into the Parlor and waited for the doors to close. Adrian's dark eyes looked back at me until the elevator finally swallowed me whole.

CHAPTER TWENTY-SIX

"Wait, are you saying this guy is the same as you?" Alexa asked as I ripped the skirt from my body.

Beth averted her eyes and said, "No, she's saying this guy is exactly what she's *pretending* to be. He was born into a human body. He didn't steal one."

"All right, I'm pretty sure that question was directed at Rose," Alexa said and handed me a pair of sweatpants.

I put them on and crashed beside her on the couch. I was finally able to sit and breathe at the same time.

"What did I tell you two about going at it?" Ben asked, looking tired. It was only a little after noon, but he looked like he could sleep a thousand years.

"Well, I was all for following instructions until I came back from my shower to find the jailbait giggling and talking over the walkie-talkies to *my* boyfriend," Alexa said, shooting daggers with her eyes at Beth.

Beth said smugly, "I can't help it if your boyfriend likes my conversation more."

"Oh yeah? Let's see how good you are at making conversation without any teeth in your mouth."

"Shut up, both of you," Ben snapped.

Alexa glared at him but didn't say anything else.

Ben sighed and shook his head. "I'm not really sure what to do right now. I want to keep going with the plan as before, but this guy, this Adrian Coallati, is making me wonder if we should just scrub this mission all together."

I said, "No. This guy is just a bump in the road, that's all. He's not worth scrubbing everything."

"You don't understand, Rose. I recognize his name."

"You said you'd never met him before."

"I'd never even heard of *him* exactly, but his last name is familiar. His family, his mother and father, I would presume, are some of the biggest names in this world. They would be the royalty if there were such a thing."

"How could you recognize his name but not know the capital?" Alexa asked, looking at him sidelong.

"I'd heard rumors about Versailles, but I'd never heard that it was directly the capital. Information like that is usually not meant for people as low as me."

"But your aura is brighter than most of the people here," I said.

Ben shrugged and said, "I am higher up around *here*, but in places like Versailles where probably everyone has a near-white aura? I'd be nothing, probably less than nothing."

"Well then, why would he tell me? I'm not anything special, at least not to them. I'm just some heiress, right?"

Ben shook his head and said, "Whether you want to be or not, you're one of them. Your aura is your ticket anywhere. Any social gathering, any government job, it's all yours. He probably told you because he assumed that's where you were going. Remember we spread the rumor you were headed to Europe? We just got lucky that it sounded like you were on your way to the capital."

Beth crossed her arms and said, "So now what? Are we giving up?"

I shook my head. "No. We're going ahead, just with caution is all. I'll think of some way to get around this Adrian guy. We got what we wanted out of him, right? The location of the capital? Now my only goal is to get invited to the ball tomorrow night where Parker and the Circle attack. Am I missing anything?"

Ben hesitated and then shook his head. "I don't know if you're going to be able to ditch this guy forever, Rose."

"And why is that?"

"I didn't want to tell you this while you two were so near…but your auras did something… Something I'd never seen before."

"What?" I asked.

"They became one."

"Excuse me?"

"When you two were dancing, I couldn't discern one aura from the other. You two were surrounded by one large, pulsating force. It was like the two of you created one super force together. Your auras were almost blinding."

"What does that mean?" I asked.

Ben opened his mouth to reply but went silent when a sharp knock came from the door. We froze, our eyes darting between one another. Beth and Alexa panicked. They looked at one another and mouthed commands, arguing and pointing, before Ben grabbed them and shoved them behind the couch. I waited until they were hidden before I went to the door.

Ben stopped me and said, "No, let me. You're not dressed right anyways. They'd wonder why you're in sweatpants."

"What? You think heiresses always wear freaking lingerie around the house?"

"Whatever. Just stay out of sight," he said without humor.

I followed him to the door. He opened it, flooding the apartment with the light from the hall. The bellhop stood in the hallway, holding a tray with a folded note on top.

"Oh, thank you," Ben said.

He reached forward, but the bellhop hesitated and pulled the tray back.

"I'm sorry, sir, but this message is for Miss Kennedy."

"Well, she's indisposed at the moment."

"But she's standing right behind you, sir," the bellhop said, peering around Ben and looking at me.

Ben turned and glared at me, the annoyance obvious in his eyes. He clenched his jaw and said, "So it would seem she is."

I stepped past him into the doorway and the bellhop cleared his throat, a goofy smile on his face.

I took the envelope and mumbled thanks, shutting the door. Ben looked at me flatly, and I shrugged.

I plopped on the couch and looked down at the calligraphy written on the paper. I hesitated, looking at Alexa, and then ripped the seal to the letter.

> Little Flower,
>   I was disappointed to see you leave the Parlor so soon. I desperately wanted a second dance. Let me have it tonight. Meet me in the lobby at nine sharp, and I'll take you out for a night you won't forget.
>
>   Adrian
>
>   P.S. Leave the boy at home.

"That was a waste of effort on his part. You're not going," Ben said, sitting back on the other couch.

"That's a joke. Of course I'm going. I could get a lot of valuable information out of him in a single night," I said, folding the note and sliding it into my pocket.

"You said it yourself. You don't need anything else out of him other than an invitation to tomorrow night's gala. That's all. No night out on the town needed," Ben said stubbornly.

"That was before I thought I'd get the chance to get anything else out of him. This could be a good thing. I could get an invitation, plus so much more. Think about it," I said.

"We don't need any information that could put you in any more danger," Ben said.

"People are dying right now," I said, thinking of Wes. I closed my eyes, and inhaled. I reopened them and said, "We owe it to everyone depending on us to get every little bit of information we can. A single piece could be exactly what we need to get the upper hand."

Ben looked at me more softly, and I knew he'd felt me thinking of Wes. He said, "I know you lost your friend, Rose, but this is war. More people will die. We can't make rash decisions because we want to save them all."

I could tell from the look in his eyes that he wasn't going to budge. I looked over at Alexa pleadingly. She shook her head and said, "I dunno, Rose. After what Ben said happened with your auras, I'm not sure you should get near him at all. Something isn't right there."

I groaned.

Ben held up a walkie talkie and said, "If you want to go so badly, why don't you ask Parker what he thinks about it?"

My stubborn nature flared. "I don't have to ask Parker, because I don't have to ask permission."

Ben shrugged and brought the walkie talkie to his lips. He said, annoyingly arrogant, "Violet rose. This is Ben speaking. I have an urgent matter I need to speak with Parker about concerning his girlfriend."

There was a five-second break where I was hopeful Parker wouldn't answer. Then he said, "Talk to me."

Ben looked at his nails as he said, "We met an exceptionally powerful host today who has become smitten with your girlfriend. He is now asking to see her alone tonight to, and I quote, 'give her a night she won't forget.' Should we allow her to go?"

"Absolutely not."

I threw my hands up in the air and sighed. Ben smiled and said, "I completely agree."

"Give me that." I stole the other walkie-talkie from Alexa's hands and brought it to my lips. I pressed down the button and said, "You know, last time I checked, I didn't have to ask any of you for permission."

Parker said, "It's just too dangerous, Rose. I won't have you—"

"I'm not asking to go. I'm telling you that I am. This guy is a gold mine of information, and I'm not passing up this opportunity because ya'll have it in your heads that it's up to you whether or not I go."

There was a silent moment on the other end of the walkie-talkie. Parker finally said, his voice hard, "You're not going, Rose. I'm sorry that you hate my protection, but you're not going."

"I am going, and I'm sorry someone gave you the idea that I need protecting, because it's going to make what I do next very hard for you."

"What do you mean?" he asked.

I turned the walkie-talkie off and threw it on the couch. I walked from the room in silence. I knew they could just turn the walkie-talkie back on and continue talking, but my point had been made. I wouldn't be there when the conversation started again, meaning that whatever they decided wasn't decided by me.

CHAPTER TWENTY-SEVEN

"You know Ben's pretty upset with me for taking your side in this," Beth said without emotion. She helped me pin back my hair

I shrugged. "Alexa's not talking to me either. They're pretty pissed that I'm going."

"It's just because they're worried about you. They don't want you to get hurt is all," Beth said.

"Yeah, well, they're just going to have to worry. This is a war. We have to start taking chances if we want to get anything done. I can't sit back letting everyone else call the shots anymore while people are dying," I said.

Beth stepped back and looked at me appraisingly. She said, "Oh yeah, you'll get what you need out of that guy tonight. You could probably get anything in that dress."

She was right; I knew she was, but it didn't make me feel any less terrible about wearing it. I pulled at it awkwardly, trying to make it cover more of my thighs. I had little success.

Beth handed me two daggers, and I slid one into each of my boots.

I let out a deep breath and then said, "All right, I think I'm ready."

She nodded and walked me to the door. I opened it and then hesitated. "Tell the other's I'm gone, and don't forget to be ready for my messages. It's harder for me to break through if you're not ready for them."

She nodded and said, "Can do."

I stepped from the room, taking a shaky breath, and shut the door behind me. The hall was jarringly silent. I stopped before the elevator and pressed the button with shaky hands. The doors opened almost immediately, and the bellhop looked at me expectantly.

I swallowed, forcing a smile, and stepped inside. I said, "The lobby, please."

He nodded and pressed a button on the wall. I could tell he was straining to look before him and not in my direction. I ignored him. I could do this. I could make it an entire night safely. I just had to focus.

The elevator doors dinged loudly before they opened, revealing the lobby. I stepped from the elevator and spotted him almost immediately.

Adrian stood by the front desk in a cream-colored suit, his dark hair curled around his face. He spotted me almost as quickly as I'd seen him.

He approached me, smiling, and said, "You're late. I was wondering if you were going to come."

I shrugged and said, "A woman makes her own time. It's just a coincidence that it somewhat correlates with the time of men."

His eyes flickered with the faintest traces of a smile. He rested his hand on my bare arm, and shocks of electricity went up my skin. I looked down at where he touched me, surprised, and found that he was looking too. He'd felt the same feeling I had.

He laughed and said, "Guess I shocked you. My apologies."

I smiled thinly, and tried to steady myself. His touch had been more than a shock, really, leaving my mind woozy.

"You look stunning, by the way," he said. He led me out of the front doors of the hotel, all eyes on us.

"You don't look so bad yourself."

He walked me to a black Porsche with butterfly doors. It was the nicest car I'd ever seen. I slid into the passenger seat, my heart pounding in my ears.

He shut my door and then walked over to the driver's side, opening the door and getting in next to me effortlessly. The car started with a soft purr that grew louder as we pulled from the parking lot.

"Does my driving scare you?" he asked, looking over at me with a smile. He was probably mistaking my overall anxiety with being nervous about how fast he was going.

I swallowed and said, "No, I like going fast."

Adrian smiled, shaking his head, and said, "You're something else, Roselyn, something else entirely."

"I was thinking the same about you."

Our eyes locked, and for a moment I couldn't breathe. Looking into his eyes was like looking into eternity. It was frightening yet beautiful. Was that how I affected people? I looked away sharply. He laughed, and his grip on the wheel tightened.

He said, "I must be honest with you, Roselyn. I think tonight is going to be something I'll never forget."

I shook my head, laughing to myself, and said, "Yeah, I'm almost positive I'll be saying the same."

He pulled into the parking lot of an upscale nightclub. Hosts crowded in a never-ending line around the corner of the building. They were roped in by a red velvet cable that shone like blood under the glow from the club's "Blood Indigo" sign, written in a fancy fuchsia script. My heart dropped in a frightened spiral that threatened to make me vomit. There were *so* many hosts.

I turned to Adrian and said almost frantically, "You want to go in *here*? With this huge crowd?"

He smiled, opening his door, and tossed his keys to a valet. He skimmed his knuckles across the hood of the car as he walked to my side. He opened the door and reached for my hand to help me out. I took it, and the electric spark of his skin against mine made my whole hand feel like hot sand.

"How do you expect us to get in? We'd be in line half…" My voice trailed. I suddenly couldn't remember what I was so worked up about. Adrian smiled back at me, squeezing my hand, and closed his car door behind me. We approached a thick-shouldered bouncer, who gave us a curt nod and then lifted the rope for us to walk in. I expected a few outraged protests, a number of glares, but instead I found nothing but warm smiles and approving glances from the ones in line.

They weren't all just staring at me, either, which was what I was worried about. A good bit of them, maybe even so much as half, were focused on Adrian. I looked over at him and found him staring at me with a bright expression.

"There's the smile I was waiting for. I was beginning to wonder if anything could impress you," he said.

I smiled broader, and he placed his hand on the small of my back, guiding me past the bouncer into the club. The immediate stench of smoke and the startling shift of lights took me by surprise.

Adrian leaned into my shoulder, his breath hot on my ear as he shouted above the music, "Follow me."

I swallowed and grabbed his arm. He led me through a swarm of dancing epidroméas. I shied away from their bodies when they touched me, their skin slick and steaming with sweat.

My stomach was in my throat, and I was so nervous I thought my heart might explode. Being here, now, surrounded by all of them, I realized how dangerous this really was. I was in a room full of epidroméas and no one even knew where I was.

That reminded me. I closed my eyes and focused on sending Beth a message. *In a club called Blood Indigo. Hundred plus epidroméas. Nothing new to report. Keep you posted.*

Adrian stopped walking, and I stumbled into his back. Everything was quiet now. He had led me to a room where we could be alone. The walls were draped in a rich, red tapestry that bled into the deep oak of the floors. A black couch lined the walls, snaking around the corners and forming a large U shape around the table in the middle of the room. A black stone fireplace roared in the corner. If not for the muffled beating of the music outside the door, I would have never guessed we were in a club.

"Sorry," I said, looking embarrassed.

He smiled and then scanned my face appraisingly. He looked at me sidelong and said, "For someone so deadly, you are so indescribably beautiful." He stroked the backs of his fingers against my cheekbone, leaving a trail of fire in his path.

"I'm no more dangerous than you are," I said, swallowing the panic rising in my veins. I had the sudden urge to break the fingers he had against my face.

He chuckled and said, "Right."

I reached up and pulled his hand from my cheek, letting it drop to his side. I gave him a sidelong smile and sat on the couch.

I stretched out and said, "Well, maybe you should define dangerous."

"That could be a long discussion. Let's start with a drink, shall we?"

He motioned to the bottle of wine sitting on the table in the middle of the room. I smiled, and he poured me a glass. I took it and prayed Ben would be right about me being immune to the alcohol.

Adrian sat at my feet, my toes in his lap and his hands resting across them. I had to make a significant effort to ignore the burning feeling his bare skin brought against my own. I swallowed and tried to clear my head. Why was it so hard to think clearly?

"Tell me, Mr. Coallati—"

"Call me Adrian."

"Adrian," I said, taking a small sip of my wine.

I asked, "How did we walk right in here? Straight into a VIP room at that?"

He smiled and peered at me through the transparency of his glass. "My family owns this place. Opened it about twenty years ago."

"Twenty years?"

"Yes. They were some of the first epidroméas to settle this area. The club was their first endeavor."

"What are they like? Your parents?" I asked, locking eyes with him. Chill bumps rose along my back.

He shrugged and said, "Ah, Martin and Andrea Coallati. They're what you would expect, I guess. Strong, moral, *rich*. They like to collect things…beautiful things. Paintings. Cars. People." He stopped and then looked at me, I guessed to judge my expression. I looked into his eyes and felt something. Not the hypnosis I had been expecting, but something sadder, something that looked more like hurt.

I spoke without thinking. "You don't like your parents."

His expression faltered, but he regained his composure and tried to smile. It didn't quite touch his eyes. He said, "It seems you're very good at reading people, Miss Kennedy."

I sipped at my wine and said, "I'm sorry. If you don't want to talk about it, I just—"

He shook his head and said, "It's all right. My parents… my parents weren't made to parent. I guess none of the epidroméas are. They lay their eggs in the mother hive, wait for them to hatch, and then insert them. But then I happened, and no one knew what to do. No one knew how to handle me. I was an oddity, an oddity no one wanted to spend time with."

His words hit me. Somehow he'd said the last thing I expected: he'd said something I could relate to. Being a child no one knew what to do with was the story of my life. I looked up at him again with his dark hair and unsettling eyes, and I didn't see a monster. I saw myself. I swallowed and said, tiredly, "I'm sorry you grew up like that."

He shrugged, taking a large gulp of his wine, and said, "It's no matter. None of them are to blame. They didn't know what they were doing."

"You said *them*. Do you not associate yourself with the epidroméas?"

He nodded, a sly smile on his lips, and said, "I'm not surprised you don't either."

I thought quickly, to change the subject. "So, uh, where are they now? Your parents?"

His demeanor shifted, and he shrugged, saying, "The capital probably. I haven't seen them in a few years. They've been pretty busy. They're getting ready."

"Getting ready for what?"

"The final strike, of course. The last step in securing earth."

My whole body went cold. I swallowed and forced myself to say, "Oh, really? When?"

He took the last sip of his wine and said, "May. Maybe June. Whenever the army is ready. It takes time to make that many sentinels. Can you imagine having to lay ten thousand eggs? I can't, and believe me, I've sowed my share of wild oats."

He winked, but I was lost to his charm. Ten thousand epidroméas. Ten thousand to fight in the end battle.

I had to tell Beth. I had to make sure the others got the message. I stood up, but Adrian stood with me, his hand on my wrist like a chain. I looked down at his hand, ready to shake it from me, but then couldn't remember why I'd stood up.

"Wait, did I say something?"

I looked around, trying to think, and said, "No, but I just remembered that I needed to get back…now."

"We haven't even danced yet."

"I know, but—"

"Please? One dance and then I'll drive you back. I promise," he said, his eyes sparkling. I bit my lower lip, unsure.

His hand was so hot on my skin; it was maddening, but also thrilling. I looked back into his eyes, and said, "All right, one dance."

"Perfect."

The pulse of the music blaring over the speakers made my eyes shake, and my heart thumped with the resonating hum of the bass. Adrian squeezed my hand tightly as he led me to the center of the room, bodies pressed up against us both. He turned to me and smiled. His enchantingly deep eyes glowed in the black light, and his smile sparkled brighter than the strobe lights overhead. He rested his hands on my hips, and I felt my pulse skyrocket. His hands felt like hot coals on my skin, warmth seeping into the deepest layers of my core, and as he moved, my hips moved with him.

He leaned into my shoulder, his face disappearing in the mass of my hair, and said, "Just feel the music. Forget everything else."

The music was unlike anything I'd ever heard or *felt* before. It seemed to come alive, to dance from the speakers and flood the room. I could feel my pace quickening and my smile growing the longer we danced to it, the notes streaming together in a never-ending current that flowed like a mighty river around us.

Adrian's lips were against my neck when he whispered to me, his words somehow making it over the *thump* of the stereo. "We're glowing," he said.

I laughed and looked around us. I could *see* our auras. They blended together, forming one massive, swirling net of pure-white light that pulsed and burned brighter than the sun. Our skin was glowing too.

Everyone in the club had shifted so that Adrian and I were alone on the floor. We were dancing in the middle of a huge circle with the entire club looking on and staring. Some distant part of me thought that I should have been concerned, maybe even frightened, but I wasn't. I threw back my head and laughed.

Adrian's hands snaked up my back. One rested on the small of my spine, and the other was just under my neck. It felt like pure sunlight was pouring into my skin, burning away every ounce of inhibition I ever had. He lifted my head to his face, and I knew what he wanted.

Our lips met with a spark. His lips sent intoxicating fire sliding down my throat. His tongue slid across my lips like flames, and I couldn't breathe. I never wanted to breathe again. I wanted to stay here, wrapped in this kiss and never let go.

He pulled me closer to him, his body pressed against mine. I wasn't sure where his body stopped and mine began. I couldn't contain the fire he brought. I couldn't hold it back. Our auras erupted, the light exploding in a fury of radiance that burned my eyes. It fell from the rafters in fits of flame, and the sprinklers burst open overhead, pouring water over everything.

Adrian pulled back, his breath deep and ragged in his chest, and he looked at me with wide eyes. The water sizzled against our skin as it hit. Steam arose from over our intertwined arms.

The rush of endorphins made me dizzy. I smiled at him anyways.

"What just happened?"

He kissed the top of my head, and said, "Come on. I'll tell you in the car."

I nodded and let him lead me through the crowd. They watched us walk by in awe. Adrian led me to the valet and said something to the dark-haired epidroméas who parked the car earlier. The guy ran around the corner and then drove back with the Porsche. He got out and opened the door for me to climb in. I held Adrian's hand, sliding into the red leather seat.

He let go of my hand and shut the door. My mind started to itch, like ants were crawling through my thoughts. I got the feeling there was something wrong. I was forgetting something, something direly important. Adrian climbed into the driver's side and looked at me. His brows furrowed.

"Something wrong?" he asked, taking my hand.

The feeling of his hand in mine brought a smile to my face. The bad feeling was gone. There was only him. I smiled and said, "Nope."

The purr of the car seemed like nothing more than a figment of my imagination as he pulled from the lot. I smiled at his face, watching him speak. His skin, like mine, sparkled as he spoke. I could feel the energy in his voice leaking from his lips like blood. I was only half aware of what he was saying, though he seemed to be saying a lot.

"I can't believe you're it, Roselyn. I can't believe this is really happening."

"Call me Rose," I said dreamily. He smiled over at me and squeezed my hand.

"Rose, I've been waiting all my life for this. I didn't think it was real… I didn't think the prophecy could be right. I-I-I just want to kiss you!"

I giggled, wishing he would, but I could see he was enjoying talking, and I wanted to keep him happy. So I asked a question. "What prophecy?"

"The oldest one I know of, really. The one that says you're everything I need, everything my race needs. The single verse that defines my life. And you're it. Dear God, I can't believe you're real."

He smiled over at me again, and my stomach dropped. What I wouldn't give to have him look at me like that every day for the rest of my life. I leaned down and kissed the knuckles of the hand he had wrapped around mine.

I felt the strange twang of disappointment as we pulled into the hotel parking lot, because I knew that meant he was about to have to let go of me again, even if it was only for a minute to open the door. I lowered my eyes, confused at my own thoughts. It wasn't like me to be so needy… was it? I couldn't remember.

Adrian put the car in park and leaned across the console. He enveloped me in another kiss, his hand soft against my cheek like flaming silk. I forgot what I'd been thinking and melted into his touch. He pulled back all too quickly, and his dazzling eyes stopped only inches from mine.

"You're perfect, Rose. Absolutely perfect."

I smiled, and he pulled away to open the driver's side door. He stopped at the front of the car and began exchanging words with the bellhop.

I looked up in front of the hood at Adrian and hesitated.

One half of me wanted to melt just by looking at him. That half wanted him to whisk me away to his room to never return. That half seemed so bright, so real that I wasn't sure what to do with the dreamy half of me that wanted to shove a knife into his eye.

A knife. I had a knife. I reached down and touched the blades in my boots as if it was the first time I'd seen them. I wouldn't have put a knife in my boot if I was going on a date with him for pleasure, would I? I wouldn't be wearing a knife at all if I weren't in danger, right?

I looked back up at him and furrowed my brows, confused. My brain was just so fuzzy…so blank. I didn't like the feeling. It wasn't right. There had been a purpose for tonight…a reason I was with him that would make me bring a knife. Someone had to know why I was wearing knives, but who?

Beth. The name pierced through my mind like an arrow, and for a moment I was unsure what to do with it. I thought, struggling to unscramble my thoughts. She was someone that I was supposed to tell something to. But what? Something about *him*? I lowered my brows and thought harder than I ever had before. I thought so hard my nails dug into my palms, piercing the skin.

It was something about him.

I looked back up at him through the window of the car. He was talking to the bellhop, laughing, but what caught my attention were the two giant bugs standing at the door of the hotel. They were massive, ugly, and, without my understanding, my knees shook just because I was near them. I was afraid of them. Adrian wasn't, though; he didn't even notice them.

I looked back down at my lap and furrowed my brows. He wouldn't be afraid of them if he knew they wouldn't hurt him. They wouldn't hurt him… because he was one of them. I looked back up, suddenly panicked. I needed to get away from him. I needed to find Beth and the others.

I opened the door of the car and jumped out faster than I'd intended. There were epidroméas all along the sidewalk staring at me. Adrian's eyes locked on me, perplexed, and he reached for me.

I jerked back from his touch like it was acidic. Every time he touched me, I lost reality. His touch made me forget.

"I need to go back to my room," I said.

"I thought..."

I dared myself to lock eyes with him. A small heat rose in my chest, but I squelched it. I said, "If you respect me at all, you won't ask me to come back to your room, Adrian."

He nodded and leaned closer to me. He reached out and touched the side of my dress. He said, "I'm really glad you came with me tonight, Rose."

"Yeah." I nodded.

Our eyes locked in a shocking electrical storm, and I forced myself to breathe. I stepped past him into the mouth of the hotel lobby.

"Rose? Will I see you at the ball tomorrow night?"

I smiled faintly, remembering that that had been my goal for the night. Now it didn't seem so important. I said over my shoulder, "Yeah, I guess you will."

He smiled, but I turned away. I didn't look back. I pressed the elevator button and waited for it to come and take me back to reality.

CHAPTER TWENTY-EIGHT

"Okay. Tell me what happened," Ben said, handing me a ceramic mug of hot chocolate.

He sat across from me on the couch beside his bed. We were alone in his room of the hotel suite. He looked at me, expectantly, his fiery eyes shifting between nervous fear and intense anger.

I looked down at the mug in my hand and said, "I don't know."

"What do you mean, you don't know?" His voice neared anger, the anxiety he was struggling to contain seeping out of his teeth like vomit.

I looked up at him, beaten, and he sighed.

"I'm sorry, it's just…this has been a night of hell for me. I don't understand how you went five hours without contacting us—"

"Five hours?"

"Yes, five hours. It's nearly two a.m."

I looked away from him and said blankly, "It didn't even feel like one."

"Just start from the beginning."

I nodded and took a sip of my hot chocolate. "I met him in the lobby a little after nine. He took me to his car… I think that was the first time he touched me."

Ben's whole body went rigid. "Touched you?"

"It was just my hand. He was helping me into his car. I mention it because…because when he touches me, it's like electricity, a dangerous, otherworldly shock. It doesn't make sense, but it's intoxicating. I should have realized then that something was wrong, but I didn't.

"He took me to his family's club, Blood Indigo. We bypassed a whole crowd of epidroméas without a single incident. It was like we were celebrities. We weren't rushed at or attacked. They just stared…at both of us."

I shook my head and looked distantly out the window, the black expanse of the city shining like fallen stars, captured and tethered to the earth.

"Well, anyways, he led me to some kind of VIP room in the back where he gave me some wine, and we talked for a little while. He told me something that freaked me out, and I got up to leave, but he talked me into one dance. That's where things get fuzzy for me."

"What can you remember?" Ben asked.

I set my mug on the small table beside his bed and said, "It's strange. I know it was tonight, but it's like it happened years ago. I-I remember the music vividly. It was so different than anything I'd ever heard. Ben, it was like it wasn't music at all, but maybe wine, or some kind of drug…"

"I should have foreseen that. Epidroméas have a very astute understanding of the brain and its workings. The music you heard was made with the sole intention of stimulating specific parts of the brain, more specifically, the pleasure centers. Most of the classier institutions don't play music like it—it's somewhat taboo—but I probably should have known he'd play it. Figures."

I looked down at my crossed ankles on his bed, avoiding his eyes.

He asked, "Do you remember anything else?"

"Bits and pieces. I remember our auras blended…and we kind of glowed. Like…our skin looked illuminated. I don't know why. And….I think I kissed him, Ben."

"You think?"

I sighed, my shoulders dropping. "No, I'm sure I did. The sprinklers went off."

Ben laughed, earning a hard glare from me that shut him up quickly. He coughed and pulled at the fitted neckline of his t-shirt. He regained his composure and asked, "When did you finally, uh, regain control of reality?"

"In the parking lot outside the hotel when he finally let go of me long enough for me to piece everything together."

"So you're saying that his touch brought on this whole drunkenness?"

"Drunkenness?"

He shrugged and said, "Yes, drunkenness. Can you describe it any better?

"I guess not."

Ben looked past me, deep in thought, and said, "I wonder if he's your Rose."

"What?"

"Work with me for a second. You know how people go wild when they see your face? How they lose sight of reality? What if he's that to you? What if your one weakness is him?"

I immediately wanted to refute it but stopped short. Hadn't I made the comparison earlier? He had every intoxicating aspect of my face, only multiplied by a million. It definitely made sense, given the circumstances.

"What good would that do, though? Why make me look like this if I only fall short in the end? That doesn't make sense. Everything done to us has had a reason, a plan. This is nonsensical, pointless even."

Ben shook his head and said, "I don't think so. If I were to guess, I'd say he's not completely unfazed by your looks either, not even close. You look like you do to draw him in. We need him. He's a major player in this war. His secrets very well could be the thing that wins this for us. I think this is just your test. You have to resist the creature made for you if you're to succeed."

"I don't know if I would go so far as to say he was made for me."

Ben shrugged and said, "I would. He seems to be your equal in every way. He takes away the hardness you have and replaces it with who you could be."

"I don't understand."

"I'm not stupid, Rose, and neither are you, so let's not pretend that the things in your life haven't made you the person that you are. If none of it had happened, you would be a normal sixteen-year-old girl, obsessing over the hot guy giving her attention and only focusing on how *you* were feeling and how much *you* wanted to be with him. You wouldn't be focused on anything else, and it seems to me that that is exactly what he did to you. He made you who you *could* have been. I'd say that makes him perfect for you."

I looked out the window again and sighed. "I just wish this wasn't always so complicated. It's like every time I start to accept another part of this crazy plan, something else is thrown at me. Can't it ever just *stay*? Why does it always have to change?"

Ben smiled lopsidedly and said, "Because that would make it all too easy."

I lay back on the bed. "I'm just ready for it all to be over with."

Ben crawled up on the bed beside me and patted my leg. "You and me both. Hey, you never told me what Adrian told you at the club."

"Oh crap!" I sat up, completely stiff. I could punch myself for being so absentminded. "The epidroméas are planning a final strike. *Ten thousand* of them against whoever is left standing."

"Ten thousand?" Ben exclaimed. The fire behind his eyes exploded, and his whole eye, even the white, turned a violent shade of red. He gasped, closed his eyes, and struggled for a moment, his forehead beading with sweat.

"Ben!" I reached out and shook him by his shoulders.

He gasped and opened his eyes. They were back to their shifty green. He coughed and wiped the sweat from his brow. "Sorry, you surprised me. It almost got out just then."

"Is it always ready to take over like that? Always waiting for the moment?"

He swallowed with a weak smile and said, "Always. Too bad I'm too hard headed to let the devil out."

I pushed the strawberry blond wisps from his face and looked at him. His forehead was damp with sweat.

"I'm sorry I went tonight. I shouldn't have."

"It's done now. And it was needed. Did he say when the final strike was?"

"May or June. He didn't say where, but I know they're gathering their troops in Versailles, France."

"I guess we should be grateful that this battle can be used to take out two birds with one stone—the capital itself and its armies. Versailles is where we'll have to go to end this."

I shook my head. "How are we going to do this, Ben? *Ten thousand?*"

"We'll figure it out. We have time, thanks to you."

"Yeah, but that all depends on if we win tomorrow." I cradled my knees into my chest as I dropped my head. I couldn't even imagine the amount of carnage that would break out tomorrow night. There would be so much death.

"Hey." Ben lay his hand on my arm, and I looked up at him. Our eyes met. I heard his voice in my head. *It's going to be okay.*

"But what if it won't, Ben? Someone I know could die tomorrow night. What if it's you? Or Alexa? Or Parker? I-I don't think I would make it."

Ben combed his hand through my hair and said, "This is what they want from you, little Cancer. They'll try to kill off those close to you, because they know it alienates you. If they get you, they get the war. You tip the scale, Rose. The others are important, crucial even, but they can't get inside like you can. You just have to remember that you're better than these bugs. You have a soul, a beautiful, beautiful soul, and they can't have it, no matter how cold and alone they make you feel. You're stronger than that."

"I don't feel stronger, though."

Ben smiled and said, "But you are. Everyone can see it. That's what makes you beautiful, Rose. Not your face or your body, it's that strength. It's blinding."

I said, "You're too good to me, Ben."

"What are friends for? But you know what you have to do now, right?"

He reached into his back pocket and pulled out a walkie-talkie. He said with a smirk, "You've got to convince your boyfriend that you're not dead."

I threw my head back against the pillow and whined. "Y'all told him I went?"

Ben handed me the walkie-talkie and said, "I didn't. Beth did after we didn't hear from you for a few hours. Last thing he heard was that you were in some club called 'blood something' full of hundreds of epidroméas and that you weren't responding."

"How long ago was that?"

Ben shrugged. "Ehh, four hours?"

I sighed and stared down at the walkie-talkie. "All right, this might take a while."

Ben left the room and closed the door behind him.

I inhaled and closed my eyes. I pressed so hard against the button of the walkie-talkie that my skin turned white. "Uh, Parker? Over."

There was a moment of static, a moment of hesitation where I wasn't sure whether to be thrilled or terrified that he wasn't replying, but then came the flood.

"Rose." It was a single word, a single syllable at that, but in it I could feel the fury of a hurricane.

"I'm, uh, back." I shut my eyes tightly, wincing at how stupid it sounded. The boy had thought I'd been dead for four hours and that was all I could say? Pathetic.

There was silence.

"I found out some stuff you'd find interesting…some real important stuff that'll help us a lot." I started rambling, my voice raising an octave with nerves. He was too quiet.

"So you're okay." The sentence wasn't kind.

My inner hardhead flared. "Yeah, I'm fine, thanks for the compassion."

"What do you expect me to sound like, Rose? You went out, against my will—"

"*Against your will?* I'm not your child, Parker."

"No, you're my girlfriend. My girlfriend who just went on a date with a bug and did *God knows what* for four hours."

"God knows what?"

"Yeah, as in only God knows what kept you out *that* long with another guy."

I tried to swallow my stubbornness and bit, "I'm sorry."

"You're sorry? That's all you can say? No explanation of what you've been doing? About what took you so long?"

I hesitated, then sighed, and said, "I'll tell you whatever you want to know. Just please, try not to let your jealousy thing get in the way of you listening."

"It's not a thing, Rose. It's you going against what I said and—"

My anger peaked. "You know what, Parker? I can't handle this. I've had a horrible, horrible night. I'm tired, and my emotions are raw. I'm terrified about tomorrow, and the last thing I need is you preaching to me. Accusing me pointlessly does nothing but piss me off."

I heard him sigh, and then he said, his voice softer, "I'm sorry, Rosie. I've just been so worried about you already, and then when Beth told me you went on that *date* with this guy... I just lost it. I'm sorry. I know you'd never kiss another guy, let alone the craziness I was imagining."

I looked down, and said, "Parker..."

"What?"

I closed my eyes and took a deep breath. I forced myself to say, "I kissed him."

There was silence on the other end.

"Parker, I'm sorry. I just didn't—"

His voice sounded disconnected as he said, "I'm in a sewer, fighting for my life and *our* future, and you're off kissing some guy you just met. Real cool, Rose."

"Parker—"

"No, I don't want to hear it, Rose. Honestly, I don't even want to think about you right now. The thought of you makes me sick."

"Parker?"

I held down the button, but no reply came. He'd turned his receiver off. I was alone. Water pooled over the rims of my eyes and slid down my cheeks. I fell back onto the pillow with my dress still clinging to me and closed my eyes to the world. The tears steadily fell.

My eyes opened slowly, heavily. They resisted the movement, trying with all their might to stay closed, but I wouldn't let them. I sat up, peeling my face from Alexa's side. She looked at me cautiously, almost as if any second she expected me to start leaking again. I pushed my hair back, feeling the wild knots forming all inside it, and met her eyes. Her gaze didn't falter. "You look like hell," she said.

"Thanks," I said and yawned.

I looked out the window over the city's landscape. The sun was high in the sky, painting a vibrant spotlight on the desert city.

I turned back to Alexa and asked, "How long have I been asleep?"

She shrugged, smoothing her shirt, and said, "Most of the day. You didn't fall asleep until nearly three this morning, and it wasn't exactly an easy night. None of us wanted to wake you."

I nodded. Not any easy night? What a frickin' understatement. "Has he, uh, called?"

"No, but I did talk to Brad this morning, and he assures me that everything is still ready for tonight. Assuming you're still up for it?"

"Oh, I'm up for it. Believe me, all I really feel like doing right now *is* fighting."

"Good. That's the insane Rose I know how to deal with. I didn't know what to do with that crying Rose from last night. Honestly, she had me a little scared."

"Yeah, well, she had me scared too."

"Well, all right, black Dahlia, nice to know you're back. Go and get a shower, please."

"Black Dahlia?"

She reached forward and wiped my cheek. A thick black residue came off on her finger as she smiled. "Didn't anyone tell you not to sleep with this crap on?"

"Oh, I forgot about the makeup."

"Yeah, well, it's hard for me to when you look like a horrified clown. Go clean yourself up. Then we'll talk."

She left, closing the door behind her. With her gone, I could assess what state I was in. After every battle it was important to check for injury. Now was no different. I was stiff. My back popped when I stretched my hands over my head. I could move, though, so the music from last night hadn't damaged anything irreparably. My mouth was dry, and I had a killer headache, but that would fade quickly; they always did.

What I wasn't sure would heal, even for me, was the gaping empty feeling in my chest. When I let out a breath, I felt nothing—numbness, emptiness. It felt like something was missing, something vital and important.

I took a deep breath and made myself gain control. It was done; the situation was past help. People needed more of me today than to fall apart. I could confront these emotions later, fall apart *after* tonight. I took a deep breath and wrapped all my thoughts in a little box inside my head and stored them away for later, just as Ben had taught me.

I climbed out of bed, my joints popping, and stumbled to the bathroom. The cold tile floor raised goose bumps on my skin, and

I shivered. I reached the tub and turned on the water. I watched the huge tub fill, steam rising from it, and peeled my clothes off.

As soon as I sank into the water, my chest opened, and I could breathe. I smiled sadly, thankful for the small respite, and then sank under the water. Tiny bubbles snaked across my skin in their escape to the surface. The muffled roar of the faucet was the only thing I heard.

I fumbled along the tub's rim for a bottle of shampoo. I massaged it into my hair and closed my eyes. If only I could wash away the dirtiness I felt inside as easily.

I fumbled with my toes to turn off the water and then washed the shampoo from my hair. I stayed under, listening to the sound of the bubbles around my ears. When did everything become so complicated? When did my life turn into the mess that it was now? I was drowning in the weight of it all. In less than ten hours I would be fighting for not only my life but for the lives of everyone I knew. I was afraid. When did I become the kind of girl who was afraid?

"Rose, you still alive in there?" Ben asked from the other side of the door.

"Yeah, sorry, just soaking."

"Well, could you soak a little less? We're all waiting."

I closed my eyes and leaned back against the edge of the tub. I swallowed and then said, "Alright. I'll be out in a second."

I sighed and lay there a moment longer. I had to get up, though. I knew that. I forced myself to stand and climbed over the rim of the tub. I wrapped myself in a towel and opened the bathroom door. Someone had left me clean pajama pants and a new t-shirt—one that hadn't belonged to Parker. I made myself numb to the thought and put them on.

When I finally made it to the living room, everyone was sitting on the couch. All of them stared, analyzing me. I looked away from Beth and Ben, because their looks were nauseatingly concerned.

Kinda creepy, isn't it? Walking out and seeing us all staring at you? I feel like I should say something really creepy like, "We've been watching you," Alexa said to me. She was smirking, and I had to smile back. I was glad she was here. She knew me well enough to know not to pity me.

"So," I said, breaking the silence and sitting on the couch facing everyone.

"Are you all right?" Beth asked, her expression soft.

I thought seriously of hitting her. "Look, I'm fine. Now can we please just talk about what needs to be done tonight and stop worrying about me? We have too much to think about without throwing my emotions into the twist. Believe me when I say that I can, *and will*, deliver tonight. Okay?"

"Alright," Ben said and nodded, wiping his hands on his cream-colored linen pants. Dark bags hung under his eyes, and I wondered how long he'd been awake.

"What's the first thing that needs to get done on our end?" I asked.

"For you? Brushing that rat's nest you're trying to pass as hair," Alexa said.

"I like it. It's like bed-head sexy," Ben said and winked.

Alexa rolled her eyes and said, "Of course you do, but for a formal occasion?"

"That's all? The major objective here when we're about to go into battle is how I'm wearing my hair?"

Ben shrugged and said, "For you it is. For the rest of us, it's more strategic. I've got to call room service to get the trolley, deal with that epidroméas who brings it, get the weaponry together, divide it, and then get in touch with someone on the other end to see how their progress is going. We might have to create some type of diversion to ensure that all the forces get into the subway tunnels before we enter the ballroom."

"They're not all in the subways yet?" I asked, my brows lowering. They were supposed to have finished that yesterday.

"Oh, they are, but they've got to navigate their way to the basement of this hotel. That requires a short amount of time above ground. I don't foresee them getting caught. Most of the epidroméas are going to be trying to get into that ball. However, a great deal of this plan is just playing it by ear."

"I just hope it's not too much of the plan," I said, biting my lip and crossing my legs. This seemed too big to let anything take us by surprise.

Ben leaned forward and said, "Look, Rose. It's better if we don't have every little detail planned out. This way we're flexible. We can do this. Trust me."

I held Ben's gaze for a moment and then nodded. "All right. I trust you. I guess that means you don't need me for a while, though?"

"Why? What are you going to do?" Ben asked.

I motioned at my hair and said, "Apparently I need to tame my rat's nest. It could take some time."

Ben laughed, and I shrugged, standing up. Alexa and Beth stood with me. I gave them a questioning look.

"What? You think *you'd* know the first thing about making yourself look good?" Alexa said, grabbing me by the elbow and pulling me toward our room.

Beth sighed and then followed us.

I stopped cold when we entered the room.

"What the hell is that?" I said, gaping at the abomination lying on the bed.

Alexa grinned wickedly and said, "That is your dress."

CHAPTER TWENTY-NINE

"Alexa..." I said, shaking my head. I had no words to convey what I was feeling. The dress was beautiful, but it wasn't *me*. I stared in the mirror and didn't know who was looking back at me.

"Stop looking like you're about to shatter. It's a dress, not a dying puppy," Alexa said.

I pulled at the red fabric and sighed. "I guess my armor's a little different than yours, huh?"

Alexa shrugged and said, "I like yours better. You can at least tell you're a girl."

"Here, put these on," Beth said, stepping past Alexa to hand me a pair of red gloves.

As I was putting them on, Alexa handed me two small daggers. "Here, put these in your gloves. There're little compartments right by the seams. Yeah, there." She nodded as I slid the knives into their slots.

I reached out and took my familiar leather knife belt from her.

I ran my thumb across the worn leather and exhaled. I'd had that belt from the first few weeks living on my own. That belt had been my safety and the sign of my resilience. I adapted. I grew. I was scared. There was a time that I wouldn't even have considered taking my knives off, yet now, as I held their belt, I didn't want to put it back on. "Rose?" Alexa asked, touching my elbow with a concerned look on her face.

I shook my head and let out a heavy breath. I made myself unbutton the sheaths from the belt and attach them to two garters around each of my thighs. Two knives and two daggers. Four blades. That would be the only thing saving me from the mass of epidroméas in the ballroom. I swallowed and tightened the leather straps around my thighs.

"All that's left now is the shoes," Alexa said, smirking.

I put them on and then stood back up to full height. My hands shook from my nerves. I breathed out and said, "This is it. This is the first time we're really fighting back, isn't it?"

Alexa said, "It's been a long time coming, but yeah. We're starting a war tonight."

I nodded, breathing out heavily. Our plan of attack for tonight was good, as good as it could get really, but I had an increasingly bad feeling about it. After tonight, we'd be one step closer to getting to Versailles and taking out the mother hive. We just had to win here first. The war was finally starting for real, and we were at the center of it.

A knock came at the bathroom door, and I jumped. Ben entered the bathroom and looked at me. He lost his composure, and his jaw dropped.

I shifted uncomfortably, crossing my arms over the dress. I walked past him out of the bathroom. I stopped in the living room and looked back at all the furniture. I said, "This is the last time I'm going to see this place, isn't it?"

Ben said, "You sound almost sad."

"I guess I am. It's always hard leaving someplace."

"No, it's not. It's hard leaving the memories made there."

"I don't get why I'm sad leaving here, though. It's not like a lot of spectacular memories were made here. Nothing good happened, really."

"Maybe that's why. Maybe because it's one place you don't have any bad memories of?"

I shook my head and laughed solemnly, "You know your life is screwed up when you count not having any traumatic memories in a place as a blessing."

Ben said, "Or it could be a sign of a life full of adventure."

"What good is a life full of adventure if you never get to choose which adventure you take?"

Ben lifted my chin with his hand and said, "That's where you're wrong, little Cancer. We don't choose the adventures we take. The adventures choose us. It's up to us if we rise to the occasion."

I turned from his hand, a soft smile on my face, and said, "Careful there, Ben. If you keep talking like that, someone might mistake you for caring."

He laughed. "We wouldn't want that, now, would we?"

I tried to smile, but couldn't muster it. We fell silent, the tension heavy and apparent. The room was dark, the night sky over the city filling the window. We both looked out over the landscape, and I was afraid.

My voice was barely above a whisper as I said, "It's time, isn't it?"

"You can still back out, Rose."

I didn't trust my voice, so I shook my head and took in a deep, shaky breath. Ben walked me to the door and opened it. We both stood, staring at the empty hall. I could feel my stomach in my throat. I'd never been so afraid in my life. I couldn't go back. As soon as I stepped out of that door, I was alone.

I turned and gave Ben the hardest hug I'd ever given anyone. Tears threatened my eyes, but I prayed they wouldn't pour out. I said frantically into his shoulder, "If tonight…doesn't…go well, I want to thank you for being my friend. Thank you for being my friend even though you never had to. I just—"

"Shh," Ben said, gently stroking my hair. I didn't even care if he messed it up. "This isn't good-bye, not even by a long shot, little Cancer. We'll both make it out tonight. You'll see."

I nodded and forced myself to step away from him into the hall.

"Hey, Rose? Do me a favor and don't think about anyone other than you tonight, all right? No playing hero. You just get yourself out of there."

I nodded again and started walking away. My feet were heavy as lead. By some miracle I made it to the end of the hall and pressed the button for the elevator.

The shiny doors dinged open, and I stepped into the small elevator. The bellhop's eyes widened to disks, and he took a drunken step toward me.

I stepped back from the corner and straightened my dress. "Stop looking at me like that."

The bellhop's dull eyes shifted, confused, and I was suddenly annoyed by him. My nerves were on such edge, I couldn't even decide what I was feeling.

I pinched the space between my brows and said, "Take me to the ball."

He turned back to the row of unlit buttons on the wall and pressed G for ground floor.

The only way to start a revolution is from the ground up, I thought.

The elevator stopped moving, and the light over the doors glowed green. I took a deep breath, my stomach already churning, and stepped from the elevator when the doors opened.

The room was massive. Soft band music filled my ears. Tables covered in white cloths and decorated with candles clung to the walls. Ten chairs, all blood red, were tucked under each table. Some already had elegantly dressed hosts sitting in them, eating and conversing with others.

A swarm of hosts, infinitely more than I'd seen in Blood Indigo, buzzed in the center of the room. They were clumped in pairs, swaying softly with the music. Others traveled along the seams of the room, talking with those they knew and then nodding at those they didn't.

The lighting of the room was odd. It took me a second to understand that the orangey light filling the room wasn't from the massive chandeliers but rather the collective aura of everyone in the hall.

I felt my anxiety escape me and instantly I was calm. That could only mean one thing, though: Adrian was near. I cursed under my breath and closed my eyes. I thought hard to connect with Alexa.

I said to her, *I'm in. Adrian is nearby. Tell Ben to call the bellhop. Don't forget, eleven o'clock. Don't be late!*

"There's my Rose," Adrian purred, appearing like a dream beside me. He was clad in a classic black tuxedo, his hair slicked back in a "007" style.

My breath caught in my throat when I looked at him. I drank him in, practically feeling my eyes dilating.

A waiter stopped him a couple feet from me, and I took the opportunity to barricade my mind. I shut my eyes and visualized brick walls, barbed wire fences, anything that would be treacherous to anything trying to seep in. Even with all of my mental defenses, I could still *feel* how beautiful Adrian was. I had enough control not to run to him and melt into his grasp, but he still had a pull on me like there was some invisible rope between us. I opened my eyes and saw him staring at me. The look on his face said he felt it too.

"You look…" he said, his eyes melting over me like oil, greasing every ounce of exposed skin.

"I'd ask you to finish that sentence, but the drool on the side of your mouth answered for you," I said.

Even though our skins weren't touching, I could feel the pulsating electricity through the fabric of my glove as he grabbed my hand. I swallowed and steadied myself.

Adrian smiled. "Should I waste my time telling you how spectacular you look, or is my sneaking suspicion right and you already know?"

"Some people believe a woman should always be reminded of how beautiful she is."

He leaned into me, whispering softly, "That's for the women who are *only* beautiful. All the eyes focused on you now should be proof that you are beyond that."

His breath on my neck made goose bumps rise along my skin. I looked up, away from him, and noticed that he was right about the staring. The room still moved, buzzing with conversations and music, but everywhere I looked I could find at least one pair of eyes trained on me.

I looked back at Adrian and saw that the air around us shimmered like it was buzzing with electricity. I rolled my eyes with impatience. The air could just go on its merry little way, because there would be no connecting auras tonight.

"You roll your eyes at your admirers?" Adrian asked with a half-smile.

"I roll my eyes at those stupid enough to be caught staring," I said.

He smiled and reached for my other hand.

I stepped out of his reach and said over my shoulder with a smile, "I want a drink. Get me one."

His eyebrows rose, but he nodded. He reached out and touched my elbow, which was clad in the satin glove. My heart stopped. I was afraid he'd feel the dagger hidden in the fabric, but he didn't.

"What would you like? Bacardi? Dom Perignon? Maybe the house special?"

"Surprise me," I said.

He bowed and kissed my knuckles. The whole room stilled when his lips met the fabric. I looked around me self-consciously and saw the faces were stunned speechless. It seemed that the prince of the Infestation didn't bow to others too often.

I sighed in relief when Adrian's dark head completely disappeared into the crowd. I didn't even bother to register the people around me, their faces unwavering from individual to individual.

I scanned the room, looking for a head of strawberry blond hair and fiery green eyes. What would I do if Ben didn't come? There were countless things that could have gone wrong. The bellhop might not have brought a buggy, the bellhop was too strong to overpower, and they'd somehow overpowered the bellhop but then were caught on the trip down... I forced myself to breathe and empty my head. I could do this.

I looked into the crowd for somewhere to disappear. Losing Adrian was the first half of my plan. The second half required me getting to the other side of this gargantuan ballroom without picking up a tail so I could let in Parker.

Parker.

My chest ached, and the empty feeling inside me swelled unexpectedly. The surprise of its intensity knocked my mental guard down. I felt the instantaneous pull to my right, my body yearning to move in that direction. I cursed a stream of profanity under my breath and wrangled my subconscious back, The damage had been done, though. With my guard down, my mind had called to Adrian, and now I could *feel* his presence responding. I cursed again.

I turned and dove into a swarm of bodies. Women in expensive dresses stopped talking as I passed. Some even bowed and dipped their heads in curtsey. I cursed and pushed passed them. The last thing I needed was a trail of curtseying morons for Adrian to follow.

"Stop bowing." I spit out, extending my mind to theirs.

Their faces blanked, and they stood back up.

I could feel that I was putting distance between Adrian and me.

I wasn't stupid enough to believe he was out of the picture completely, though. There was no doubt he was following me. I only had so much time to do my part before he caught me. It was ten fifty. I had ten minutes.

I focused on finding the left side of the ballroom where the doors to the basement would be. The elevator was to my back left, wasn't it? Or was it my right? I didn't dare turn around and look for fear that Adrian would catch up. The anxiety bubbled in my chest. Time was ticking. Each second that passed was like a stone thrown at my back. I had to get to the door in ten minutes, or everything would be disastrous. If one side opened before the other, that half of the army could get swarmed by the masses, overtaken, and defeated in the minutes it would take for the other half to make it through the doors. Timing was everything.

And I was running out of it.

I made a sharp left and nearly screamed when I saw the elevator. How had I gotten back to where I started? Seven minutes were left.

I looked around, pausing, and a cool sensation started to tingle in my peripheral. I panicked, feeling Adrian getting closer, and grabbed the man to my right. His expression startled as he looked at me closely.

"Where is the left entrance to the basement?"

He merely looked at me in shock. I groaned and shook him, saying, "Tell me where it is."

People were staring, but I didn't have time to acknowledge them. I needed this answer, and I needed it now.

"There." He pointed a little to the left of the center of the room. I could barely make out a mahogany door,

"Thank God. You never saw me. None of you did," I said and dove back into the crowd. I was nearly running. The clock ticked down to five minutes.

I had over forty yards to go, forty yards separating me and what could decide this war, and I wasn't moving fast enough.

Four minutes. My pulse sounded like drums in my ears. I pushed myself harder, my hair flying over my shoulders as I walked as fast as I could,

Three minutes. I was halfway there. I could just make out the door between the dancers' heads bobbing in and out of the way. I was going too slow. I broke out into a run, beyond caring who saw. It didn't matter anyways; they were all about to die.

Two minutes. I started shoving hosts out of my way. I heard gasps, and people covered their mouths as I blurred past them.

One minute. I came crashing out of the mass of bodies to the door, breathing heavily. I opened it and ran down the dark staircase that folded back on itself.

Thirty seconds. I went crashing down the stairs, my flimsy heels clacking wildly on the unadorned concrete steps.

Ten seconds. I crashed into the door at the bottom of the steps and threw it open.

A rush of bodies went past me, clapping me on the back and filing out the stairs. I sighed with relief and found myself raked with some sort of delirious laughter. I'd done it. I got them in.

I watched as the humans, both men and women, went past me, dressed in warrior's garb. I saw something in their expressions that I hadn't noticed amongst the epidroméas. These people had hope. I never thought I could have put hope in visual form, but there it was in the eyes of all these people.

My whole world stilled, and gravity lost its hold on me. Parker hesitated in front of me, our eyes locking. I opened my mouth to call to him, but he stepped past me, unsheathing one of the swords at his waist, and disappeared up the stairs. My legs shook, and my whole body threatened to collapse. It was too much. I leaned back against the door frame for support and tried to find my breath. I didn't have time for this, not now, not today. I swallowed and made myself stand up. I climbed the steps, one by one, into the battle.

CHAPTER THIRTY

My ears rang with the cries of those dying and the ringing, metal-on-metal twang of those still battling for their lives. I was frozen, shocked by the carnage all around me. Blood pooled everywhere; I was even standing in it. People were dying, I watched as a man's head was ripped from his shoulders and then eaten by the bug who'd detached it. Another man plunged his knife into a bug's face, detaching its pincers, only to be skewered by a host who'd found a sword.

It wasn't real, I told myself. It wasn't really happening. My hands felt dumb and useless at my sides. My eyesight shook. This wasn't real.

A girl cried out, and I turned to see her. Her knife was thrown out of her hand by two bugs in hard, roach-like skeletons. They closed in on her, and she searched frantically around her for a weapon. Part of me was detached, watching her and wondering what would happen, but then she looked at me. Her eyes, as big as my fists, settled on me, and I felt her fear.

I shook my head, regaining myself, and reached for my knives. I pulled them from their sheaths and ran toward her. I used a corpse as leverage, jumping from its back into the air. I landed with a hard *thump* on one of the creature's backs, digging my knives into its torso.

Black juice seeped out. I pulled my knives and stood in front of the girl. I locked eyes with the other bug and smiled. "You know what sucks about being a bug?" I asked. It cocked it head to the side and I smiled. "I've never thought twice about squashing one underneath my boot."

It opened its pincers to sound, but I spun, roundhouse kicking it in the face, and knocked its pincers straight from its head. Black syrup sprang from the wound.

It leaped forward and caught me on the shoulder. I felt the bones crack, and I screamed out. My hand went slack, and I dropped my knife. The girl behind me shrieked, but I ignored her. I danced around the bug, grimacing with every move of my arm, and evaded its hits. Finally my skin began tingling, and the broken bone healed.

I feinted left and then spun right. I used my other knife and stabbed into its back, slicing down and ripping open its torso. It fell to the ground in a pool of its blood. I turned back to the girl, and she was staring at me in horror.

"I watched it break your shoulder, but you—"

"Yeah, I know. Here, try not to get yourself killed," I said, handing her one of the daggers.

She took it, dazed, and I left her to throw myself into another fight.

At one point I saw Brad and called out to him. He waved and then turned and kicked a bug so hard that its exoskeleton actually collapsed in on itself. I gave him an approving nod but stopped when warm, black blood dropped onto my shoulder.

I spun and saw a host standing behind me with a sword raised where my head should have been. It would have killed me had the golden arrow protruding from its forehead not killed it first. Alexa ran past me, laughing, her dark hair flowing free like an Amazon woman. She was firing her bow, shooting targets in the distance, and when someone got too close, she swung it like a club, knocking them to the ground, and then stabbed them.

That was in the beginning, though, before the fatigue set in. I could feel my body slowing, my movements not as precise as the time passed. I noticed more and more scratches on people I knew when I came across them. The problem was that for every bug we took down, three were there to take their place.

I looked up to see that I hadn't even made a dent in the mass. I got the first real taste that we might not win, then. I had to get to the others and be with them in case we had to make a final stand. If it came to that, at least I would make it with them.

I dove into a swarm of epidroméas, swinging my knives like a metallic windmill. I made contact with every stroke. A host with dark hair jumped before me, and I kicked its legs out from under it. I plunged my knives into its chest and felt the life flow free from it.

"Such a beautiful dress for such an ugly night, would you not agree, little Dream Wanderer?" I heard the voice from above me, and chills ran down my spine. I would have recognized it anywhere.

"Rayon," I said, pulling my knives violently from the corpse beneath me.

This was it. He would finally pay for what he'd done. I stood, raising my blades, and he smiled. He lifted his hands and a swirling ball of fire appeared between his palms. Of course he was a fire user.

"One little flame ball isn't going to stop me from ripping your heart out," I said.

"Ah, but what if I were to throw in a wild card?"

Wes Deluka stood before me. Only, it wasn't him, though. His face was void of expression, and he held a sword longer than my arm in his hands.

"Like my new pet? I must admit, he was a hard one to break, but now I've earned myself quite a little lap dog," Rayon said, grinning.

"I'm going to make you die slowly for what you did to him and Lila."

He stepped in front of Wes, and said, "One moment, little Dream Wanderer, why don't you hear me out? I represent a very important family. One, for whatever reason, has taken a *very* strong interest in you and is willing to do whatever it takes to get you alive. Do you understand?"

I said, "Speaking of the Coallati's, where is Adrian? I haven't seen him since the fight broke out."

Rayon shrugged. "A battleground is hardly the place for a prince. He's been safely relocated."

"Of course," I said dryly, circling around him hoping to catch him off guard.

He moved with me, foiling my attempt. "So I'm guessing your insolence means you're not going willingly?"

"Nope. You can tell Adrian that the next time I see him, I hope one of us is dead."

Rayon shook his head and stepped behind Wes. "How foolish you are, child. You face annihilation. Do you expect to face me alone?"

"She's not alone," Parker said from behind me.

I turned. He was standing beside me with his sword out and ready.

He gave me a soft smile and said in my head, *I'll have your back, Rosie. Now you get Rayon and leave Wes to me.*

I nodded and turned back to Rayon. I crossed my blades before me. He laughed and said, "You think your knives can take on flames?"

He scowled and then turned, quicker than I'd thought possible, and shot an orb that glowed like the sun at me. I rolled, missing the fireball by inches, and came up behind him, slicing down with my knives. I cut his hamstring and he dropped to one leg. Blood seeped from the wound. "This is for Lila," I whispered and raised my knives, ready to come down on his head.

"Rose!" Parker screamed.

Cold pain erupted in my stomach, and I fell forward. A sword stuck from my gut, the pommel in Wes's hand. I looked up to him, my eyesight flickering, and he dug the blade in deeper, spinning it so that I actually *felt* my organs shift. He pulled the sword out, his eyes hard and emotionless, and I gasped. I raised my shaking hand to my gut and fell to my knees. I looked down at my hands and saw red blood gushing from my body.

I won't heal from this, I realized. My body was already failing, my sight dimming far too quickly. I felt tired too, tired and cold. I fell onto my back, my legs folded strangely beneath me. It wasn't uncomfortable, though. I couldn't even feel them. I didn't feel anything but the coldness, the mind-numbing chill that wouldn't let go.

My chest began to rake with shudders, and I was struggling to breathe. Warm blood rushed in my ears, trickling from my mouth. I could feel its warmth everywhere. But it wouldn't satiate the cold.

"Rose!"

I opened my eyes and saw an angel's outline. He had beautiful brown curls and startlingly blue eyes. He looked too sad to be an angel, too sad to be so wonderful.

I tried to smile at him, but a cough raked my chest, and more warm blood bubbled out. *I'm dying,* I thought. It didn't scare me, not really. It was natural. People are born. People live. People die. It was probably the first purely human thing I'd done in my life. That really did make me smile, though my whole body deplored the movement of those small muscles.

The angel was crying, his tears falling on my face. I wanted to comfort him, tell him it'd be okay, but I couldn't find my voice. Then the mist that clouded my mind and made me so tired and so, so cold parted for a second, just long enough for me to form a coherent thought.

I love you.

It was the only time I said it to him while I was alive.

POSTLUDE

I
t was beautiful.

I was standing in the middle of a forest of dogwoods in the midst of winter. Icicles hung from the trees, reflecting the orange light of the setting sun like tiny mirrors. Snow silently fell from the sky, blanketing the ground in an ethereal carpet that was so pure, it almost hurt my eyes to look at it. There were no sounds, no clank from swords hitting one another, and no cries of dying men. There was only the snow and the trees. The world was silent and calm, and I was safe.

I looked up at the sky, at the snow falling slowly down on me, and I smiled. I stretched my arms out and opened my mouth, catching the snowflakes on my tongue. I laughed, easy and unworried, spinning in circles. Someone appeared in my peripheral and I stopped spinning to look. It was Lila. She was standing on a cobblestone path that looked as if it was cut from the snow. She wore a long, white dress and no shoes, though the cold didn't seem to bother her, either. She was exactly how I remembered her, if not better. Her blonde curls hung perfectly over her shoulders, and her pale skin was without mar. No bags hung under her eyes, no sadness filled her expression. Comfort had finally found her. She was safe, too.

She stared at me, and I smiled. I ran to her, my feet leaving foot prints in the snow, until I, too, made it onto the path before her. She didn't reach for me or even move in my direction. She merely stared.

"Lila," I called to her, still smiling.

Her expression didn't change. Doubt filled me. Something caught my eye behind her, and I squinted into the tree-line to try to make it out. Faces. I was seeing faces, I realized. They peeked behind the trees, staring at me in both wonder and fear. My brows furrowed. If this was heaven, why were they hiding?

"This isn't heaven, is it?" I asked, staring past her.

She shook her head.

I stumbled over my words, "But…this has to be heaven. I died. I died, and I woke up here."

She shook her head again, and I faltered.

"What is this, then?" I asked, my voice only a hint of a whisper.

Lila's eyes settled on me, and fear rose up my spine. She opened her mouth and said, "This is only the beginning."

ACKNOWLEDGMENTS

There are so many people to thank! This book was truly a journey that was a couple years in the making. During that time, there were so many people that encouraged, inspired, and believed in me, and without them, Rose's story might have never begun. I could never list every one of them here—there are truly too many!—but there are a few that I can't leave out. So special thanks to the fans of the blog from the beginning: Kat White, Daniel Barber, and Mrs. Nicole McKinney. Thank you to all the members at Tate Publishing who put up with my craziness like true professionals. A big thanks to my closest friends: Calah Reynolds, Maria Evans, Kristina Kosogorova, and Tyler Erb, who listened to my psychotic ramblings about the plot good-naturedly and even managed to give me ideas. Also, I must say thank you to two of the best English teachers I ever had: Mrs. Kristi Sayers and Mrs. Melissa Dixon, who both pushed my understanding of the English language even further. There were countless more teachers, family members, and friends that made this journey possible and to all of you, I say again from the bottom of my heart, "Thank you, thank you, thank you!"

LIVE

listen|imagine|view|experience

AUDIO BOOK DOWNLOAD INCLUDED WITH THIS BOOK!

In your hands you hold a complete digital entertainment package. In addition to the paper version, you receive a free download of the audio version of this book. Simply use the code listed below when visiting our website. Once downloaded to your computer, you can listen to the book through your computer's speakers, burn it to an audio CD or save the file to your portable music device (such as Apple's popular iPod) and listen on the go!

How to get your free audio book digital download:

1. Visit www.tatepublishing.com and click on the e|LIVE logo on the home page.
2. Enter the following coupon code:
   07c2-e985-21be-93d9-4ae8-8e03-647f-56d2
3. Download the audio book from your e|LIVE digital locker and begin enjoying your new digital entertainment package today!